# HABITS

By
Kevin Bryan

FRANK —
ALWAYS GREAT ON THE BASS.
WHAT A JOY TO WATCH YOU GROW
IN THE LORD!

Kevin Bryan

This book is dedicated to my fabulous and
faithful wife, Marsha Wood Bryan.
Thank you for believing in me.

I want to thank Angela Smith and Sarah Nichols for being such supportive fans. And a special thanks to Detective Faith Bryan for lending authenticity to the police scenes. I couldn't ask for a better trio of daughters!

You may also enjoy 'Horse Sense', another
Christian Suspense novel by Kevin Bryan

# 1

The high desert sky was ebony, but the robins had begun their early morning routine. The roosters jumped from limb to limb in the young ponderosa pine trees. Their tweet and trill calls at dawn reminded their neighbors of where the territorial lines were drawn. The hens sang as they preened and prepared to leave their grass and mud nests for a few minutes of frantic foraging.

The ambitious song birds weren't the only ones who got an early start in the high desert. Gabe Green sat at his breakfast bar, squinting at a passage in his well worn New International Version of the Bible. He was preparing for next Sunday's lesson in the Adult Education Bible class. It was his habit.

He read a sentence or two, scratched his grizzled gray beard, mumbled a little, scribbled a note and linked a couple of words with a semi-straight line, then read another sentence. When he thought he understood the meaning of the passage he checked his thoughts against the half-dozen commentaries that were strewn around the slate green Formica countertop. As often as not, his 'paper brains' as he called the thick books, reinforced what he was thinking; but, this morning his thoughts were diverging from those of his favorite theologians.

The passage he was studying was in Matthew 13; the parable of the yeast. To Gabe, it looked like yeast was a positive thing in this story. But the commentators held the position that yeast *always* had a negative connotation. He flipped through his Bible, to all the other passages he could find that talked about yeast, and it looked like the commentators had a point. Still, he was sure that, in this case, the yeast was the good news of Jesus. How could that be bad?

Though he was confused and frustrated about how he was going to present the passage to the class, Gabe continued his normal routine and got on his knees to pray. As usual in his prayer time, he was trying to visualize being in the presence of the holy controller of the universe. At times, obtaining that vision was easy; on other days, it took a lot of discipline.

That vision became impossible when Gabe heard the metallic click of a door opening followed by the sound of sticky bare feet crossing the hardwood floor.

This was not part of the routine. Gabe and his wife Meg had been the only two bodies rattling around this house for the past fifteen years, ever since their daughter had moved out. Meg was not an early riser, so his morning prayer was normally uninterrupted.

That had changed two days ago when they had met their grandson up at the airport in Redmond, and brought him home for a visit. Gabe was having some difficulties with the changes that arrived with the boy. Not that thirteen-year-old Zach was creating problems. It was just different. Gabe did not have an easy time with different. He was not accustomed to being disturbed when he was on his knees; but, he knew that there were going to be some questions to answer.

The boy had a million questions.

Gabe had a fleeting thought about getting his sorry bones up and into a chair before Zach found him, but he knew that he there wasn't time. The boy was as quick as a cat on caffeine and Gabe wasn't.

"What are you doing down there, Grumpa? And who was the huge guy with the shiny clothes?" Zach asked as he came around the corner.

"What shiny guy? Are you makin' fun of my bald head?"

"Is that guy going to go fishing with us? He looks kind of creepy."

Gabe's knees creaked as he hoisted himself up from the floor, but he kept the groan to himself. He didn't want to set off an additional round of questions. "I don't have a clue what you're talkin' about with this big shiny guy stuff."

"I'm talking about the guy who was walking across the lawn when I looked out the window just now. He was a big dude and his clothes were really bright, even in the dark. He freaked me."

"You musta been havin' some kinda weird dream. There weren't nobody out there. The dogs would've been barkin' their fool heads off if there was."

"Nute and Ace walked right past him. They acted like they didn't even know he was there."

Gabe went out on the deck and scanned the yard. The two big labs immediately ran up to him, wiggling and whining. "Who's out here with you bruisers?" Gabe asked the dogs, as if he expected a verbal response. "Go get 'im." At the command, the dogs leapt off the deck and raced around the yard with their noses on the ground. Finding nothing, they came back and sat on their haunches in front of him. Their tails were beating a perfect four/four cadence on the two-by-six decking.

"Now that's real curious. I don't know who or what you saw, but there ain't anybody out there now. What are you doing up so early anyway?"

"I thought I heard you out here and thought you were going fishing without me. But there was a guy out here just a minute ago. I swear I saw him!"

Gabe thought it best to change the subject. "Zach, I told you last night we was goin' fishin'. Why would I get up and leave without you?"

"I don't know. Sometimes people forget what they promised. What were you praying about? Is something wrong?"

"No, nothing's wrong. I just like to check in with my boss first thing in the mornin'. And I would *not* forget and leave without you. I need your help in gettin' some of those ornery old trout out of that crick."

"What do you mean about checking in with your boss?" Zach asked as he scratched through his sleep ratted hair with his short fingernails. "Who's your boss? Aren't you retired?"

"Well, when I became a Christian, about a hundred years ago—when I was 'bout your age—the fellow who was my Sunday School teacher told me that Jesus was gonna be my boss from then on. I try to start out every day by askin' him what kind of jobs he has for me to do. There ain't no retiring from the Lord's work. Shoot, we get to keep on working for him for eternity."

"Working forever? That doesn't sound like heaven to me."

"Ah, but working for the King of the Universe is better'n anything!"

Zach gave a confused shrug and said, "I don't have a Sunday School teacher."

"You go to church don't you?"

"Yeah, sometimes. But I don't go to the classes with the other kids much. They kind of pick on me."

"They pick on ya? What about?"

"Just stuff. Hey, when we going fishing?"

"Tell ya what. You go get dressed and washed up and I'll cook us up some grub for breakfast. Soon as we eat we'll head out!"

"Okay. But what'd he say?"

"What'd who say, Zach?"

"You know. Your boss."

"Oh. He told me to go have a great adventure with my grandson!"

"Are we going to have an adventure? That'd be awesome!"

"Zach, it's always an adventure when you get to go out in the woods. We'll likely see some deer or elk. Maybe some antelope. A bunch of birds and squirrels and stuff. Yup. It's going to be an adventure alright. Now you go get out of those jammers and into some adventure type clothes. It'll be getting daylight soon and we got places to go, things to see, and stuff to do. So get a move on! Oh, and dress in warm clothes. The weather 'round here hasn't heard that it's spring. The high today will likely only be around fifty degrees."

Five minutes later, Zach was back in the kitchen, and he had traded his flannel pajamas for jeans and a plaid flannel shirt. The outfit looked like it had just jumped off the pages of a Cabala's catalog. There was no sign that the boy's face had seen any water or that his hair had been combed.

"Hey, them's some fancy duds, Zach. Did your ma get them for you special for this trip?"

"Yeah. She said I needed some warm stuff to wear while I was here. Nobody wears flannel shirts and jeans in

Phoenix. We all just have tee shirts and shorts."

"No I'd guess. You'd cook in the Arizona sun wearin' this stuff, wouldn't you? But they should be perfect for here. By the way, have you got a coat? You'll likely shiver your hair off without one."

Gabe placed a plate of bacon, eggs, and hash browns in front of Zach and sat down beside him. The boy picked up his fork and prepared to dig in to the hearty breakfast but his grandfather stopped him, fork in mid-air. "Hadn't we ought to say a word of thanks before we start to get this grub on the inside of us?"

So they sat, a young city boy's soft almost fragile white hand lost in the grip of the ham-sized, gnarled and scarred, old man hand. They bowed their heads and Gabe spoke words of thanks for the nutrition the food provided and a request that the day be a blessing to their souls.

"Grumpa, do you really think that there's a God that hears you when you pray? And if there is...do you think he cares? I mean, with all the people in this world, how is God going to hear *you*?"

"You bet I do! I know there's a God. How else could this wonderful world be here? Hold out your hand, Zach." When Zach stretched his hand out, Gabe said, "Now open and close your fingers as fast as you can. Do you think that just happened? The action of your fingers demonstrates some amazing mechanics. And the engineering involved with your hand is child's play compared to the design of some of the rest of your body. Like say your heart. Oh, there's a God alright enough, no matter what them idget evolutionist tell you!"

# 2

The diamond-plate toolbox that rode in the back of the four-wheel drive Toyota held all the gear that Gabe felt necessary for a foray onto the logging roads of Central Oregon's National Forest Land. It held a set of tire chains, an ax, a shovel, a tarp, a fifty foot coil of rope, and a bunch of other odds and ends.

Gabe made a quick check of the additional gear that he had loaded into the pickup the night before. He didn't want to drive for an hour and a half only to find that something critical had been left home. There were fishing poles and bags of tackle, a Styrofoam container of night crawlers, boots, a Ruger 10-22 rifle and its corresponding ammo, coats, and an ample lunch that Grandma Meg had packed for them.

Satisfied that the necessary stuff was in the truck, Gabe inventoried his pockets. He had the waterproof match case, his folding jackknife, and the wallet that held his fishing license. "All set," he said.

"You got your fishin' license with you?" he asked Zach.

"Yes."

Zach sat in the passenger's seat, examining the three-inch folding Buck knife that his granddad had given him the afternoon that he had arrived. He turned the knife over and over in his hands, examining the shiny blade and knife's black handle.

"Better fold the knife up and slide it deep into your pocket. Remember, that's a tool, and it's razor sharp. It'll take your finger off in a blink if you aren't careful with it."

The boy reached back to put the knife in his hip pocket and Gabe said, "I'd carry that in my front pocket were it mine. They slide out of a hip pocket too easy."

"Grumpa, I don't think that Mom would like me having a knife, especially not one this sharp."

"Well, a knife sharp enough to split frog hair is way safer in the long run than a dull one, and that's a fact. And you're not going fishin' with your ma now are you? Besides, you're going to need that toad sticker to help clean all the trout we're gonna catch today."

"Do you really think I'll catch some fish? I caught a couple of little bluegills out of Lake Powell last summer, but my dad made me throw them back. He said that cleaning them was too much trouble."

"Well, bluegills is hard to clean. You have to scale the little varmints, and they're not really worth the bother unless you got a good mess of 'em. They be dee-licious though. But, yeah, I think we should be able to get enough brookies for a good fish fry, and they're mighty fine eating in their own right. Yep, we should really rip some lips if we find the right crick."

8

# Habits

The first rays of the morning's sun brightened the eastern sky as Gabe and Zach drove out of the pine-forested area of Rosland and lost elevation as they went south where sparse junipers and sagebrush replaced the pine trees and bitterbrush.

Long-eared jackrabbits made the most of the semi-darkness that marked the beginning of the day. One or two zipped across the road in front of the pickup every few minutes. Gabe and Zach laughed and cheered for them as they zigzagged across the asphalt that was illuminated by the pickup's headlights.

"Grumpa," Zach asked, "do you think the other animals tease the rabbits because of their big floppy ears and monster feet?"

"Nah," Gabe replied, "I don't think critters are into teasing. They chase one another some. And, of course, coyotes 'ill eat the rabbits should they git the chance. But, I don't think they notice if some other varmint has big ears or feet."

After a few minutes of silence, Zach quietly said, "I think I'd like to be an animal."

Gabe took off his Ducks Unlimited baseball cap and scratched his balding head before he replied, "I don't think they got it too awful easy, Zach. They got no warm house to live in. They can't go to the grocery store and buy vittles. No pizza or soda pop neither, ever. And having to look over your shoulder to make sure a coyote ain't putting the sneak on you, or an eagle isn't swooping down to have you for lunch don't sound like too much fun to me."

"Yeah, but at least you'd know that the coyote and eagle were going to try to hurt you. You wouldn't expect them to be your friend, then find out they weren't."

"'That's true enough I suppose. But, Zach, who was it that you thought was your friend but then turned around and hurt you?"

"I really don't want to talk about it, Grumps. How much longer 'til we get to the creek?"

"About half-an-hour."

Man, Gabe mused silently. Where is this stuff coming from? "Lord," he prayed silently, "I'm in way over my head here. I'm going to need you to send me some wisdom. This boy needs some counsel, and I have no earthly idea what to say. A heavenly idea would be better anyway."

While Gabe drove he watched Zach out of the corner of his eye. The boy was looking out the passenger side window, mouth downturned in a sad arch; his shoulders were slouched, and his eyes were way too vacant for someone so young.

Maybe a good fishing trip would begin snap to him out of it.

# 3

The air was frigid when they parked on an old landing that had been left behind at the end of a long ago logging operation. To get to this spot Gabe had been forced to drop the Toyota into low range four-wheel-drive. That was the only way to bust through some of snow drifts that were lingering with stubborn determination on the northeast slope of the hills.

Zach hadn't said a word since they had left the paved highway and started up the gravel logging roads of the Winema National Forest. Gabe wasn't sure if the boy was excited, or scared, or both.

There wasn't any water in sight when Gabe and Zach climbed out of the pickup. The youngster looked around and said, "What're we doing here, Grumps? I thought we were going fishing."

"We are, Zach. We just have a little walkin' to do first. If you want to get to the good spots you have to hoof it.

Anybody can fish the holes right by the road, but most folks aren't willing to hike very far."

"How do you know where the stream is?" Zach asked.

"Well, I checked the topographical map yesterday, and if it's anywhere near accurate, Coyote Creek ought to be two ridges over; about a mile to the west of here. We should be able to follow the skid road to get over the first ridge. Then we'll hafta find a deer or elk trail from there."

Zach stood in front of the pickup and slowly scanned the panoramic view with a look that could only be interpreted as panic. As far as you could see in any direction, there were just ridge after ridge of trees. Some of those ridges were covered with a variety of pines—lodge pole, sugar pine, ponderosa, with an occasional white fir thrown in. Others had been clear cut and were in various stages of reforestation. The undergrowth, where you could see it, was predominately Manzanita, grease wood, and bitterbrush. The boy stood looking away from the sun for a couple of minutes. "A mile's a long ways. How do you know there is a creek over there?"

"Oh, it's there to be sure. God put it there and it can't get away. I reckon that the map I was using might be a skoash wrong in spots, but I bet it is close enough that we'll find the crick without much trouble. And a mile isn't far. We'll be there before you know it."

The boy had grown paler as his grandfather spoke. "But what if we get lost? Or what if some wild animal— like a bear or mountain lion—gets us?"

"Those critters 'ill have to watch out for theyselves. If the bears and cougars ain't careful we'll roast 'em over a fire and grease our chins with their fat. And you couldn't get lost on a bright sunny day like today if you tried. All we have to do is pay attention to where the sun is and getting back will be easy. Come on, let's get a move on. There're fish over there that're depending on us to give 'em some exercise!"

"Are you sure about it being safe, Grumpa? I saw a show on television where people got lost in the woods and a bear came after them." A whine had crept into Zach's voice.

"Stop the whining. I got no time for whining." There was a bit of teasing in Gabe's voice, but it was obvious that he was more than half serious. "And you don't have to worry, Zach I fish around here a lot, and I've only seen a couple of bears in all the times I've been out here. They were scart to death of people. When you do see one they are goin' so stinkin' fast that it's hard to tell what you're seein'

"And I've never been lost. Well, not for more than one night anyway.

"Come on, let's get moving. Remember to keep the end of your fishing pole pointed up. You don't want to poke it into the ground and break off the tip."

The morning was perfect. It was still too early in the year for the mosquitoes to be a problem, but the rising sun was warming the air. Flickers were drumming and calling from snags on opposite sides of the clear cut. Chickadees were harvesting some type of insect from the leaves that were beginning to sprout on a patch of currant bushes. A flock of geese were questioning something's intentions in the distance. Golden mantels jerked and jagged from stump to stump while they hunted for seeds and pine nuts and just felt good about their long winter hibernation being over. And the man and boy walked side by side down a skid trail, dust puffs coming up from their feet at each step.

When they reached the bottom of the slope, Gabe stopped and said, "Zach, stop for a second and look back up to where we left the truck. Can you see it?"

The boy turned and scanned the horizon for a second before spotting the rig. "Yeah, I see it."

"Now look around and pick out some landmarks that will be easy to recognize even if you are looking at them from a little different angle."

"Like that dead tree?" Zach asked, pointing to a tree about thirty yards from the pickup.

"Well, look around a little. Is there anything about that dead tree that makes it look different from all the other dead trees around here?"

Zach looked around for a couple of minutes. "It has a funny white stripe down the side of it. Oh, and it has two tops!"

"Okay. That's good. That white stripe is from a lightning strike. That's likely what killed the tree. Now try to take a picture of the tree in your head. Got one? Now close your eyes and look at the picture." Gabe looked at Zach and watched him squeeze his eyes shut. A wave of love coursed through his heart. The emotional tie to his grandson would never cease to amaze the crusty old man. "Now open your eyes. Does the tree look like the one in your picture?"

"I don't know. I guess so. Why are we looking at trees? I thought we were going fishing."

"You have to make sure that you have some landmarks saved in your head if you want to keep from getting lost. When I go through the woods in a new place I always stop and look around, taking pictures in my head every hundred yards or so. You 'specially want to turn around and look at things that you walked by. Everything looks totally different when ya look back at it then when you're walking toward it."

"Why don't you mark the trail with flags or something so you can follow them out?"

"That'd be a lot of fooling around for nothin'. And you don't want to be advertisin' where you're at or where ya been anyway. In fact, I don't like leavin' anythin' in the woods when I leave. Besides, there are plenty of natural markers out here if you just pay attention to them. But you have to be watchin'. Come on, I'll show you as we go."

At the bottom of the first slope they, stopped to look around for a good path through the limbs and slash that the loggers had left when this section had been cut over. They moved up the slope at a much slower pace than they'd walked down. At an elevation of over seven thousand feet, the air was a little short on oxygen.

Gabe tried to find things that he could point out as landmarks. There was a triple-topped ponderosa and three boulders that a bored skidder operator had stacked on top of each other, then a stump from a tree that had barber-chaired when it was cut. They were little things that were duplicated throughout the area, but put in sequence, they were enough to provide direction on the way back. When they reached the top of the ridge, they paused to catch their breath and look at their back-trail.

"Look, you can still see the pickup," Zach said pointing at the truck. "Boy, it looks little! And look at the road we drove in on, it looks like a ribbon."

"Yeah it does, doesn't it? But look on past it. Can you see way off there to that next big bluff? See that big shale rock slide? You should be able to see that landmark from a high point anywhere around here. If you get turned around, go to the highest spot you can find; then, start walking back toward that slide. It'll bring you back to the road we came in on."

Zach just stood staring. "You're not going to leave me out here, are you, Grumpa?" Panic had crept into his voice.

"No, I just want you to know how to get around in the woods is all. You might want to come out here by yourself someday. Anyway, let's get to the crick before all the big fish die of old age."

The clear-cut ended about a hundred yards past the top of the second ridge. From the ridgeback, looking north—back toward the truck—the shale slide stood out like a beacon. To the south, trees swayed in the morning breeze looking like a sea of green. The slope fell off sharply, and while the water wasn't visible, a grassy meadow, and a row of willows, marked the stream's course.

"See that meadow down there, Zach? That's where we're going to fish. All we have to do is get down there."

The boy stood looking down the steep slope. "How are we going to get back up from down there? It looks really steep. And are there bears or cougars down there?"

"Oh we'll get back up just fine. Might have to zigzag a little in the steep spots, but we won't be in any hurry. And I thought I told you not to worry so much about the critters. I keep telling you, they're afraid of you. Hey, I saw some elk sign back there a ways, let's see if we can find an elk trail that'll take us off this hogback. Those big fellas should be movin' back and forth from the water to the bedding grounds in the timber and up into this clear-cut to browse. There has to be a good trail here somewhere."

"Will the elk get mad if we use their trail? Aren't they really big and have really big horns?"

"Yeah, they're big critters, and the bulls sometimes have big horns, but they won't hurt you. If we're lucky enough to see some elk they'll run like crazy...away from us."

They cut a trail fifty yards later and Gabe started following it. There were fresh tracks from five or six head of elk on the trail and he was so intent on the tracks that he didn't notice that Zach wasn't with him until he had gone about thirty yards into the trees. He stopped to point out the biggest set of tracks to the boy, but discovered that the boy wasn't there! Gabe's heart kicked up to a staccato beat as he headed back up the trail, hoping that his grandson hadn't had time to get out of sight. When Gabe got back to the clearing, Zach was sitting on a stump, his knees were pulled up under his chin and his head was resting on his knees. His fishing pole was lying off to the side across some huckleberry bushes.

"Zach, you liked to scart me half to death. What're you doing?"

Zach jumped at the sharpness in Gabe's voice, but he sat where he was, the sun lighting up the red highlights in his brown hair. Gabe stood looking at the boy. He was skinny in spite of his height, all elbows and knees, looking like an ill-kept orphan, not because his clothes were old or worn; in fact, they were the latest in urban-straining-for country-fashion, but they just didn't seem to fit right.

For that matter, nothing about the boy seemed to fit correctly, not his ears or his nose or eyes. He looked like he had been put together from spare parts. No wonder he's been having trouble at school, Gabe thought to himself with a bit of guilt. There sure are enough things to make fun of him about. But didn't every adolescent look like this? It's such an awkward age. They were no longer children, but certainly not adults, kids caught between worlds.

That seemed especially true in the American society that demanded rapid development in athletic ability and sexuality but fostered a lack of responsibility in every other facet of life. What are we doing to our kids? Gabe wondered to himself.

"Come on, Zach, what's the matter? What're you doing?" Gabe asked again.

The boy didn't look up when he responded: "Won't those elks be upset if we go into their forest? I don't want them to get me."

"Zach, they will not hurt you. I doubt we'll even see any of 'em. And if we do they'll just run away. They're afraid of people, son. Come on, let's go see if we can get down to the crick and catch some trout! I'll be right behind you."

The boy reluctantly climbed off the stump, picked up his fly rod, and started down the trail into the trees. He was moving slowly with his head down and shoulders slumped.

"Hey, Zach, elk are about the prettiest critters in the woods. They're big powerful animals but they don't hurt people. I love it when I see a herd of 'em, though that doesn't happen very often. They're sneaky and shy and they do their best to stay away from people."

"That's not what I saw on TV. There's a town in Wyoming or somewhere where elk attack people and hurt them. They even smash into cars and stuff. One of them threw a man into the air with its horns and trampled over a guy that was trying to take pictures of it. They were all over town, and they were not afraid of the people at all."

"Oh, the elk 'round here aren't like the ones you saw on television. Ours are wild and they're scared of people 'cause people try to shoot 'em every fall durin' hunting season. Those you saw on the television were half tame and have lost their fear of man. It ain't the same out here. You don't have to worry 'bout 'em coming after you, 'at's fer sure."

The boy kept moving, but Gabe could tell he was expecting to get run over by a herd of rogue elk at any second. Here's another reason to dislike TV, thought Gabe.

18

To Zach's relief, they made it through the quarter mile of trees to the water without encountering any animal attacks more vicious than a pine squirrel who sounded none too happy about having his territory invaded. Though the little guy weighed less than ten ounces, he acted like he thought he was king of the woods as jumped from limb to limb in a lodge pole pine tree, chattering and scratching the tree's bark, posturing and expressing his displeasure to the trespassing humans.

When they intersected the stream it was at a spot that was shallow and fast flowing, running over round rocks that were, on the average, about the size of softballs. About fifteen to twenty feet wide, but in most places less than four inches deep, the water along the stream's banks was lined by long, coarse, grass that was left over from the previous summer, and smashed down by the weight of the winter's snow.

Gabe knew from experience that schools of feisty brook trout were hiding at the edge of that grass, but that same experience told him that it would be tough for the boy to present a hook or fly to those fish without getting snagged in the grass. He thought the best way for Zach to gain confidence in his ability to catch fish, was to move downstream until they came to a deeper, slower, stretch of water. If they could find a place where the water hit an eddy, or boulder, or log, anything to slow the water down, or move it into a deep hole, they'd find fish that were in greater numbers and more easily enticed then those that would be hiding along the edges of the fast, shallow water. The hard part was being patient enough to pass water that Gabe knew held a lot of fish, to get Zach into position where the trout would be more cooperative.

Before moving downstream in search of a deep spot, Gabe turned to Zach and said, "Okay. Now that we've found the crick, we need to find a couple of good holes to fish. I think it'd be a good idea to head downstream until we find a good spot. So how do you think we'll know how to find our way back to the truck when we're done fishin'?"

The boy looked around for a couple of seconds, and Gabe could tell that Zach had no idea how to get back to the rig now, let alone when they finished fishing, but he let him talk his way through it. "Well, we could just walk back up stream to here; then, follow the trail we made through the grass to the elk trail we used to get here."

"That's good thinking, Zach. But how are we going know if the trail through the grass is what we made or if some wild animals made it?"

"I guess we better mark this spot somehow."

"Right. How are we going to do that?"

"How about we make a little pyramid from some of the stones from the stream?"

Gabe nodded, "Not a bad idea, Zach. But can you think of a way that might be just as good, but easier?"

"Eh, I guess not. What do you think we should do?"

"Look across this grass to the tree line. You see that tree with the little yellow piece of metal nailed to it? A surveyor nailed that up there when this area was being surveyed for a timber sale. Our elk trail comes out of the trees right at the base of the tree that sign is nailed to. Why don't we use it for our marker?"

"That little piece of metal isn't very big, Grumpa. What if we walk by it without seeing it?"

"Oh, I think we'll see it alright. See, there's a tree that the wind blew down right next to it, and then there's that clump of willows between here and there. If we pay attention, it should be easy to come right back here when we're ready to leave."

Zach didn't look very convinced, but started moving.

"Zach," Gabe said, "if you were ever to get lost in the woods, say you couldn't find the truck and you didn't know which way to go, the best thing to do is to stay put. The more you wander around the harder it would be for a search crew to find you."

There was a well worn game trail that paralleled the stream, and the pair took advantage of it to make walking easier. Off the trail, the brush and grass made for slow going. It took only a few minutes of walking downstream to find the flow of the water slowing down and deepening. The bottom went from rock to mud and, at a bend in the stream, a deep hole formed. Gabe liked the looks of the spot and told Zach, "Okay, this looks like what we're lookin' for. I bet there's a bunch of hungry fish swimmin' around in there, so let's get you baited up."

Gabe preferred to use flies when fishing these streams. Zach's inexperience, however, made Gabe think that worms would work better. So, though the boy was packing a nice eight foot fly rod, the fly line loaded on the reel had about twenty-five feet of six pound test monofilament line as a leader, and terminated in a size six hook, beneath a couple of small split shot weights.

In this small stream, the boy could strip an arm's length of line off the reel and flip it into the water. The current would take the bait to the fish. After threading about an inch and a half of night crawler onto Zach's hook, Gabe demonstrated how to toss the line into the water. He then handed the rod to the boy.

"Now, just hold the line in your left hand and keep the tip of your rod up out of the water. You should be able to feel the fish add tension to the line when they pick up the worm. These brookies don't bite hard like a rainbow or red band, but if you pay attention…oh, man your line's moving I think something is after your bait!"

**21**

Zach snapped the rod back like he was trying to set the hook on a twelve pound steelhead, and the line, lead, and hook went flying by Gabe's head like they'd been shot from a slingshot. "Oh, rats," Zach said, "I felt him biting, Grumpa, but I let him get away."

"Hey, don't worry about it. There are a lot more of 'em in there just waiting for their chance at that tasty piece of worm. Here, let's bait you up again and see what happens."

When the boy's line was back in the water, Gabe continued the instruction. "Now, when you feel him bitin', let him play with the bait for a minute before you try to set the hook. These guys like to roll a worm around a couple of times before they take it into their mouths. And don't jerk too hard. You have a nice sharp hook on there, so they'll pretty much hook themselves if you just tighten up the line."

Gabe had no more than said the word than Zach's line went taut, and the boy was playing a fat, ten-inch brook trout. Things got a little confused in the ensuing action, and the line got tangled up in the grass at the edge of the stream. The fish went back into the hole while the hook stayed snagged in the grass.

"Oh, man! He got away, too. I'm no good at this," Zach said, exasperation filling his voice.

"Don't worry 'bout it, Zach. It takes a few tries to get the hang of this type of fishin'. The good news is there are plenty of hungry fish to practice on. You'll get your share, you'll see. Here, throw your line back out there and see what grabs on this time."

Within fifteen minutes, from that one hole, Zach hooked eleven fish. He managed to get five of them into the canvas tote that Gabe had given him to hang on his belt. Obviously proud of his catch, the boy kept peeking in the tote to admire the fish.

# Habits

The pair of smiling fishermen moved downstream in search of a new sweet spot. As they moved, Gabe let a fly drift ahead of them. With the sensitive tip of his nine foot fly rod, he steered the imitation leech through the swift, shallow water, keeping it as close to the grass-draped bank as he could without getting snagged. Several nice trout, including one fourteen incher—a monster in this stream—and scores of fry came out of their hiding holes to attack the black feather on a hook, that had been tied to look like a water worm. By the time they had gone down the stream seventy-five yards, Gabe had enough brook trout in his bag to provide a good mess for the smoke house.

Gabe also caught a bull trout and gently held it out for Zach to examine. "See this, Zach? This is one of the species of trout that is protected in these streams. He looks an awful lot like a brook trout, don't he? But look 'ere at his dorsal fin. See how there ain't any spots in it? Take one of those brookies outta your tote and compare 'em. See how the brookie's dorsal is spotted? 'Ats the best way to tell 'em apart. Here, let me get this fella back in the water," Gabe said as he released the small fish. "If you catch any of those just put 'em back as gentle as you can."

As they approached the next bend in the stream, they started past a clump of willows at the edge of the water. The color of the trees showed that the sap had moved up the branches of what was more a shrub than a tree. The bark was yellow, and gray pussy willows lined the slender limbs. Leaves were just waiting to explode with the help of a few warm days. From the snarl of the brown remnants of last year's growth of dense grass a mallard hen launched herself into the air in an explosion of wings, and a startling series of quacks. The racket stopped both the fishermen in their tracks and got their heart rates up for a few seconds.

When the racket was over Gabe moved slowly and cautiously into the willow. After gently moving the grass at the center of the willow aside, he smiled and called Zach over. "Take a look at this, Zach. Move in real careful. See right here, that's a mallard hen's nest. That lady we sent squawking into the air is buildin' her family right here."

Zach edged over beside his grandfather and peeked into the grass. At least a dozen tan-to-gray eggs were piled in a grass nest that was lined with feathers and down. "Wow, that's awesome. How many ducks are putting their eggs here?" Zach asked, his eyes round with excitement.

"Oh, just the one hen, more'n likely. She's setting on 'em now. It'll take 'em a total of twenty-eight days to hatch. No telling how long she's been at it already."

The look of pleasure on the boy's face turned to concern as he asked, "Will she come back to her nest now that we've disturbed her?"

"Sure. She'll be back to finish the job. We haven't done any harm, but we should get out of here and let her get back to work so the eggs don't cool too much. Let's get back to fishin'."

Zach said, "Man, that duck scared me almost to death when she came out of there. She was making a bunch of racket!"

Gabe laughed and said, "Me, too! What a neat treat."

Bag limits weren't an issue on this stream. The State of Oregon Fish and Wildlife Department had decided that the bull and red band trout populations in this creek, and in the other streams in the vicinity, needed protection from the more aggressive brook trout. In an attempt to equalize the populations, anglers were encouraged to take as many brook trout as possible. Any bull or red band trout taken were required to be released. That was fine by Gabe. He considered the brooks to be the best eating fish of the three anyway.

On a bend in the stream, a huge old ponderosa log had fallen length-ways into the creek some years earlier. Heavy runoffs, created by spring snowmelt in the years since the tree had fallen, had carved a deep channel under the log. The water slowed and eddied as the stream flowed under the log. The combination of the deeper water, and the protection the log provided from predators like blue heron, osprey, and kingfishers, resulted in a near perfect environment for trout.

As soon as Gabe spied the spot, he knew if they approached this stretch of water with enough stealth, they should be able to snake twenty or more fish from beneath the old log.

"You see the way the water boils where it goes under that ole' log, Zach? That makes the water nice and deep by washin' out a big hole in the rocks and mud under there. There's going to be some lunkers hidin' in this spot I'll wager, ah, you betcha. Come over here, I'll show you where to flip that worm to get the best shot at the big toothy varmints that are lurking in that hidey hole!"

Zach sensed the excitement in his grandfather's voice and, wanting to get a fish as big or bigger as the one that Gabe had caught earlier, he hurried to get up to the hole before his grandfather did. While he was rushing forward to get into position he stubbed his toe on a rock, tripped, and fell headlong into the stream. The fast moving current instantly swept him downstream. He bounced and slid toward the log like he was on a slide at a water park. When he was midway down the log, the current took him under it, sliding him roughly between the creek bottom and the log's slick surface.

Instead of relaxing and going with the current, Zach struggled and fought trying to keep from being swept further downstream. His struggling only caused him to be pushed further under the log where the force of the current wedged him between the log and the stream bed.

For a moment, Gabe expected to see Zach pop out in the current below the end of the log, but when he realized that his grandson was stuck, Gabe threw his rod aside, splashed into the stream, reached under the big ponderosa, and grabbed the boy's coat. Pulling him out was another story. Zach may have weighed all of a buck-thirty, but add the water-soaked clothes, and the force of the current, and it was all the old guy could do to pull the boy out from under the log.

The boy struggled to get his breathing under control. He'd filled his lungs when the shock of the cold had hit him. His grandfather pounded on his back while Zach coughed and hacked up water. Both of them were as wet as a bullfrog in a Willamette Valley rainstorm.

As Zach's coughing began to subside, and his breathing returned to normal, Gabe said, "Well, I guess that kind of took care of that, didn't it? I don't reckon the fish in this spot are gonna get tricked into biting today. We managed to stir things up pretty ..."

Gabe was in mid-sentence when Zach let loose with a wail loud enough to silence every critter within two hundred yards. "Ahhhh! I ru...ru...ruined the best fishing spot ever! I'm sorry, Grumpa. I didn't mea...mea...mean to! I just can't do anything right. That's why nobody likes me. I hate fishing! I want to go home." Zach broke down, his whole body jerking in racking sobs.

"Well," Gabe said slowly and evenly over the boy's crying, "I doubt it was the best fishin' spot ever. And yup, you ruined it...for today. But I don't think you kilt the fish or anythin'. They're kind of used to bears and such swimmin' with 'em so I don't think the two of us bothered 'em that much. We'll just have to come back and snake those slimy rascals out of here another time. Unless, of course, you're gonna hate fishin' for good. Which I hope ya don't, 'cause I kind of like you for a fishin' partner."

Zach was beginning to shake uncontrollably and whined, "I'm cold. Can we go home?"

"Yeah. You'll warm up while we're walking." Gabe gathered the rods, and the assorted gear that was strewn around the stream bank. "Come on, let's get moving."

Their hiking boots squished with each step and their pants stuck to the back of their legs.

The climb up the forested slope leading away from the creek was shaded, making it cool, and Zach continued to shake as if fevered. Gabe set as fast a pace as he thought the boy could tolerate.

The air was noticeably warmer when they got out into the clear cut where the sun could hit them. Steam rose off their shoulders as they walked. Gabe's attention was split between watching Zach for signs of panic or hypothermia and finding the shortest way back to the rig.

They were moving slowly and quietly in the loose dirt when they crested the first hill. Movement caught Gabe's eye. A herd of Rocky Mountain Elk were moving through the clearing between them and the pickup. Seventeen cows and calves, a spike and a branch antler bull were feeding on the new growth that was sprouting up in the open ground left by the logging operation. The big animals were grazing away from Gabe and Zach and were about a hundred yards distant. Gabe stopped and whispered, "Zach, look, see those elk? Aren't they beautiful?"

The boy's eyes went wide with fear; then, as he focused on the animals, awe replaced the panic. "Why is that big one with the horns so yellow?" he whispered.

The branch antler bull's body was almost a yellow color behind the dark chocolate-brown cape. The big fellow looked like he would glow in the dark. The rest of the animals were a rich tan. "That's the herd bull. I don't know why he's that color, but a lot of times bulls are like that."

About that time, the lead cow—the true leader of the herd, except in the fall when they were in the rut—apparently caught wind of Gabe and Zach. She threw her head up, looked over her shoulder, and started running. When she went into motion she gave a warning 'boing' and the whole herd followed her lead. Within seconds the air around the animals was filled with dust as they galloped for the stand of timber on the far side of the clearing. They moved across the rough steep terrain with a combination of grace and power that had to be seen to be appreciated, or even imagined. They were gone from view in an instant and all that was left was a cloud of dust that lingered in the air.

"Wow," Zach said, "Why'd they run so fast?"

"Like I told you, they're afraid of people."

"But where'd they go?"

"Oh, they have a lot of hidey spots. They're probably hunkerin' down in a good dense pine thicket right now, listening and watching to see if we're gonna try to follow them. They'll hold tight 'til they know we aren't a threat, then they'll go about their routine. That's how it is with most of the critters out here. I don't know if you want to call it instinct or what, but God has designed each type of animal with pre-disposition toward a certain way of actin'. Inside a wide parameter, their reaction to a set of conditions is fairly predictable, if you know enough about the particular critter, that is. "

"Grumpa?"

"Yeah, Zach."

The boy was kicking at a root that was sticking up out of the trail, looking down as intently as if a buried treasure was hidden under the piece of wood. "My mom says that you're smart about a lot of stuff, but you try to cover it up by the way you talk."

"Hmm. Is 'at so. How did she say I talk?"

"She says you sound like an uneducated hick. "

"Is that a bad thing, Zach?"

"I don't know. Mom just thinks you don't need to act like that. I heard her talking to Dad about it. She wonders if you're going to be a bad influence on me. She says that she doesn't want me to start to talk like someone without an education. And she really doesn't want me to learn to hunt. She says that shooting animals is barbaric."

"Well, son, I am just a country boy. I grew up kind of poor, out in the country on a little farm, and I didn't go to much school. In fact, I barely got through high school. So I guess I might just as well sound like an old redneck, seein' how that's pretty much what I am. It really ain't an act you know, and I don't see how it's such a bad thing. It's how my daddy was, and his daddy before him. And when she was a kid, I sure don't remember your ma backing away from the trough when it was full of wild meat I'd shot. I don't recall that my less than perfect handling of the English language bothered her neither. Not at least, before she took up with your dad the doctor. What does your dad say about all this, anyway?"

"He usually just laughs and starts talking about something else. He says you're harmless, except for your religious fanaticism. That worries him."

"Ha," Gabe laughed with obvious mirth. "So, I'm an uneducated wild man *and* a religious fanatic. I'm surprised that your parents sent you out here and risked having your young mind corrupted by someone as dangerous a reprobate as me. "

"Grumpa," Zach said, looking worried, "I don't think I was supposed to tell you any of that. Please promise that you won't tell them that I told you. Anyway, they sent me out here to get me out of the house while they worked on their marriage."

"What'd you mean, 'worked on their marriage'?"

"I don't think I'm supposed to tell you about that either. In fact, I'm not supposed to even know. But, they're talking about getting a divorce. I heard mom tell one of her friends that if she and Dad can't get some things ironed out this week, she's going to move out."

The news knocked the wind out of Gabe's lungs like a punch to the stomach. He knew that his daughter didn't have the best marriage and he had long agonized over her apathy toward Christianity. But, he hadn't realized that the relationship had come to the brink of divorce. Not knowing what to say about this revelation, he started walking toward the pickup and simply said, "Come on, Zach, let's get to the truck and get the heat on before we both catch p-namonia."

"Grumpa? Who's that up by the truck?" Zach asked when the rig came into view.

"Where? I don't see anybody."

"I don't see him anymore either. He was all dressed in black; a tall man," Zach answered. "Didn't you see him? He was wearing a black baseball cap and one those suits like Air Force pilots wear, you know a jumpsuit. He was right there alongside the pickup, looking at us."

"Did you hit your head when you fell back there, Zach? There's not very apt to be anybody besides us out here in these woods. Do you see any rigs here besides ours? Anyway, if there was someone else here he'd likely

30

have spooked that herd of elk before we had a chance to get a look at 'em."

"Well, I saw him," the boy answered.

When they got to the rig, Gabe made a careful search of the dusty ground around the Toyota. There wasn't a single man track around the rig other than the ones that he and Zach had made when they had arrived.

# 4

They both stripped off their wet coats, boots, and shirts and climbed into the truck in their T-shirts, jeans, and socks. Gabe had the pickup's heater cranked up to full-furnace-blast as they meandered out the spider web of logging roads toward the highway, eating their lunch as they rode. For a long while neither of them said anything, and, since Zach had finally quit shivering, Gabe expected him to fall asleep before they went much further. It startled him when Zach quietly said, "That's my fault, too."

"What're you talking about, Zach. What's your fault?"

The boy left the question unanswered for so long that Gabe had begun to think that the boy had fallen asleep after all. But after about a mile of silence Gabe realized that instead of sleeping, the poor kid was quietly crying.

"Hey, buddy, what's wrong? You can talk to me about whatever's buggin' you. I won't tell your ma. I understand that sometimes a guy just has to unload." Gabe left it at that. He suspected that the boy needed to talk and he thought that he'd be more apt to open up if he wasn't pushed. They drove on. The only sounds were from the gravel coming off the tires and the hum of the pickup's engine.

After a couple of miles, Zach started talking so quietly that Gabe had to struggle to hear him. "Dad was a really good basketball player. He even had a scholarship to the University of Oregon. He wants me to play, too. He says with my height I'd be a star. But I'm no good at sports, and I don't want to play that stupid game, anyway. I don't really like playing any kind of ball. Dad says I have to, but Mom always says that I should be able to do what I want to do. Sometimes they yell about it. They yell about a lot of stuff."

"Zach, Zach. You know if your folks are havin' trouble it doesn't mean that it's your fault. If they want to argue they're gonna find something to argue about. I'd bet that you are just one of a bunch of convenient subjects."

Zach didn't respond so Gabe said, "If you don't like ball, what do you like?"

Zach remained silent for several minutes, and Gabe had decided that the discussion was over, but then the boy blurted, "You'll laugh if I tell you."

"No I won't. I'd like to hear about it. What hobby would you choose if you could do anythin' you wanted?"

More silence, then, "Well, I like to read, and I like video games, but my favorite thing is music."

"That's not weird. Lots of people like music, especially young people. What'd you like? Rock and roll is out of style isn't it? You like that rap stuff?"

"Rock and roll or even rap would be more acceptable to Dad than what I actually like. I mean it's not only him, everyone thinks I'm strange. I like Classical music. Stuff like Beethoven and Bach and Mozart. I guess that... like...that makes me a sissy, doesn't it?"

"If that's what you enjoy, what's wrong with it?"

"Dad says that it's old lady music. He says that guys don't listen to stuff like that. They play sports and listen to loud stuff."

"There must be some of your friends who like the classical style. Don't cha ever get together with them and listen to your music together?"

"I told you. I don't have any friends. And if I told anyone that I wanted to play piano, or listen to violin music, instead of playing basketball, they'd laugh at me even more than they already do."

"Have you told your dad how you feel?"

"I've tried, but he just tells me that I'll grow out of this stage. He says that in a couple of years, after I discover girls, I'll want to be a ball player. But according to him, by that time it'll be too late. Everybody else will have a bunch of experience and skill, and I won't be able to ever catch up. He doesn't believe me when I tell him that I don't care."

"Why don't you like sports?"

"I told you, I'm no good at them."

"Okay. But you don't have to be Lebron James or Brett Favre or Ichiro to enjoy playing a little ball, you know. I wasn't the greatest athlete when I was your age, but I still loved to play."

"Did everyone call you things like twinkle toes, and clumsy-dumsy? Did they laugh at you every time you shot the ball over the backboard or dribbled it off of your toe?"

Gabe drove, tapping the steering wheel with both hands. It was his turn to retreat into silence. After about a mile he finally said, "No. Nobody made fun of me much.

But I did shoot the ball over the backboard and more than once I bounced the ball off my shoe—that happens when you wear size thirteen when you're in seventh grade. But, nobody made fun of me 'cause they knew that their nose would soon be well acquainted with my right elbow if they did. I know now that it wasn't right, but back then my philosophy was that violence was the answer."

"How'd you keep from getting beat up all the time? Or kicked out of school? If I started punching guys, first I'd get pounded to dog doo. Then I'd get kicked out of school for fighting. Then, Mom would kill me when I got home."

"Your mom would probably kill *me* if she knew I was tellin' you this, but I'm old, so I guess dying wouldn't be so bad. Anyway, I figured out a very important fight strategy when I was just a tadpole. I noticed that guys would always strut and yell for a while before anyone ever threw a punch. So, whenever I thought a fight was gonna erupt, I'd skip that ritual. I'd just grab, or punch, or elbow the other guy as quick as I could.

"Most times it only takes one good shot to the nose to take the fight out of an average guy.

"My favorite thing was to grab 'em by the shirt with my left hand and jerk them forward while my elbow went out to meet their face. Punchin' guys with your fist seems to work good in the movies and on TV, but I learned real quick that it hurt my knuckles too much. Elbows are all kinds of tough.

"As for getting kicked out a school, things were different when I was your age. Teachers and principals expected a few fights. They'd pretty much turn the other way—unless someone was in danger of gettin' seriously hurt—and most of the brawls ended too fast for anyone to suffer anythin' worse than a bloody nose or black eye.

In fact, I think there were times when the teachers wanted me to wallop some kid that was giving 'em grief."

"Didn't you get in trouble at home? Mom would ground me until my eighteenth birthday if I ever got in a fight at school."

"Well...like I said, things were different back then. Most the time, word never reached my parents. And if it did, the main questions were about who started the fight and who won. If the answers were them, and me, in that order everythin' was fine. And your great-grandparents never heard of grounding. Sound thumpin's were more the order of business."

"Grumpa, could you teach me to fight?"

"Well, I could teach you a few tricks, but things *are* different now than they were back in my day. Like you said, if you get in a good old fashioned punchin' match, you'll likely end up in juvvy hall or somethin' and then your ma would turn me and you into dog biscuits.

"Anyway, wouldn't it be better to try to make some friends so ya don't hav'ta fight?"

Zach sighed, "I already told you, nobody wants to be my friend. I'm an uncoordinated nerd. If you don't want to teach me to fight maybe you could teach me how to make people like me."

"That would be a huge challenge for me," Gabe admitted. "And I don't mean because of you. See, I never managed to learn how to make friends either. To be honest, I never really cared. I've always been a bit of a loner. Havin' close friends is more your grandmother's thing. I never had any friends when I was a kid. Since I've been grown up, any friends that I've had have been by default."

"What's default mean?"

"It means that they're my friends only 'cause they're your nanny's friends first. Maybe she could give us both some advice on how to make friends with people.

"Or, hey, maybe you could work out some kind of a deal with your dad. Tell him you'll go out for the basketball team next year if he'll let you get some piano lessons now. He *was* a fantastic ball player ya know. I remember watchin' some of his games. Man, oh man, he could *shoot* the ball. You must have gotten some of those genes, and you sure are tall enough for it. Has he ever tried to teach you to play?"

Zach's voice sounded like he was on the verge of tears again when he answered, "Nah, doctors don't have time to play with their kids. He's always at work or in some kind of a meeting. When I do see him, he just wants to know how good my grades are and stuff like that. And nothing is ever good enough to suit him. Just because he was athletic and smart doesn't mean that I ever will be. But, if he's so smart, why hasn't he figured that out?"

Gabe looked across at Zach and said, "Hey, I don't think you're givin' your dad enough credit here. It looks like he's a pretty good dad to me."

Zach just shrugged and said, "Yeah, whatever."

# 5

Zach's visit with his grandparents ended before he was ready to leave. While he was at their how he felt wanted, at times, even needed.

He and Gabe had cut a couple of cords of firewood and Zach had even run the chainsaw a little bit, which was cool. Getting acquainted with the splitting maul was not quite as enjoyable or exciting.

They also built some bird houses that were suitable for chickadees and nuthatches, from some plans that Zach found online.

He had a great time with both of his grandparents and wished there was some way to extend his stay. But he refused to enter into any more serious talks, even though Gabe tried to draw him out on a couple of oc-casions. Trying to get him to talk to Meg about tech-niques of developing interpersonal relationships—aka, friendship making—was like pushing rope. Zach was afraid that he had already revealed too much of himself to his grandfather and was afraid that if anymore of his personal thoughts were brought into the open he would no longer be accepted or loved.

When the week was up and they took the boy to the airport, Meg and Gabe stood hand in hand watching their grandson inch along in the line leading to the security gate. From a distance, he looked like any other young teenage boy trying to look cool and mature. He was decked out in the most up to date clothes that started with the designer sneakers on his feet and ended with the high-dollar sunglasses that were riding on top of his Arizona Diamondback's baseball cap.

As they watched him move toward the metal detector they were both silently praying for him. Their prayers were less for his physical safety on the flight than for his spiritual safety when the flight was over.

They were shocked when he was ordered out of line by the security guard, and stunned when the guard examined Zach with the hand-held wand and then led him to a detention room. Gabe and Meg looked at each other feeling helpless. Not only were they unable to assist Zach, they couldn't even find out what was going on.

"Oh, man," Gabe moaned. "I told that knucklehead to put that knife in his suitcase and not try to carry it on board the plane."

"What knife?" Meg asked.

"I gave him an old folding Buck Stockman. Just a little pocket knife for cleanin' fish and whittling. But a nice knife, and now he's gonna lose it because he didn't pay attention to what I told him."

"I can't believe you gave him a knife in the first place. Honestly, you know Becky—"

"I didn't think Becky would even have to know about the knife. And I *sure* didn't think he'd try to carry it on the plane. But whatever, he's lost it now. And it was a nice knife."

"You don't suppose he's going to be arrested, do you?"

"Nah. They'll just confiscate it and send him on his way."

About that time, the security guard let Zach back out of the booth that he'd pulled him into, and sent him down the corridor. As the boy disappeared into the mysterious bowels of the post 9/11 airport, Gabe turned to his wife of thirty-five years and said, "Let's go eat. He's gonna be fine."

At their favorite restaurant, Gabe said, "Meg, do you have any ideas about what we can do to stop Zach from feelin' like such a misfit?"

Meg riffled the ends of the packets of sweetener that were stacked in their chrome nest while she formulated her answer. "You and I both know that the only way those things are going to get fixed is if God gets a hold of that boy. All we can do is pray, and, when we're blessed with an opportunity, show him the love of God through our hands and feet. I've heard you say it at least a hundred times in the Bible Studies you lead, 'You are not the Holy Spirit and you cannot change a heart.' So why all of a sudden do you think things are different when it involves our grandson?"

"Yeah, yeah. I know. But I just want to fix things so much. It's frustratin'. If he'd just throw himself on God, life wouldn't be easy, but at least it would be doable. Doesn't he seem a little too young to have already built so many barriers to allowin' God, or anyone else, close to his heart?"

She was still messing with the little pink packets when she replied, "I don't know. He hasn't had the best example from his parents. Dave is an absentee dad; his work schedule doesn't allow him any time at home, let alone any opportunity to get involved with Zach. And Becky, well I hate to say it of our daughter, but it looks to me like the size of her house and the brand of her vehicle, not to mention the label on her clothes, is more important to her than spending time being a mom."

The waitress put their food on the table. She was a young gal who had waited on them on several times before. And she understood when her customers wanted to chat with her and when they wanted swift, unobtrusive, service. She had arranged the plates and quietly made her exit.

Meg and Gabe linked hands across the table and Gabe prayed, "Lord, we wanna thank you for this meal. And we wanna say 'thanks' for letting Zach catch his flight. Now, Lord, please keep him safe as he flies, but more, Lord, help his mom and dad be the parents they need to be. Please, Lord, pull all three of 'em close to you. Help us know how to help. We'd like to rush in and try and fix the whole mess, but we know that you're the only one that can do that. So, we're just turnin' the whole mess over to you. Thank you, Lord for your mercy. Amen."

After taking a couple of bites Gabe put down his fork—an oddity since he loved to eat—and quietly said, "I carry a huge load of guilt over Beck's spiritual shallowness. I can't help but agonize over havin' sacrificed my family on the altar of my job, my duties at the church and worse, fishin'. If I'd been a better example maybe her life wouldn't be such a mess and Zach would have more of a chance."

"Come on, Gabe. Aren't you taking too much on yourself? I don't remember you being such a rotten father. And how 'bout me takin' a little of the blame? I *am*

Becky's mother for goodness sakes. Besides, you know as well as I that everyone makes their own choices. Sure, parents and everybody play a part, but in the end don't we all have to decide our own paths?"

"Yeah, sure, but I still wish that I'd been a better father. Becky just doesn't seem to be able to grasp the importance of the spiritual side of life and I can't help but think that I'm to blame for that. But I don't see any of this bein' your fault."

"Gabe, you did the best job that you knew how to do."

"What I haven't told you is..." Gabe hesitated while he rolled small bite of his dinner around in his mouth, "Zach told me that his mom and dad fight about what's good for him right in front of him. It's tearin' the poor kid apart."

Meg had tears in her eyes when she responded, "I don't think Dave and Becky have ever been very happy together. I honestly don't know how they stay married. Dave's always at work and Becky is as independent as a hog on ice. But, you have to admit that they have tried to give Zach everything he needs or wants."

Gabe shook his head. "Yeah, everythin' but the love and acceptance that he needs way more than all that stuff. Dave wants Zach to be an athlete like he was. And I can't really blame him. Those days of being the big man on campus were probably the best days of Dave's life. But that's not what Zach wants. I guess Dave just doesn't believe it, or at least he won't accept it. He enjoyed those things so much that he's sure that everyone should.

"And to make matters worse, Becky uses those differences as a wedge between father and son. It seems like she thinks that keepin' Zach at odds with his dad will keep him close to her."

Meg and Gabe pushed their food around on their plates. Finally, Meg said, "Well, God is still in control. We'll just have to spend more time in prayer, worry less, and leave the whole mess to him."

Gabe looked across the restaurant and out the window while he dropped the next bomb. "Zach told me that he heard Beck talking about leavin' Dave. Ain't that a fine thing for a kid to overhear? In fact I guess that the reason Becky and Dave wanted him to stay with us this past week was to give them an opportunity to work at resolvin' some of their differences. If they aren't successful they're threatenin' to throw in the towel."

Meg's shoulders slumped and she sat staring at the hardly touched meal on her plate. "Well, I guess it shouldn't come as a surprise, but hearing it makes me sick to my stomach."

Gabe nodded and said, "That's for sure.

"And as long as I'm gettin' things out in the open, there's one other thing, too."

"Oh, Gabe, what else?"

Gabe hesitated for several seconds before answering quietly, "There's somethin' wrong in Zach's head."

"Now that is ridiculous," Meg huffed. "That boy is sharper than a whip and you know it!"

"Oh, I know he's smart, but he sees things. Hallucinates."

"What do ya mean? What kind of things does he see?"

"Well, the day we went fishin' he saw two people who weren't there, one guy in our yard before we left, and another out in the woods. It was ... creepy."

"Maybe he really did see someone. You know your eyes aren't as good as they used to be."

"If he saw someone in our yard, the dogs didn't see him. You know as well as I do those hounds don't let

**44**

anybody on the place without raisin' hob. And you also know how likely it is that someone would get by them without being noticed. And if there was someone out in the woods, he sure didn't leave any tracks. My eyes haven't gotten so bad that I can't see man tracks in a dusty road."

When the waitress interrupted the conversation by bringing them the check, Gabe remembered that she had shown them a picture of her twins the last time they were in and asked, "How're your boys?"

His interest bought a smile from the harried looking young mother, "They're good. But you know boys, they keep me busy. They'll be five next week."

"I bet they *do* keep you jumpin'."

"You know they do!"

A few minutes later they were walking to their car and Meg said, "I don't know how you do that."

"Do what?" Gabe responded.

"Start personal conversations with complete strangers. Isn't that a little awkward?"

"Not really. Just seems natural to me. And that girl isn't a stranger; she's waited on us half-a-dozen times. People like you to remember details of their lives. Besides, what's it cost to offer a little concern? I'll bet there are plenty of folks that give her grief. I like to try to even it out."

"I know," Meg said climbing into the car. "I just have a hard time striking up conversations like that."

"I try to remember what's at stake. I don't know of a single soul – and I've known some pretty nasty folks – that I'd want to see go to hell. Besides, if a person dies without the Lord, because I was too frightened or intimidated to speak up, am I gonna have ta answer for them endin' up in hell?"

"Do you really think it works like that?"

"Ezekiel chapter 33 sure does read like that."

"I don't understand how heaven is going to be paradise if God is holding us accountable for things like that?"

"I dunno. Maybe I take things to literally. But God obviously wants those of us that have a relationship with him to share that love with other folks. That's all I'm tryin' to do. I'm sorry if I embarrass you with it."

"You don't embarrass me. You just continue to surprise me time to time, even after thirty-five years."

"Well, I hope that that's a good thing, 'cause I'd like to take a shot a surprisin' ya for about thirty-five more years."

"Then how come you're always telling me that you're ready for God to take you home? You know, all that talk about hearing the angels tuning up their trumpets."

"I'm ready all right. Wouldn't mind havin' God pull me outa this game right now. But if I gotta hang around on this earth, I wanna do it with you."

Meg shook her head. "Thanks, I think.

"But, you know, I really think that this deal with Zach seein' stuff that isn't there has you half spooked."

# 6

When Gabe and Meg arrived home the phone was ringing.

"I'm glad he's home safely," Meg said. "Yeah, we saw him get pulled aside, but we couldn't tell what was going on. You mean to tell me that the metal detector picked up the little bit of aluminum foil in the wipes he had in his pocket for cleaning his sunglasses? I didn't know those machines were that sensitive, even if he did have half a dozen of those packets. Well I'm glad that's all it was and he made his flight okay."

When Meg turned the phone off, Gabe asked, "Well, what'd she have to say?"

"Oh, you know how Beck is. Everything is great. Thanks for keeping Zach. That sort of thing. She never really says anything about what is really going on."

"Yeah, I know. But I was hoping that she might have given you some clue as to whether she and Dave were still together."

"I hope she'd tell us if they split up. But I don't know. It'd probably be two months before she told us. Then it'd be, 'Oh, by the way, Dave and I are divorced. How's the weather up there?' It's just so frustrating!"

"I know. She takes after my family. My parents never talked about the problems in their lives. They thought it was a sign of weakness to admit that you weren't completely in control. Everyone else is allowed to—even expected to—have problems, but not a Green."

"Well, that may be how the Greens think, but it's still ridiculous. Everybody has problems. What good does it do to pretend you don't? And where does that leave room for God?"

"I know, I know, you're right. But it's hard to break those thoughts and conceptions that you've carried with you from childhood. You know that. You have a couple of your own."

"Yes, I do. And I've passed a few of them along to our kids, too. But this whole deal with Becky has me about stretched to the breaking point. And now it looks like this stoicism thing has been passed down to Zach."

"Yeah, I can see it shaping him. When we were out fishin' I almost had to drag anything that had to do with what he was feelin' out of him; and, he's still young. He did let his guard down a few times and told me some the things that are buggin' him. But, if he keeps practicin' for a couple more years you won't be be able to get anythin' important out of 'im."

Meg was scurrying around like a squirrel that feels fall in the air, straightening this and cleaning that. She didn't make eye contact with Gabe when she said, "Well, you should know. It's only been in the past couple of years that the Lord has softened you up enough so that you're able to show any emotion other than anger. Or talk about anything important to you, other than self-criticism."

"Meg, why don't ya tell me what ya really think?" Gabe said sarcastically. "Yeah, I know I haven't been good at talkin' about, or showin', how I feel. But I am changin'. In fact, sometimes I think my stinkin' tear ducts have busted. I catch myself cryin' over the stupidest cockeyed stuff! Next thing ya know I'll be huggin' people at church. And crying over television commercials."

Meg stopped fluttering and went and put her hand on Gabe's shoulder. "I know you're changing. And I understand that you learned stoicism from your parents, who learned it from their parents. And Becky learned it from you and she's passing it on to Zach. But maybe, now that you're changing, just maybe you can set a different example and the pattern can be stopped before it gets another generation up the family tree—at least on this branch. But if you're gonna start hugging folks at church, just make sure that it isn't only the pretty young women!"

"Huh? Ya noticed that, did ya? And here I thought I was bein' so sneaky. Seriously, that whole thing about 'God visiting the sins of the fathers upon the children to the third and fourth generation,' I think that it's talkin' about the consequences of the sins that we hang on to and accidently train our kids to fall into. And I'd really, really, like for this one to stop with me. But I'm not sure how to make that happen.

"But, on the positive side, I'm pickled tink to know that the knife wasn't the cause of the airport pat-down, and that it wasn't confiscated. Now if Becky just doesn't catch wind of it, he should have that knife for life."

"You and that stupid knife! Man, you'd think it was some mega-treasure."

"You just don't understand, Meg. Heck, I well remember my father givin' me my first knife. It was nowhere near as nice a knife as the one I gave Zach. And I was

**49**

a far sight younger than Zach is; in fact, I think I was the ripe old age of five. Anyway, I was so stinkin' excited to get it you wouldn't believe it. I did manage to cut myself pretty good, though. I'm still carryin' the scar to prove it," Gabe pointed to a white line bisecting his index finger. Then I lost the durn thing within a year, but I'll never forget the way that knife made me feel."

"What do you mean? How'd it make you feel?"

Gabe rubbed at the bald spot on the back of his head before he answered. "I don't really know how to explain it. There was a sense of pride in knowin' that I was being trusted with somethin' potentially dangerous. But it was more than that. It seemed that there were so many things that I was gonna be able to do with that knife. I know it sounds weird, but it just made me feel grown up somehow."

"Is that why you gave Zach the knife? So he'd feel grown up?"

"I guess. Mostly I just wanted to try to give him somethin' positive to think about. He seemed so depressed."

"Gabe, I'm not going to pretend to know whether or not giving Zach the knife was a good idea or a bad one, so let's not argue about that anymore. And I don't have a clue whether or not Becky and Dave are going to be able to salvage their marriage. But what I do know is that I have an overwhelming feeling that we should be praying for that family like we have never prayed before. In fact, I'm going to do something that I have never felt led to do before. I'm going to set aside tomorrow, and every Tuesday until God tells me otherwise, for fasting and praying."

The announcement left Gabe a little stunned. For the thirty-five years they'd been married he'd watched Meg be the perfect, submissive wife when it came to spiritual matters. She had always followed his lead with a solid

**50**

and steady faith. Now she was stepping out of character and taking the lead. And what surprised him even more was that he was glad to see it. And he was going to follow her lead for a change. "Ya know, I think that's a great idea. Let's do it!"

"I don't expect you to fast just because I'm going to. I'll still cook your dinner and everything, but I think God is asking me to do this thing."

"No, I wanna do this together. I think it's a great idea." Gabe patted his round stomach and said, "Maybe it'll even help me lose some table muscle."

Their first Tuesday fast was an experience, and really not much like either of them had expected. Sure, there were some issues with hunger, especially in the morning, yet they were not nearly as intense as they had anticipated. They spent meal times praying together instead of preparing meals and eating, but aside from that they went about their normal routines.

Both of them were surprised on Wednesday morning when they awoke with no more appetite than on any other day. Talking about it, they agreed that they didn't feel anything magical about the experience, but they also concurred that they had found it easier to focus on the petitions that they were presenting to God while not being distracted by food. So they committed to repeat the exercise the next week.

# 7

It was so odd for the phone to ring before eight in the morning in the Green house that Meg and Gabe sat at the breakfast bar and looked at each other through the first two rings. Gabe finally got up and answered, "'Ello?

"Beck, slow down. I'm not understandin' anything you're sayin'!"

"Daddy, it's Zach. The police have him!"

"What'd d'ya mean the police have 'im?"

"He got arrested at school!"

"Whoa, whoa, whoa. Arrested for what for cryin' out loud?"

"I'm not sure. I'm headed to the school right now to try to sort this whole mess out. It has to all be some kind of gigantic misunderstanding. The principal said something about a knife. I don't know what they're talking about. There is no way that Zach would have a knife at school! He doesn't even own a knife. And I am quite confident that he would not resort to violence under any circumstances. Anyway, I just called to ask you and Ma to be praying that this whole thing gets sorted out. I need to disconnect now; I'm almost at the school."

The phone went dead, and Gabe was left holding it to his ear, gazing out the window while he tried to make sense out of what he'd just heard. Suddenly he realized that Meg had him by the arm and was shaking him saying, "Gabe, what *is* going on? Did Dave get arrested?"

When Gabe turned and faced her he was white as a sheet. "No, *Dave* didn't get arrested. Apparently, *Zach* did."

"What? That's insane! Why would Zach get arrested?"

"I dunno. I didn't get many details. Becky just said that the school had called her and said that the police were holdin' Zach. It has somethin' to do with a knife. That's all I know. Becky was callin' from her cell phone to ask us to pray."

"Oh, Gabe, that stupid knife that you gave to Zach has got him into trouble just like I knew it would. Do you suppose he was showing it off to some kids at school and everyone overreacted? You know how paranoid everyone is about weapons at school these days."

"Yeah, I know. But I can't imagine the police bein' brought in just because a kid showed his friends a knife. I hope Becky calls back pretty quick with some more details. Meanwhile, I think we better spend some time prayin'."

As they knelt in front of the couch in their living room and clasped hands, Meg said, "I don't know what's going on, or what else is going to come from this, but the bright spot right now is that Becky asked us to pray."

"That's a positive thing alright. I hope it's still positive when she finds out where Zach got the knife," Gabe muttered.

Three hours later, Gabe had mown the lawn and raked about a quarter of an acre of pine needles while he waited for more news about Zach. While Gabe was occupying himself outdoors, Meg was inside cleaning and doing laundry. They had both gone through the cycle of peace, frustration, anger, and distress at least twice before the phone rang again. This time Meg answered, "Hello. Hi, Becky. Oh. Emmhmm. You're kidding. No, that most certainly does not sound like Zach. Okay. Sure. Just let us know as soon as you can. Thanks. Love you. Bye."

As soon as Meg put the phone down, Gabe started the questioning. "Well, what's goin'on?"

"Things are still a little confused. It seems that some kids were picking on Zach, and Zach stood up to them. According to a teacher's aide who witnessed the conflict, Zach was holding his own against one of the bullies when a second one joined in. That's when Zach supposedly brought out the knife. So now the police and the school administrators are trying to hash it all out and reach a satisfactory solution. Becky is going to update us as soon as she knows more. Right now the police are holding Zach at the school."

Gabe started pacing again. "Now that's just about absurd. Do they think he was gonna hurt people with that little toad sticker. Why would they get that excited about a playground scuffle; and what about Dave? Where's he in all this?"

"Becky didn't say anything about Dave, and in all the turmoil I didn't think to ask. And she didn't say anything about where the knife came from. But you know, as soon as she has time to think about it for a while, she's going to clatter to where Zach got that knife. Then there's going to be hob to pay.

"You didn't encourage him to get physical with the bullies at school, did you, Gabe? I mean, I know that

**55**

you had the reputation for settling things in the Clint Eastwood style when you were a kid. Please tell me that you didn't suggest that it was a good idea."

"Well, I wouldn't call it encouragement exactly. Zach did ask about how I handled bein' picked on when I was a kid, and I answered honestly. I told him that I never got picked on much, because them that was doin' the pickin' usually got a fat lip or bloody nose for their trouble. But I never told him that he should start settling things with violence. And I certainly did not give him any indication that I thought knives were a good way to take care of things."

"Man, Gabe, are you saying that you didn't make it sound like you approved of violence? You know how much Zach wants to be like you. All that fighting you did as a kid wasn't the best idea, even back in the day, and it certainly isn't going to help anything now. In fact, you'd never have made it out of junior high if you were in school in this century!"

"I dunno. I might have given some hint that a guy has to stand up for himself...and I think you do. I don't care what century you're livin' in, ya can't just let folks walk all over you. But that's a far cry from encouragin' him to get in a knife fight. But, if those kids were gangin' up on him, it seems to me that he had a right to defend himself."

"See, you do think that things can be straightened out with a punch or a kick! And I know good and well that those feelings show through when you're telling Zach about your childhood."

"What? So I guess you think that it'd be better if a couple of big goons beat the feathers offen the boy, eh?"

"I didn't say that, Gabe. But there has to be some way for him to protect himself without resorting to violence.

I mean, couldn't he tell a teacher or something? Or, maybe just try to reason with the other boys?"

"Meg, it's been a long time since I was a boy, but not so long that I don't know that tattlin' 'ill just get ya a worser beatin' later. And reasonin'? Reasonin' don't get ya nowhere with a bully. A bully only recognizes one thing: pain. And they don't like it. Hurt a bully a little and they'll leave *you* alone and go pick on someone who won't stand up to 'em. But our pansy society doesn't understand that, so we let the bullies run everythin' 'cause anybody who tries to stand up to 'em is the one what gets in trouble. The whole thing's enough to make me puke."

"Not everyone sees it in such vivid black and white as you do, Gabe. And do you think that Jesus would have gone around punching people in the nose; even if they were bullies?"

"Well, I don't know, but when I read the gospels I see a Jesus who sure didn't let the Pharisees and Sadducees run rough shod over ever'one else. Think about it, isn't that true? And old King David was a man after God's own heart, but ya don't have ta read too far to see that he was a pretty stinkin' violent man. The way I see it, sometimes circumstances require that a person defend themselves—and their friends and family."

"We aren't ever going to agree on this issue, Gabe. But, you have to admit that it looks like Zach has gotten himself in a bunch of trouble by resorting to violence. I just hope that Becky and Dave can get it sorted out without there being too many long term consequences."

"I'm not gonna admit to anything about what happened until I talk to the boy his self. Things like this get so twisted up, it's almost impossible to sort out the facts. Did Becky tell ya anything about when she might be able to call us back with some more information?"

"I'm sure she'll call as soon as she has more to tell us. Man, I wish I lived closer to those kids. I grateful for being able to talk on the phone but it would be so much better to be able to put a huggin' on both Becky and Zach."

Gabe got up from his stool and paced a circle around the living room before coming back to Meg to say, "I think we maybe otta get down there as soon as we can get a flight. I know it'll cost a fortune to get tickets on short notice, but don't you think we need to be down there?"

"I don't know, Gabe," Meg answered. "With the problems the kids are having with their marriage, I not sure they need us adding to the turmoil by being underfoot."

"Yeah, I suppose 'at's true. But maybe we could offer to take Zach for the rest of the school year, that'd give this whole fight business time to blow over."

"The school year is about over. In fact, I think there are only four or five weeks before school is out for summer."

"Well, how 'bout we offer to let him stay here for the summer? He could help me with the yard work and stuff, and we could do some fishin'. You could give him some help with his social skills. And maybe if we got 'im plugged in with Pastor Ben and the church's youth program Zach would gain a little bit of self confidence through God reliance."

"That would suit me fine, but I think we better let this issue at the school play itself out before we make any offers, don't you?"

"Yeah, I suppose, but, man, I wanna *do* somethin' *now*. But I still can't imagine Zach doing anythin' violent. When he was up here, he was afraid of his own shadow. There is no way that kid would start a fight."

# 8

Years of watching the six o'clock news and reading the newspaper had given Becky the perception that the wheels of justice moved incredibly slowly. Now she was learning firsthand that if you involve a couple of children, a school ground, and a knife, the process sped up to warp speed. School District policy, as mandated by Arizona State law, required the immediate expulsion of any student using a weapon on school property. Therefore, Zach was immediately expelled. Being re-enrolled would require that she or Dave request a hearing before the school board and convincing that board that Zach was not a threat.

The principal explained that the decision of whether or not criminal charges were filed against Zach was up to the District Attorney's office.

The assistant to the D.A. advised Becky that Zach would be released to her custody but would be required to appear for questioning in the morning. The young lawyer explained that whether or not charges were brought against Zach would depend on what was determined through examination of the evidence, interviewing the three boys that were involved, and talking to any witnesses that could be located.

Becky couldn't keep from staring at the young man's shoes. They were scuffed and dusty, and she was certain that they hadn't seen any polish since he took them off the department store shelve. She found it nearly impossible to concentrate. How can the system expect anyone to take this process seriously, she thought, when the people they send to talk to you are so blatantly disrespectful of proper decorum?

It was only with the greatest effort that she was able to listen long enough to hear that, since Zach was a juvenile, bail would not be required. He stressed again that Zach was being released to her custody with the understanding that she would be held accountable if he did not appear in court as scheduled.

Of course they were seeing her as the one responsible; certainly no one else was going to step forward. The boy's father was always too busy playing the almighty doctor to involve himself in such trivial matters. And the boy could not be expected to be accountable; he was too young. Why, he was hardly able to take care of his own personal hygiene. Although, she thought, he did do better than this bohemian from the District Attorney's office.

Zach spent the trip home staring out the passenger side window. With the exception of an occasional loud dramatic sigh, Becky drove without comment.

As they pulled up in front of the garage and waited for the automatic door to go up, Becky turned to the Zach and asked, "What in the world were you thinking, young man. Are you no better than a common thug, fighting and brandishing knives. When are you going to realize that you are a better person than those despicable children that behave like animals? What are my friends going to think when they hear about this? It's a complete embarrassment. Have you no sense of proper behavior?"

Zach sat through the ranting without any outward sign of acknowledgment. When his mother stopped her railing, he opened the door and climbed out of the car. His posture communicated nothing but indifference.

This is great, Zach thought. The school and the cops act like I just shot the principal or something. Here I am catching all the blame when the whole deal would have been avoided if those jerks would just have left me alone. And my good old mom; leave it to her to care more about her precious reputation than about what's going to happen to me. But at least Mom showed up; that's a lot better than my hero of a father whom couldn't even be bothered enough to come and get me. If I wasn't such a worthless misfit, I bet none of this would be happening.

His father was in the kitchen preparing a salad when Zach entered the house. "Well, young man, what is all this nonsense about an altercation at school? How can you be competitive enough to get in a fight and yet not have enough spirit to compete in sports?"

Zach did not acknowledge the question or glance in his father's direction; instead, he headed toward the stairs that would take him to the sanctuary of his room. Dave barked, "Hey, don't you walk away from me! You get back here and answer me. I will not tolerate this disrespect!"

Zach stopped, cocked his head to the side, and looked at his father from beneath his brow. But he said nothing, communicating by locking eyes with his angry father for the eternity of twenty seconds before continuing toward his room.

The display left Dave furious. He was not accustomed to insubordination either at work or at home. And especially not from this son who had, until this moment, always maintained an attitude of submission. He hardly recognized the boy that had just tried to stare him down. Until today, Zach had never so much as flirted with any type of rebellion. Oh, he occasionally refused to comply with Dave's suggestions about getting involved in sports, but that was primarily a byproduct of Becky's objections to the 'crass atmosphere surrounding athletics.' The personality that he had just glimpsed in his son's eyes was not mere insubordination. It was defiant. That was unnerving. Dave did not like it even a little.

When Becky came into the house, Dave vented his anger on her. "What is going on? You leave a message at my office saying that our son was involved in an altercation at school, then you bring the boy home and he acts as if he would just as soon kill me as look at me. What kind of poison are you pouring into him now?"

"Oh, so it's my fault is it? You're the one who is always encouraging him to be more 'of a man' and not waste his time with sissy music and books. So he finally takes your advice and acts the part of some athlete with a Neanderthal mentality and then you say that it's me that's poisoning him. That's just what I've come to expect from you! Anything positive is a result of your influence. Anything the least negative is my fault.

"The real question is not what I have been doing with Zach, but where you are when we need you. Would it have been such a major inconvenience to you to interrupt you precious routine in order to react to a family crisis?"

"I don't see you complaining about my 'routine' when it comes time for you to spend the money I earn. You seem more than content to throw away every dollar, plus ten percent more, on maintaining your frivolous lifestyle. Do you know a doctor that has a practice profitable enough to provide the income necessary to supply the spending habits to which you have become accustomed, that doesn't spend a lot of time in his office? It requires a lot of sacrifices. And believe me, I don't like it anymore than you do."

"The only sacrifices I have witnessed you making are the sacrifices of our son and our marriage. But, apparently, they are of so little consequence to you that would not recognize them as sacrifice."

Zach's reappearance, a full duffle bag style suitcase in each hand, halted the verbal battle taking place between his parents. "You two can stop yelling at each other now. You both get what you want. I'm leaving," he declared in an unemotional monotone.

Becky was the first to recover from the announcement enough to respond with, "Where do you think you're going? You are in so much trouble that you won't be going anywhere for a very long time! So you can just march right back to your room and put that stuff away." She angled to get between the young man and the door as she spoke.

Zach reached out with the duffle bag that he was carrying in his right hand to push her out of his way. The action infuriated Becky, and she launched herself at her son. To her utter surprise and astonishment, Zach leveraged her away from him with one of the bags.

She grabbed the duffle and shouted, "How dare you use violence with me! Stop this insanity this instant!"

As he had with his father a short time ago, Zach just looked at his mother with an unemotional stare, released his grip on the bag, and continued for the door leaving her holding the bag. "Dave, do something!" Becky shouted. "Do not let him out the door!"

Dave yanked Zach toward him and pushed him on the couch and ordered; "Now you sit there! I have had enough of these insolent theatrics. I don't know what has gotten into you, but this behavior will end, NOW! Do you understand?"

Becky moved to an armchair across the room from the couch on which Zach had been placed. Dave sat, too.

The room grew quiet as the three glared at each other. As the seconds turned into minutes, the trio felt more and more like strangers forced to sit together, each waiting for the other to begin a dialogue.

Becky broke the silence: "Zach, what is going on? Are you using drugs?"

Zach's stoicism melted and tears started to stream down his face as he responded, "What is going on? I don't know what's going on! All I know is that I am sick of living. I'm sick of living in a family where nobody loves me, and I'm sick of living in a world where everyone expects me to be someone that I can never be. Why don't you just leave me alone? And, no mother, I am not using drugs! I'll leave that for you."

Zach's emotional outburst left Becky hurt and confused, and David embarrassed. Then, in the first unified act in a very long time, they both spoke at once, "Zach, we love you."

"Yeah right! You say you do, but if you loved me you wouldn't always be trying to make me into someone I'm not. And you wouldn't fight every time we're together. And you wouldn't be talking about getting a divorce. Maybe if I'm gone you won't be reminded all the time of what a disappointment I am, and you will quit feeling like this family is so bad that you have to put an end to it."

Zach stood up and grabbed his bags and had made it about one step toward the door when Dave was up and had his arms wrapped around his son. "Zach, this is ridiculous."

As soon as Dave stopped speaking Becky started. "Zach, your father is right. We love you more than anything. So, please sit down and let's discuss what happened at school today that has you so agitated."

"I don't want to sit down. And nothing happened at school today that doesn't happen every day. There isn't a day goes by that some big important jock, or some other popular kid, doesn't start harassing a kid that the teachers think is a nerd. The teachers don't care, just as long as it doesn't get violent. Well today it got violent. And guess what, big surprise, it isn't the big old football player who knocked my books out of my hands that is in trouble, it's me."

David had released Zach and backed up a step before he asked, "So what happened? This guy knocked the books out of your hands, then what?"

"This big bully was right in my face glaring at me, daring me to say something and hoping I'd start crying. So I bent over like I was going to pick up my stuff, but, instead, I came up really fast and swung my elbow into his jaw. He went down, flopping like fish. Everything got really quiet for a minute, and I thought I was home free, but then a couple of his buddies couldn't leave it alone and ran over to help.

"They said they were going to knock me down and kick the stuffing out of me. I knew that they would because I've seen it happen before. So I took out the knife to show them that I didn't feel like getting beat up. That's when all the kids that were watching started going crazy and yelling and screaming. It was alright for the nerd to get pounded, but nobody wanted the cool kids to get hurt. Anyway, the teachers heard the racket and came running to see what was going on and I ended up in the principal's office being grilled like I'd shot the president."

David looked down at his toes. "If this pack of punks ganged up on other kids and beat them up prior to this, how come they're still in school?"

Zach sighed and shook his head before answering. "Dad, nobody tells. If someone asks you how you got bruised or whatever, you know you have to say that you wiped out on your skateboard or crashed your bike. If you tell the truth it'll only get you whooped ten times as bad."

"I can't believe this stuff is going on in this school. I spend a lot of money to get you in the best school available and this is what I get for it?"

Zach threw his hands in the air and shouted, "See, this is exactly what I expected. Dad, it isn't about your money or the school you chose. In fact, it isn't about you at all.

"Just let me go."

Becky got up and moved between Zach and the door and asked in a low voice, "Where are you going to go? You can't just leave home. Where do you think you would live? What are you planning on eating? Be realistic, Zach, you can't just leave."

"I'll hitch a ride back to Oregon. Grumpa and Nanny will take care of me."

Dave exploded when he heard Zach's plan. "Oh, I get it now. *Grumpa* is behind this whole mess, isn't he? He's filled your head full of that 'stand your ground' baloney and has probably even given you fighting lessons. I bet that's where you got the knife isn't it? I don't understand how that old coot talks all that religious mumbo jumbo one minute and then promotes a life of violence the next. I've had it with that old nut!"

"David!" shouted Becky, "you're talking about my father. I will not tolerate your belittling him."

"Becky, you know as well as I that your father is not a stable man."

"I know nothing of the kind! And I will not stand for you talking that way about him, especially in front of Zach."

It wasn't in front of Zach, though. He had gone to his room and closed the door while they were arguing. He could hear their heated tones, though the well insulated walls of the expensive home distorted most of the words beyond recognition. That was typical, he thought; his parents arguing over what was best for him while neither of them cared enough about him to notice that he had left the room. His mom would notice soon and come in dramatic fashion to see if he was alright. She would flutter about like a mad hen for a minute or two and not have a clue of how to connect with him. In her mind, it really was all about her.

He lay in his room with the blinds on the windows closed, staring at the strange shadow the light fixture made on the ceiling in the dim light. He put his ear buds in and began listening to one of his favorite Mozart CDs, beginning with Piano Concerto Number 4 in E-flat, waiting for his mother to make her theatrical entrance, but wishing that there was someone who understood him well enough to tell him what he should do, and how to do it. He wished that there was someone who didn't *think* they knew what was best. Someone who *knew* what was right. He was so confused. Being in trouble at school had certainly not been his intent when he got into the fight. He was simply tired of being harassed.

Right on cue, the door to Zach's room flew open and the light came on. He rolled onto his side with his face to the wall as his mother burst in. "Zach, sit up. Take those things out of your ears!" She turned his music off and sat down on his bed beside him.

"We need to talk. I've decided that as soon as this misunderstanding with the police is straightened out, we're going to Oregon. We'll spend the summer with your grandparents and by fall we'll know what to do about where to enroll you in school. There are plenty of good schools in the area; there is no reason that you should have to be associating with that bunch of bar- barians. So it's settled. You don't need to go running off. As usual, Mother will fix everything. You just stay put and let me take care of it."

Zach didn't turn over even when he heard the light switch snap off and the door click close. He stayed on his bed as the dim light in his room grew darker with eve- ning. He listened to his parents go through another heat- ed exchange and then he heard the purr of his father's Mercedes as it pulled out of the driveway. As the house went quiet, Zach got up and turned the music back on. His mind began to slow and he found himself wondering what it would be like to be able to communicate with God like his grandfather thought he could. If he could talk to the being that was in charge of everything he'd ask why his world was such a mess.

He hadn't thought much about God since he was in fourth grade. His science teacher was talking about the big bang theory of how the universe came into existence. Zach had raised his hand and said that he thought that God had created everything. The teacher had made fun of him and said that only uneducated and ignorant fools believed in creation. Everyone in the class laughed.

Zach didn't think that his grandparents were stupid or ignorant, so he silently asked God to strike the teacher dead. But nothing had happened. So Zach figured that if God, if there *even* was a God, didn't care enough about his own reputation to intervene, then there wasn't much sense in trying to defend him. He hadn't really prayed much before that, and never since. As the music of two and a half centuries earlier soothed his nerves, he fell asleep.

He dreamed of being at his grandparents'. He was standing on their wrap-around deck on the east side of their house. On the emerald green lawn two men faced off like gunslingers in the old west. One of the men was the shiny guy that Zach had seen out the window when he was at his grandparents', the other was the man that had been near the pickup when Zach and his grandfather were walking back from their accidental swim in the stream.

When he realized that Zach was watching, the man in black began firing words from his mouth like explosive projectiles. The shiny man was deflecting the force of the words with a strange silver sword.

The blade of the sword was broad and sharp, and there was a large cross piece above the weapon's handle. Each of the men kept glancing at Zach as if they expected him to assist them. But he didn't know how to help. He didn't even know which of them he *should* help. Neither of these adversaries seemed able to gain advantage over the other, though the one with the sword appeared only to be moving defensively. The word-flinger tried every angle and varied the velocity and frequency of the small bombs that were leaping from his tongue; none, however, made it past the sword.

# 9

Zach awoke and was relieved to realize that he was in his room sleeping not at his grandparents' home witnessing a battle. He glanced at the green glow coming from the alarm clock and was surprised that it was only a few minutes after midnight. He felt like he had been watching the battle for hours.

He was drenched with sweat and he was thirsty. He rolled off his bed, removed his ear buds, and intended to go down the hallway to the bathroom to get a drink of water. When he got to the bedroom door it wouldn't budge. The knob turned, but something was preventing the door from opening. He rattled it a few times thinking the latch had stuck, but, when it still refused to open, he began to feel a slight sense of panic.

He jerked and pulled on the door knob. By bracing his feet and pulling, he could feel the door give a little. It had opened about an inch when the knob suddenly came off, and Zach went flying across the room and crashed onto the floor between his bed and dresser.

"Mom, Dad! What's going on? I need out of my room." His shouts echoed through the house. Even though the door opened into the room, in his fear he backed up and hit the door with his shoulder, then again, harder. All he got for his effort was a sore shoulder and deeper fright.

There was no way that his parents could sleep through the racket he was making he thought. He shouted again, louder, "Hey, Mom, Dad! Wake up! This isn't funny, you guys. Let me out of here!"

When there still was no response, Zach turned to the window. His room was on the second story, but the roof of the porch was an easy step right outside. He thought he could crawl out on the roof and find a way to the ground.

Zach was relieved when the window opened and he was able to get outside. Though the night air was far from cool, it felt better than the stale air-conditioned air in his room, and he felt the growing feelings of claustrophobia taper off.

The clay roof tiles were slick and hard to walk on. He cautiously made his way to the edge of the roof and looked down. It was further to the ground than he expected. A light from inside the main floor of the house illuminated a rectangular patch on the lawn that didn't look like it would provide a very soft landing. He picked his way around the house looking for a better way to the ground.

Even under the circumstances, being on the roof provided an unusual and interesting view of the neighborhood. Each of the other eight homes that shared the cul-de-sac was dark, but the roadway was lit by street lights. Everything looked familiar, yet strange. It was like seeing one of those old photos of Phoenix with all the old cars from fifty years ago; things looked familiar, but not quite right.

Motion in the shadows of the nearest yard caught Zach's attention. The hair on the back of his neck stood on end and an ice cold tremor ran down his spine in spite of the heat coming off the roof tiles.

As he studied the area where he had seen the movement, the man in the black jumpsuit stepped away from the shadows of the neighbor's house and onto the sidewalk. The man didn't appear to be in a hurry but just casually walked away. Before he turned the corner, he stopped to look back and tipped his head up in order to look out from under the bill of his black baseball cap. He looked directly into Zach's eyes. Over the distance of more than half a football field and in lighting that was too dim to be able to see into anyone's eyes, Zach could, and he felt pierced to the soul. Their eyes locked and the man grinned as the blood in Zach's veins turned to ice.

Finally, the man broke the spell and turned and walked around the corner. Just before he went out of sight, the man flipped something into the air with his thumb, caught the object in his right hand, and slipped it into his pocket.

Terrified, Zach searched for a way down from the roof.

His parents had planted a small Australian Bottle tree just off the northeast corner of the house when they had first moved in to their new home. The tree had grown fast, and it had soon become obvious that it had been placed too close to the house. Though it should have been removed, they enjoyed the shade and the tree had been spared.

Zach looked around the neighborhood and down the cul-de-sac but didn't see the man in black. He decided to try to climb down.

He got on his belly and slid to the edge of the roof; then, he bent at the waist and felt for a large limb, which he had noticed was growing parallel to the fascia board, with his feet. He located the branch and scooted further down the roof tiles until most of his weight was on the limb. He pushed down with his legs a couple of this and once he felt satisfied that it was going to support his weight he started climbing down. A slight creak was the only warning before the branch snapped and he landed in a heap in the yard. A big "woof" of air escaped his lungs on impact, and the clatter of the broken wood set the neighborhood dogs to barking. Pieces of limbs, twigs, and leaves covered the ground around him.

Zach struggled to get some oxygen back into his lungs and felt the terror of not being able to breathe squeeze his chest harder. His diaphragm finally pulled in some air and he began to calm down.

He made a quick inventory of his arms and legs and was relieved to find that everything was intact. The combination of youth and adrenalin allowed him to struggle up and head for the front door.

It didn't surprise Zach when he found that the door was locked. What he had not expected though was the spot above the window, which normally held the spare key, to be empty. Running his fingers back and forth across the rough wood at the top of the shutter produced nothing but dust. He stepped back to the door and pushed the door bell. He could hear the chimes, but, once they stopped, everything was quiet. He pressed the button again, stepped over to the window, and peeked in as the annoying tune was repeated. Again, there was no response.

He moved around the house looking in windows and rattling doors hoping to find one that was unlocked.

Each room that he could see into was empty and every potential opening was secure.

Where was his mother? He couldn't remember the last time she had gone somewhere with his father. He'd heard only one car leave and she never walked anywhere. Confused, he stood in the yard beside the debris and tried to decide what to do next.

He was looking up at the quarter moon when a stray thought about how much brighter the moon had looked in Central Oregon fleeted through his mind.

As he turned to go back and renew the search for the hidden key, the blinding beam of a flashlight hit him full in the eyes.

The roar in his ears was nearly deafening as a fear-induced spike in blood pressure gripped him. It was *almost* deafening, but the orders to, "Get on the ground and put your hands behind your head!" roared through the foggy consciousness and into his comprehension.

Zach went down like he'd been shot.

While his body was complying with the orders, Zach's mind was struggling to catch up. He was startled and confused, wondering why someone was shouting at him while he was in his own back yard. And why was he being roughed up? None of this was making sense.

He couldn't be arrested for the second time in one day.

With handcuffs securing his hands behind his back, he was jerked off his stomach and onto his knees. The flashlight was back in his eyes and the staccato questioning began. "You have any weapons we should know about? What's your name, boy? What'd ya think your doin' tryin' to break inta this house? Ya got any I.D. on you?"

The questions were coming so fast that Zach didn't know how his interrogators expected him to be able to answer. But, as his fright began to subside, insolence began to surface. His parents had systematically, if un-intentionally, instilled in him the idea that the police were an incompetent group of cavemen. This was done through routine comments about the lack of intel-ligence, diligence, and education of any officers they happened to see. Now, the effect of the accumulation of those comments began to come out when Zach said, "Excuse me, but I don't think we have any donuts in the house. This house right here. This house in which I just happen to live." The inflection and tone was a perfect echo of his mom, and the posture was a reflection of his dad.

Officer Evans was neither intimidated nor impressed by Zach's performance, but he was more than a little irritated by the boy's lack of respect. The officer's voice was filled with a large dose of sarcasm of its own when he softly stated, "To the neighbor that called 911 you looked like an intruder. When my partner arrived, you looked a lot like a burglar. To me, right now, you look like a chump that's going to take a ride down to the station. Unless, that is, you lose the snot-nose punk attitude and start explaining to me what's goin' on here."

When he finished the speech, the officer stood shining his flashlight in Zach's eyes, waiting for a response. The boy held his ground for all of fifteen seconds, which was about thirteen seconds longer than Todd had expected.

First, tears started welling up in his eyes, and then the boy was trying to talk through some chest racking sobs. While Zach was struggling to regain his composure and try to explain what was going on, Officer Evans' part-ner approached them after completing an inspection of the house.

"Everything's locked up tight on the ground floor, but it looks like there's an upstairs window in the back that's open," the second officer said. "I'd think our suspect here was attempting to break out, not in, if I hadn't seen him sneaking around trying all the doors and windows."

"What do you say, boy?" Todd asked. "Were you trying to get into or out of this house?"

"Kind of both," Zach managed to squeak out in a little boy voice.

"What'd you mean by both?" Todd asked.

"Well," Zach said, "somehow the door got stuck closed and I couldn't get out of my bedroom. I couldn't get my parent's attention so I came out my bedroom window. Once I got down on the ground, I discovered the outside doors were all locked and the key wasn't in its normal hiding spot. I tried all the doors and windows but everything is locked."

Officer Evans had shifted the beam of the flashlight away from Zach's eyes as the boy talked. "So, how long do you think it will be before your parents get home to verify this baloney?"

"I think my mom is home but I can't get her to answer me."

Both officers were heading to the front door, pulling Zach along with them when Todd asked the next question. "You think your mom's okay and everything? I mean, is she like sick or anything?"

"I don't know. My dad and I and mom had sort of a fight this evening. I went to my room and I heard them yelling at each other. Then, Dad drove away, and I haven't heard or seen Mom since."

"You're sure she didn't go with your Dad?" Todd inquired as they reached the front door.

"If she did it would be the first time in a long time. They don't go anywhere together, and I don't think that would change when they are mad at each other."

Ringing the doorbell brought no response, so Officer Evans removed his Billy Club his from his belt while he asked, "What's your mom's name, son?"

"Becky Mertz," Zach answered.

Rapping on the door with the nightstick, the officer hollered, "Becky! Becky Mertz!" Pausing for about fifteen seconds, he tried again, pounding louder. Again, no one came to the door or answered.

"Are you sure that your ma is in there? What's your name again?"

"My name is Zach Mertz. And, no, I'm not positive that Mom is in the house, but I don't know where else she'd be. I can see her car through the garage window."

"Buck," Todd said to his partner, "get a hold of dispatch and find out any history on this address."

Pounding on the back door was no more successful than the attempts at the front. The officers met on the side of the house. "I talked to dispatch and got some interesting information. It seems that our good buddy, Zach here, was already arrested once today. For assault."

"What?" Todd said as he turned to Zach, "You've had a busy day haven't ya? Would you care to fill us in on that little detail?"

"That was a complete misunderstanding at school. I was just trying to protect myself."

"Oh, yeah, it's always a misunderstanding, isn't that right, Buck?"

"Always," Buck agreed, "but how 'bout you tell us how this misunderstanding came about?"

Zach's voice was going back to the pronounced whine when he responded, "I'll be glad to give you all the details about that if you would just get into the house and see if my mom is okay. I'm really worried about her. Please, can't you break in or something?"

"You know, Zach," Todd answered shifting back into lecture mode, "we don't get to break into houses anytime we want. We are required to have a search warrant, and there isn't anything to justify that."

"Well, my mom is in trouble in there," Zach replied. "I know something's wrong, or she'd answer the door!"

Todd ignored the boy's whining and turned to his partner and asked, "Buck, did you get any history on this address that would collaborate the boy's fears about his mom bein' in danger?"

"Yeah. We responded to an attempted suicide at this address about three years ago. It seems that Ms. Mertz tried to off herself with a bottle of sleeping pills. Her husband came home and found her in time for the EMTs to get her to the hospital and save her."

Officer Evans turned to Zach, "You remember anything about that, son?"

Zach was staring at the ground and answered in a mumble, "I remember that Mom had to go into the hospital for a while when I was about ten. I went and stayed with my grandparents in Oregon. They just told me that she was sick. I didn't know that she had tried to kill herself."

Todd turned to Buck and said, "Do you think that we are justified in goin' in?"

Buck replied, "Man, I'm just not sure. Her car's here, there's a history, and she has reason to be upset, normally I'd think we need to go in. The problem is, the folks that live in this neighborhood are not shy about complaining that we overstep our authority and infringe on their rights. Maybe we should get Sarge on the radio and see what he thinks."

"That's a good plan. He makes the big bucks. Let him to make the decision and suffer the fallout."

On the radio, Buck nodded his head and said, "Okay, boss."

Once off he said, "He wants us in the house ten minutes ago. And he's on the way over. Apparently Zach's dad is a big shot doctor who plays golf with the mayor. We better get 'er done!"

"Great," Buck said with obvious disgust. "See if you can pick the lock on the back door. It looks like a lot cheaper lock than the one on the front. I don't think we want to be responsible for kicking down the door of a friend of the mayor's." Turning to the boy he asked, "So Zach, once we're inside, where do you think your mom is most likely to be?"

"I think she'll be in her bedroom. It's at the rear of the house. If you go through the mud room and then turn right at the hall way, her room is the first room on your left."

Buck had the door open in under a minute.

"You better stay here with the kid until some backup arrives," Todd told Buck. "I gonna go in and see what I can find."

"Hurry please. I'm sure that Mom is in there."

Sticking his head in the door, Todd yelled, "Police, Ms. Mertz. Are you in here?" When there was no answer, he tried again, louder. "Ms. Mertz, this is Officer Evans of the Phoenix Police Department. Are you here?" Then, "We're comin' in!"

Todd headed for the room that Zach indicated was Ms. Mertz's bedroom. He made his way past a laundry room that was as neat and tidy as the living room of most homes, and then he stopped at the doorway that led into Zach's mom's bedroom. The bed was neatly made and the adjoining bathroom was empty and clean.

The big officer continued through house, moving more like a cat than the bull that he physically resembled. He heard the jets stirring the water in a tub or Jacuzzi as soon as he got to the door of the master bedroom. He shouted, "Ms. Mertz, you in here?" as he headed in.

80

Again there was no answer and he was in the bathroom before he had time to shout again.

A petite dark-haired woman was in the big tub. Her head was resting on the headrest while the water roiled around her. She looked peaceful, a little too peaceful. Officer Evans crossed the room in two steps and immediately checked for a pulse in the woman's neck. He found a heartbeat, but it was faint. She did not appear to be breathing.

Looking over at the vanity counter top he spotted a pill bottle, cap off, lying on its side. He quickly keyed the radio on his shoulder and called for an ambulance, explaining to the dispatcher what he had found. Todd had just gotten the woman out of the tub and onto the floor to begin CPR when his sergeant burst into the room. The two of them tried to resuscitate her for the ten minutes that seemed like six hours until the ambulance crew arrived and took over.

While the paramedics were checking Ms. Mertz's vitals and preparing to load her on the gurney, the sergeant was giving Todd orders to get pictures of everything. On his way out to get his camera from the patrol car, Todd saw Zach and Buck sitting on a marble bench beside a water feature in the center of the circular driveway. Both of them looked up when they heard him approaching. He gave them a quick synopsis of what was going on.

The lights from the numerous emergency response vehicles parked in the loop were producing enough light for them to see each other clearly. Zach's eyes were wet with tears and filled with panic and for just a second Officer Evans's professional detachment began to erode.

"Your mom's still alive, Zach," the big cop said. "The paramedics will take her to the emergency room where the doctors will pump her stomach, and whatever else needs to be done. Have you got somebody to call and ask to take you to the hospital?"

"I'll try my Dad's cell, if I'm allowed to go in the house to use the phone."

"Okay. Buck, why don't you take him inside? Maybe his dad'll answer if he sees a call coming in from his own number. I've already tried to reach him but he may have been afraid to pick up when the display showed 'unknown'.

"Is there anybody else that you need to let know about what's going on? Do you have any uncles or aunts or anything in the area?" he asked Zach before continuing on his mission to retrieve the camera.

"No. Dad doesn't have any family and Mom's is in Oregon."

"How about friends?" Buck asked. "Have you got any friends or maybe a pastor that we can try to reach if you don't get an answer from your dad? Somebody needs to be with you in the waiting room while they work on your mother."

"I don't know. Can I see Mom?"

"Buck, after he makes the phone call, why don't you take Zach over and wait by the ambulance," Todd answered. "Maybe he can say something to her as they load her."

After taking a bunch of photos in the master, bathroom, Todd met his sergeant, in the hallway. "What's it looking like Sarge? They think she's going to be alright?"

"I dunno. Depends on how much of that crap's in her system and how long it's *been* in her. They got her breathing and her heart's beating but they won't know how much organ damage has been inflicted until they can get her in the hospital and start running tests."

"What'd you want us to do about the kid if we can't raise his dad? He doesn't seem to have anybody to call."

"You an' Buck can take 'im up to the hospital. We should be able to reach the dad before too long; if we can't find him, we'll have to call in Children's Services. They deal with this crap day in and day out, they can handle him."

"You got it boss. And hey, you don't think there could be any foul play here do you? I mean it looks like a cut and dried suicide attempt, but the boy said he heard his parents having a loud argument earlier this evening."

"Oh, I'm pretty sure that it was self-inflicted. There is no sign of any struggle. We'll still do the full investigation and we'll want to have a chat with the husband when we find him, though but I doubt we find much beyond a jumbo batch of stupidity mixed with a sizeable douse of dispair. The only really odd thing that I've found is that two rooms upstairs had their doors tied together with a length of rope. Make sure you get good photos of that before you go into those rooms."

The conversation of the two policemen was interrupted by the paramedics wheeling the gurney carrying Becky Mertz down the hallway. They stepped into the laundry room to give the crew room to get their patient past. Her eyes were closed and there were wires and tubes hooked up all over her. Todd was a little surprised when he found himself wishing that Zach didn't have to see his mother like this. He'd been doing this job for almost twelve years and his hide had gotten pretty thick, but for some reason this boy was getting under his skin. He just seemed so *lost*; but didn't they all? Why was this one hitting him in the heart?

They followed the gurney down the hall and out onto the porch. Todd was watching Zach when the boy looked up and saw his mother and all the medical paraphernalia that the EMTs had on her. A renewed look of panic washed across the boy's face, and then just as quickly, that expression was replaced by resolve. This wasn't the boy's first rodeo, thought the officer.

"Come on, Buck," Todd said to his partner, "Sarge wants us to take Zach and follow the bus to the hospital." They put the boy in the back seat of the patrol car and waited for the ambulance to head out. The EMT's didn't mess around once they had their patient on board. They took off with their lights filling the night sky with red, amber, and white light. The trio in the patrol car spent the twenty minute ride to the hospital in silence.

When the police car pulled into the 'no parking' zone in front of the hospital's emergency entrance, the officers got out and Buck opened the rear door of the car. Zach sat staring through the wire mesh and out the windshield. "Let's go Zach," Buck encouraged. "We'll get inside and see what the doctors have to say."

"What if they say that my mom's not going to make it? She's not is she?"

"Come on," Todd said, "you don't know any of that. Let's go inside, maybe you'll get some good news."

The boy climbed out, but his expression made it obvious that he was not buying into the cop's optimism. It was hard to believe that this was the same kid that was giving them so much grief not much more than an hour ago.

The officers led him to the reception desk and explained the situation to the receptionist. She suggested that they take a seat in the waiting area while she checked on whether or not Zach could go back and see his mother.

After about a twenty minute wait, Officer Evans got antsy and said, "I'm going back and see what the hang up is."

He came back a few minutes later and said, "She's in real serious condition. The doctors are working on her so you can't go back there right now. We might as well settle in, it looks like we're in for the long haul."

Buck groaned and stretched his legs out in front of him, trying to find a comfortable position for his six-foot four-inch frame in a chair built for people that were five-nine. He and Todd had come on duty at three in the afternoon. Their twelve hour shift was supposed to be over in about half an hour. But it was pretty obvious that this was going to be an over-time shift and staying awake was going to be tough in this waiting area. Maybe that's why the furniture was designed to be so uncomfortable, he thought, to keep dopes like me awake. Where was the person from Children's Services?

Zach sat with a blank look on his face, his eyes glued to a TV that was hung on the wall. The program was one of those wildlife documentaries that the public broadcasting stations are always airing. The sound was muted, so it was difficult to understand the point the producers were making from the footage of a herd of elephants that were pushing over trees to get at the upper leaves. The boy wasn't really processing what he was watching anyway. His eyes were merely attracted to the movement on the screen while his thoughts were focusing on his mother.

# 10

Dr. David Mertz burst through the doors of the emergency area of Saint Joseph's Hospital. He took in the people in the waiting area in a glance. His eyes hesitated on his son for only a moment before he moved to the reception area and addressed the woman behind the desk. "I'm Dr. Mertz, and I understand that my wife, Becky Mertz, has been brought in by ambulance. I need to see her immediately."

The receptionist politely and professionally responded, "Dr. Mertz, please step over into the waiting area— I believe your son is over there with those two police officers—while I relay the fact that you are here to the attending physicians."

David cleared his throat and his voice was lower and louder when he continued. "Look, I think you misunderstood. I'm a doctor and my wife has been admitted to your facility. I demand to be allowed to see her. Now!"

The hospital's security guard heard the angry tone and moved to intervene, assessing the situation as he walked. When he was about twenty feet from David, he said, "Sir is there a problem here?"

"Oh, there's a problem alright. And it's going to be all yours if you attempt to interfere with me. My wife was brought in by ambulance earlier this evening and I *will* be allowed in to see her!"

The receptionist tried to regain control of the situation by saying, "Yes, I understand that your wife is here, Dr. Mertz. And as I stated, if you will please step over to the waiting area, I will gladly find out whether or not the attending physicians wish to grant you access."

Due to the rage that was rampant in him, David was unaware that the security guard had moved within arm's length. When he began to berate the receptionist and demand to speak with her supervisor the guard didn't have to move far to respond. The rent-a-cop wasn't particularly young or strong, but he had just enough training to think that he knew how to handle a middle-aged doctor. What he failed to take into consideration was that this particular middle-aged doctor was, by genetic blessing, incredibly athletic *and* made it a point to keep himself in good physical condition through a regular workout regimen.

The guard planned to persuade David to calm down by twisting his arm behind his back just enough to produce some discomfort. Unfortunately for both parties, as soon David felt the other man grab his arm, he pivoted on his left foot, leaned in, and whipped his right elbow against the side of the other man's head. It wasn't a move he had practiced, and it wouldn't have gotten him many points in a serious brawl, but it was certainly effective. The instant that the elbow connected, the security guard went to the floor like a pole-axed steer.

The two cops who were waiting with Zach had been content to watch the drama until the blow was administered. Before the security guard had time to recover the pair was on their feet shouting, "Stop! Police! Get on the floor."

Todd and Buck charged David. When he looked up after hearing their commands and saw them coming at him with their weapons out of their holsters, he hit the floor beside the security guard as quickly as the other man had fallen from the impact from his elbow.

The onlookers, including the receptionist, sat in silence and watched this insanity play out as if they were viewing an episode of *Cops*.

Twenty feet from the out of control doctor, Buck planted himself in a classic stoop-shouldered stance, with his Glock locked on David's chest in a double-handled grip. Todd had moved a little closer, and off to one side, and had his Taser pointed dead center on the doctor.

Anyone taking even a fraction of second to consider his position would have lain still and hoped for the best. David didn't take that fraction of a second. Instead, he allowed impulse to overcome reason, and he reached for the security guard's weapon that was inches from his hand. His fingers had no more than closed on the butt of the pistol than he was convulsing from a short surge of electricity coming through the fine wires that had been spit from Todd's Taser.

David's surging adrenalin had him convinced that he was invincible prior to his getting hit by the charge of electricity, but, afterward, he was more than happy to comply when the officers ordered him to lie face down and put his hands behind his back.

Once David was cuffed, he looked over at Zach. It was the only indication that he knew the boy was there since the glance he had thrown his son when he first entered the emergency room. His expression appeared more rooted in irritation then apology. Zach instantly broke eye contact and looked at the floor. The boy's expression was pure embarrassment.

Todd told Zach, "Stay put. I'll be back in a few minutes," before he and Buck led David out to the patrol car. They put him in the back seat and called in a request for another vehicle to come and take him to the detention center.

"I insist that you release me this instant," the doctor told the officers. "My wife is being treated in there, and I have every right to see her. So unless you two buffoons are eager to incur the wrath of my attorney, you will let me go."

Neither Todd nor Buck so much as acknowledged the ranting. Being ignored only incited David more and he continued his tirade, "This is unacceptable. I am not an ordinary criminal. I am an honest taxpaying citizen and I demand to be treated with respect. That guard attacked me. I had every right to defend myself. And now I have every right to go in and see my wife."

"I'm going to go in and make sure the boy is okay," Todd told Buck. "Why don't you stay out here with 'the mouth' until our back-up arrives? Then, you and whoever shows up can take the good doctor to lockup where I'm sure he will be treated with all the respect that he deserves. I'm going to stay here with the boy until this thing can get sorted out."

Back inside, Todd approached the receptionist, who looked no worse for wear for having witnessed a little police work in action, and asked, "Is the security officer going to be okay?"

"Yeah, I think the only lasting injury is to his pride. Thanks, by the way, for riding to the rescue, officer."

"Glad to be of assistance. Is there any chance that the boy might be allowed to go back and see his mother?"

"Give me a sec and I'll check her status...Ms. Mertz is still in coma. The doctors are doing everything they can for her, but her chances of recovery apparently do not look good. It'd probably not be a good idea for the boy to see her in her present condition."

Todd straightened his stance, squared his shoulders, and looked over Tina's shoulder—he'd made a mental note of her name tag while she was on the phone. The clock on the wall behind her read five o'clock. He should have been off duty, he thought. In fact, he should be home getting ready to sit down to some kind of heart-attack inducing breakfast. Instead, here he was trying to figure out what to tell a kid about his mother, whose life was teetering in some invisible balance between this life and whatever was next, and how to explain that his father was probably going to spend some time getting really well acquainted with folks that he would refuse to treat if they showed up at his office.

It didn't cheer him up when Buck arrived with another officer in tow. He liked the news that Buck brought even less.

"Hey, Todd," Buck said as he fell back into a waiting room chair. "The plan is for you to stay here with the boy. I'm leaving our unit out in the lot, and Deke here is taking me back to the precinct. Sarge doesn't see any reason for both of us to suck up all this overtime, so he's sending me home. Sorry, buddy, but you're in it for the duration. Here are the keys."

"Where is Children's Services?" Todd moaned.

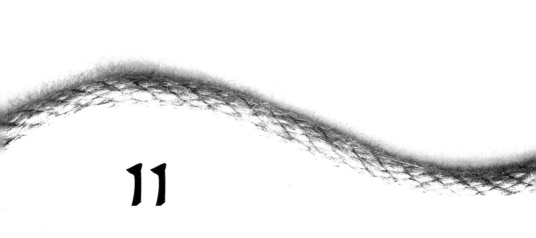

# 11

Gabe began his day as the first tendrils of dawn were stretching their fingers through the emerald needles of the Central Oregon Ponderosa. Years of getting his feet on the floor at three-thirty in the morning had forged a habit in his heart that he probably couldn't have broken if he wanted; which, so far, he hadn't. He didn't get up at three-thirty anymore, but he felt a compulsion to be up before the sun. During the winter that was easy; but in the summer it took some doing. The old golden orb didn't waste much time getting going in May and June. Not that those first rays in the morning held much heat at forty-five hundred feet elevation, but by noon the temperature would be in the seventies.

It was going to be a perfect day for putzing around in the yard.

So, just like the proverbial rooster, Gabe was up and at the breakfast bar studying his Bible as the sun began to illuminate the yard around the house. Two Labrador retrievers, one yellow and one black, were sitting outside the sliding door watching Gabe's every move. They were sure that every time Gabe made even the slightest fidget it meant he was going to come out and feed them. At ninety pounds each, the 'boys', as Meg and Gabe called them, could afford to miss a meal or two. But they certainly didn't want to.

The passage of scripture that Gabe was studying was in the New Testament book of James. He was wondering why in the world he had chosen this book for his current series of lessons in his Sunday morning Bible class. Everyone who regularly attended the class knew that they were saved by grace not by works and here the half-brother of Jesus, under the inspiration of the Holy Spirit, was making it abundantly clear that unless works accompanied faith, the belief wasn't true faith and wasn't going to save anybody at all. "Oh boy," he thought out loud, "I am six foot tall in a hole that's eight feet deep. And the water is rising fast. How am I going teach this without gettin' everyone riled up?"

His confused musings were interrupted by the shrill ring of the telephone. He glanced at the clock and saw that it wasn't quite five-thirty as he scrambled to pick it up before the ringing awakened Meg. When the phone rang at this hour it was never good news. He managed to grab the handset halfway into the second ring. "'Ello?" he barked, adrenaline coursing through his veins.

The initial silence made him think that someone had dialed a wrong number. Then, "Grumpa?" came across the line.

"Zach, that you? What's wrong, son?" Gabe said as he realized that it was his grandson on the other end of the line.

"Well, I think that I need you to come down here," Zach answered.

**94**

"Okay," Gabe replied trying to sound calm, "why do I need to come to Phoenix? Is everyone alright?"

There was a long pause, which left Gabe on the verge of hyperventilating, and then Zach finally said, "I'm at the emergency room of the hospital. They're working on Mom."

"What do you mean they're workin' on your mom? Was she in an accident?"

"I don't know for sure what happened. The police came and found her unconscious in her bedroom. Then, the ambulance brought her to the hospital. They won't let me see her, so I'm not sure what's going on."

"Okay," Gabe said as he tried to balance his panic with his desire to protect Zach from those same emotions, "how about you let me talk to your dad?"

There was another too lengthy hesitation before Zach answered and Gabe felt his chest tightening while he waited. After what seemed like an hour, Zach finally spoke in a small voice. "Dad can't talk to you right now."

"What do you mean he can't talk? He's there isn't he? Is he hurt, too?"

"He's out in the parking lot in a police car. I don't think the cops are going to let him talk to you."

"Zach, what in the world are you talkin' about? Why do the police have your dad?"

"It's kind of complicated I guess. But he hit a security guy and knocked him out. That's when the cops grabbed him and put him in their car."

"Whoa, whoa, wait a minute, Zach. Your dad knocked out a security guard; in the emergency room? Are you sure?"

"One of the police officers is right here. He let me borrow his cell phone to call you. Maybe you ought to talk to him."

Gabe could hear the phone change hands and then a deep, authoritative, voice said, "Hello, this is Officer Evans with the Phoenix police. Mr. ..., is this Zach's grandfather."

"I'm Gabe Green. And yes, I'm Zach's grandfather. Now could you tell me what's goin' on?"

"Well, Mr. Green, there's not a lot I can tell you. Your daughter...Zach's mother is your daughter I presume...has been transported to the emergency room at St. Joseph's Hospital here in Phoenix. She was unresponsive when we discovered her in her home a couple of hours ago, and the emergency room personnel are working on her now. I am with your grandson waiting for them to give us some additional information. And, Sir, I think it might be a very good idea for you to make arrangements to come down here, if at all possible."

"Do you have any information about my daughter's condition?"

"Not really, Sir. They're not being very forthcoming with the details."

"And what is this nonsense about my son-in-law bein' under arrest?"

"Yes, sir, that would be correct. We have Mr. Mertz in custody."

"Why have you arrested Dave? He wasn't responsible for my daughter's injuries was he?"

"Not that we are aware of, Sir. I'm sorry. I can't divulge any more information about that situation."

"What about Zach. Who's gonna to look after him until this mess all gets sorted out?"

"Well, I'm with him right now, Sir. And Children's Services is supposed to be on their way. Does he have any relatives in the area, an older sibling or aunt or uncle or anything?"

"No, he's an only child. And, strange as it is, he doesn't have any aunts, uncles, or cousins."

Todd looked away from the boy, wishing that he wasn't listening to this conversation. But, it was what it was. "I'll have to send him to Children Services then. They'll make arrangements for his safety."

Zach had been listening to the officer's end of the conversation without comment until he heard that he was going to be turned over to the State's custody. At that juncture, he interrupted, "I can go home. I'll be fine until my grandparents can get here. I am not going to some foster home!"

Hearing Zach melting down in the background, Gabe said, "Look, tell me how to get a hold of someone at wherever you're gonna take him. I'll be down there as fast as I can catch a plane."

Todd relayed all the details on who to talk to at the precinct to obtain the contact information then ended with, "Okay. I'm disconnecting now. Don't worry; this is all going to work itself out."

"Please let me speak to Zach again. And, Officer, thank you for everythin' you're doin'. We really do appreciate it."

As soon as Todd handed the phone back to him, Zach was frantically talking into the receiver, "Grumpa, don't let them put me in foster care. I'll be fine on my own, honest."

"I don't think that's negotiable, Zach. They have to follow the rules. Just cooperate with them and I'll be down as quick as I can. And remember, Zach, there is no way they're gonna to leave you without supervision. Remember, I love you, but even better, God loves you, and He's gonna take care of you."

That promise sounded like a trite cliché to Gabe as he said it. And *he* believed every word of it. But he could only imagine what it sounded like to his panic-stricken grandson as he faced a stay in the custody of the state, on top of having his mom in the emergency room and his dad headed for jail. He felt like he was a hundred years old as he started to the back of the house to awaken his wife, to fill her in on what was happening.

# 12

Zach sat listening to the dead air on the phone until the dial tone sounded in his ear. Then he folded it up and handed it back to Todd without saying a word. He sat forward on the impossibly uncomfortable hospital waiting room chair and let his head hang between his knees.

This entire deal had to be a terrible nightmare, he thought. He couldn't remember when he last felt that life was good, if he ever had. But, this was ridiculous. What could happen next: An alien abduction, or how about an earthquake destroying half the United States? Maybe if he closed his eyes tight enough, when he opened them again he'd be back in his bedroom and the whole mess would be nothing more than a trick of his mind.

It felt like the room was spinning. For a few minutes, Zach thought he was going to pass out. He began to hope that he would. Maybe he could suffer an aneurism and die. Anything that got him out of this incredible mess would be welcome, he thought.

The motion of Officer Evans getting to his feet brought Zach back to full consciousness. When he opened his eyes, the room continued to spin but he could see well enough to notice the lady from the receptionist's desk walking toward them. She stopped in front of the officer, glanced briefly at Zach, then said, "Excuse me officer, could I speak with you over at my desk for a moment?"

"What's going on?" Zach demanded. "Is Mom okay?"

The receptionist ignored the question and headed back to her cubicle.

"You sit down and wait right here for me. I'll be back as soon as I find out what's up," Todd ordered before following the woman to her desk.

Once back at her work station and out of earshot of Zach, she told Todd that the physician—Dr. Romero—that was in charge of Becky's care wanted to talk to him. She motioned him toward the door, buzzed it open, and instructed him to, "Go straight ahead to the nurse's station. The doctor will meet you there."

"Romero?" Todd muttered, "I don't think I know him."

"He's new to us; only been here for a couple of weeks. He came from somewhere in the Midwest. But he seems alright. Not too arrogant."

Todd had a bad feeling about this secrecy routine, and he did not like leaving Zach unattended, but he needed to find out what was going on with the boy's mother. Inside the emergency room section, a row of cubicles extended both ways from the entrance and entirely surrounded the nurses' station that occupied the center of the immense room. The privacy cubicles were sectioned off by curtains hanging from the ceiling. Todd had spent hours in this place, with various culprits and victims, but he was always amazed at the sheer volume of people that needed the services that were offered here on any given day. This was no exception. At least twenty-five of the thirty or so areas appeared to be occupied.

After a quick look around the large room, the officer headed toward the nearest nurse. He had interacted with her often enough on prior visits to be on a first name basis. She was busy working at a computer terminal, but he walked right up and said, "Hey, Darla, it looks like the crazies are keeping you busy tonight. But I guess that keeps you from getting bored."

"Oh, we're busy enough alright," she answered, looking up with a smile. "There was a nasty pile-up out on the fifty so everybody is jumping. But that hasn't ever saved me from boredom."

"I guess that must be why there isn't a chaplain around to talk to the kid I'm babysitting."

"Yeah, they're all busy with the families of the people from the accident. What are you up to?"

"I'm supposed to talk to the Doc, what's his name? Oh yeah, Romero. Tina out front said that he needed to talk to me, but that kid I've got out there in the waiting area really shouldn't be left on his own. Do you think you could scare the Doc up for me?"

"Sure thing; wait here I'll go get him. I won't be more'n a minute."

True to her word, Darla was back before Todd had a chance to pace back and forth the length of the counter more than twice. A small man in a white lab coat, worn over a neon blue shirt and tie combination, was right on her heels.

"Officer Evans, this is Dr. Romero," Darla introduced the men with an air of formality and then went back to work at her computer.

The officer and the doctor shook hands, and not wasting any time, Dr. Romero said, "Let's step over to an unoccupied exam unit." The doctor's voice surprised Todd. The guy had a deep, full voice. If he was talking to him on the phone he'd guess that the doc was a big guy, at least six feet tall, and in excess of two hundred pounds. But here he was walking behind a guy that needed lifts to reach five-five and wouldn't weigh in at more than a buck twenty. But he walked fast. Todd had to stretch out his stride to keep up as the little man crossed the open area and stepped into one of the examination areas.

Satisfied that they had at least a modicum of privacy, Dr. Romero got right to the point. "Officer Evans, I want to assure you that we are doing everything medically possible to help Ms. Mertz. However, her prognosis is not good. We have not been able to verify any brain activity. We have her hooked up to life support to keep her body functioning while we run further tests but her condition is dire. I wanted to let you know so that you would be able to take whatever steps are necessary to contact the next of kin. Unless things change very dramatically in the next twelve hours—and I'm fairly certain that they won't—the family is going to have some tough decisions to make."

Todd hesitated too long before responding and Dr. Romero was starting to fidget by the time the officer asked, "What do you think about me bringing her son in?"

The doctor simply shrugged and hurried away like a banty rooster on a mission.

Todd's head was spinning as he made his way back to the waiting room. "They don't teach you how to handle crap like this at the academy," he grumbled to himself. When he got to the stuffy room with the uncomfortable chairs, he glanced in and was relieved when he saw that Zach was still there, eyes transfixed on the silent television screen.

Instead of going to join the boy, the officer went through the automatic double doors to the parking lot. Once outside he radioed his sergeant to again ask for advice. After explaining the situation, he asked, "So, boss, what do you think? Should I risk waiting for Zach's grandparents to get here and let them make the call, or should I take the boy in to see his mother myself? The doc sure made it sound like she could kick off at any minute.

"And, oh, Boss, I'm into overtime here," Todd added, hoping that the vision of the big money flying out the window might encourage the sergeant to get someone to relieve him. Not that he minded pulling in a little O.T. but he didn't want to be the one with the kid when the news came down that the only thing keeping his mom alive was a bunch of pumps and tubes and wires.

"I don't care if you're on *double* time. This is going to be a high profile news story, what with a well known doctor involved and all. And the last thing we need is to look like is a bunch of chumps who didn't take the best of care of the boy. You've already made a connection with the kid so you're going to babysit 'til either some-one from CSD, or his grandparents, make the scene and take over. And no, I wouldn't advise taking the boy in to see his mom. We'll just hope that Ms. Mertz holds on long enough for her parents to get there."

*The sensation was one of rapid movement, like a ride on an electric train or elevator, but without the jarring and bumping. A single source of light ahead was all that was visible. It was intense, bright, and white. Becky was being pulled down a vortex toward that light as if a gi-ant magnet in the core of her was responding to its polar opposite.*

**103**

# 13

After checking all the available flights, Meg and Gabe decided that driving to Phoenix would be quicker than flying. They loaded the necessities into their car and headed south.

Half an hour after merging onto Interstate 5 off Highway 58, Meg said, "Do you think Becky is going to be alright?"

"Sweetie, I have no idea. I want her to be with all my heart. I'm prayin' she will be. But I just don't know. I keep telling myself that God knows what he's doing; but, I have to confess, I'm having trouble believin' it this time. What do you think?"

"I'm not sure what I think, but I know what I feel, and I what I feel, is guilty. I keep wondering what I did wrong as a mother. I mean, I must not have been a very good example of a follower of Jesus, 'cause I sure didn't make her want to follow me as I followed him."

"Hey, Babe, don't you think you might be bein' kinda hard on yourself? You were, and are, a great mother. Like I told you before, it was my fatherin' skills that were suspect."

"Ah, Gabe, you might not have been perfect, but you are a fantastic father and husband. No, I'm sure that this has got to be primarily my fault."

"You know, Meg, we might both be to blame. Or maybe *neither* of us is the cause of Becky's rebellion. I don't know, but didn't you remind me recently that at some point a person becomes responsible for their own behavior, no matter how good a job their parents did or did not do?"

"I suppose. I don't know either. I'm just really worried. What if she isn't alright? I don't know if I can stand to lose her, especially not knowing where she stands with the Lord. And please, God, not by suicide. I don't think I can stand that. Wouldn't that disqualify her from going to heaven?"

"Now don't start going there. It seems to me that you're gettin' all worked up about things that might never be. And no, I don't believe that committin' suicide automatically means you can't go to heaven, though a lot of people think so. Sampson killed himself, and I'm positive that he's going to be there. And King Saul, he intentionally fell on his own sword, and I'm expectin' to see him up there, too."

Meg was trying to keep from crying, but her voice cracked and Gabe knew that she was almost to break down when she said, "But what about Zach, what's going to happen to him, Gabe?"

"Zach's gonna be just fine. If need be, he can come live with us. Anyway, we're borrowing trouble here."

Meg went silent, and Gabe's response was to push a little harder on the accelerator, hoping to coax more speed out of the Toyota's six cylinder engine.

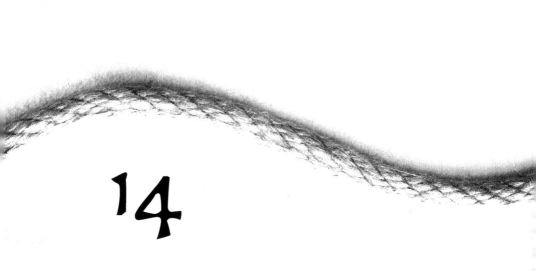

# 14

As he sat next to Zach, Police Officer Todd Evans felt his cell phone vibrate against his thigh for what seemed like the fiftieth time. Half of the calls were routine, and came from the precinct's dispatcher. He took those calls, and was aware that Zach was listening in, either intrigued by the police business or trying to discern details about his mother's condition. The other half came in flurries, and the number that came up on the screen belonged to the cell phone of Zach's grandparents. He didn't have anything to say, that he hadn't already said, so he ignored them.

"Hey, kid," Todd said, "I need to visit the men's room. You sit here and behave yourself. I'll be right back." Leaving Zach even briefly made the officer nervous, but he didn't have a choice, and the boy *had* stayed put during Todd's conference with the doctor.

When the officer came back down the hall, he was irritated, but not too surprised, to discover that his charge was not where he had left him. He didn't see the boy with a quick glance around, so Todd went to the receptionist desk and said, "Excuse me, Tina, did you happen to see where the kid went?"

"Yeah, right after you left he got up and took off down the hall toward the cafeteria," she answered, pointing down the hall.

Todd threw a quick, "Thanks," over his shoulder and headed in the direction the receptionist had indicated.

He was walking fast, and his irritation was growing, when he stuck his head into the small cubical that served as the waiting area for the X-ray department and saw Zach huddled in the corner. The boy was as white as a sheet, and trembling, when Todd approached and said, "I thought I told you to stay put! What're you doin' down here?"

"I'm hiding from that weird guy in the black jumpsuit. Did you see him?"

"What guy? I didn't see anybody in a black jumpsuit, and I don't expect that I am going to, considering it's about a hundred degrees outside. What are you talkin' about?"

Zach rubbed his face with both hands, and his voice was quivering when he answered, "Last night, just before you and your partner found me, I saw this dude leaving my yard. He was wearing a jumpsuit - you know, one of those one piece things like overalls - a black baseball cap, and army boots; he wears the pant legs inside his boots. I saw him up in Oregon, too. Well, I just saw him again, and he creeps me out!"

Not knowing what to think about Zach's story, Todd grabbed the boy by his left elbow, lifted him off the chair, and said, "Come on, let's get back to emergency. If you see this guy in black again let me know."

108

They had been back in their chairs for less than fifteen minutes when the doors of the emergency treatment area opened and Dr. Romero walked out. Todd knew as soon as he saw the doctor that it was not a good sign. Todd stood up and Zach got up, also. "Sit down, and this time wait here," Todd ordered in his most authoritative voice, and he walked toward the doctor. In three strides, the policeman had the doctor's upper arm in his hand and used the frail limb to guide the small man out of earshot of Zach.

When he recovered from the initial surprise, Dr. Romero barked in an offended tone, "Let go of me. What do you think you are doing?"

"Don't get your shorts in a wad, Doc," Todd said in his ear, "I just need to get you away from the boy before you share the information that I'm expecting you to share."

"You could show some respect! It's no wonder that the police department has such a terrible reputation in this city, the way you shove people around like we are so many cattle."

"Sorry, Doc, but what were you coming out to tell us?"

Todd had released his hold on the doctor's arm when he thought that they were out of Zach's earshot. Before answering the question, the doctor made a show of straightening the wrinkles in his shirt sleeve and rubbing his bicep. Then he said, "We performed another brain scan on Ms. Mertz, and there is still no evidence of brain activity. My initial assessment is that she is suffering from an overdose of prescription medications. I expect that once the blood screens are back, they will confirm that. Of course, we won't know for sure without performing an autopsy, which I am sure your department will request, once the family decides to disconnect her from the life support machines."

Todd's mind was in overdrive trying to think of how he was going to present this news to Zach. This kind of thing was the worst aspect of his job. When he turned to go back to Zach, he saw that he wasn't going to have to be creative. The boy had been standing behind him and judging from the look of shock on his face he had heard the doctor's statement. Maybe it was just as well. Todd had been on duty for almost twenty hours and his abilities at creativity were largely impaired by fatigue.

"I'm sorry, Zach," was the best that Todd could muster.

The boy responded by turning and walking slowly toward the exit.

When Zach went through the door, Todd followed. Once outside, to Todd's amazement, the boy made a sharp right turn and started sprinting. Todd hit the mike on his shoulder and requested backup while he watched the teenager crossing one of the soccer fields in the park across the street from the hospital. Too tired to give chase, and not caring if the boy got away or not, Todd just watched him run.

Dispatch informed him that there were no available cars in the immediate area. Todd responded that he didn't think it was urgent; the boy was not apt to go anywhere but home anyway. Someone could pick the kid up there when he arrived back at his house. Meanwhile, Todd was going to go home, eat, and crash. He'd had his fill of this whole crazy deal. When he pulled his phone from his pocket to turn it off, he saw the string of messages from Zach's grandparents waiting. As much as he did *not* want to contact them, he knew there wasn't much choice.

# 15

"Ms. Green, this is Officer Todd Evans of the Phoenix Police."

Gabe was slowing the car and pulling to the side of the highway, not wanting to drive out of the phone's area of reception, when Meg started to sob. By the time they had stopped rolling, Meg was crying uncontrollably. Gabe reached around her with his right arm and pulled her to himself as best he could with the car's console between them. He took the phone from her and held it to his ear. In as modulated a voice as he could muster, he said, "Hello, this is Gabe Green."

"I'm sorry, Mr. Green, I know that this information should have been relayed to you in person, but under the circumstances, it is obvious that that was not possible."

Though Gabe knew what the information was without being told, he found himself saying, "What? My wife has been unable to tell me what you said."

"Well, again, I am very sorry, but the medical personnel have been unable to find any brain function in your daughter."

Gabe was amazed at his own calm demeanor as he continued the conversation. "Thank you for your kind concern officer, now may I speak with my grandson?"

"Well...Mr. Green...actually that is why I'm calling. It seems that there is another problem. Zach took off on foot as soon as he heard that his mother was considered to be brain dead. We were unable to catch him but expect that he is headed back to his house."

Gabe sat in stunned silence for half a minute as he tried to make sense of what he had heard. Finally, he said, "I'm having a little trouble comprehending what you just said, officer. Am I to understand that Zach is runnin' around the city of Phoenix on his own, right after learning that his mother was unlikely to recover?"

"Yes, unfortunately, that is the case, Sir."

"And what exactly is the Phoenix Police Department doing about that?"

"Well, we are waiting for him to arrive back at his home."

"You understand that he is thirteen years old and that he is undoubtedly in a state of shock? What's gonna keep him from gettin' run over in that crazy Phoenix traffic."

"Yes, sir, I spent the whole morning with him. I know his age and have a fairly good understanding of his mental state. He appears to be a competent young man, and I am quite confident that he will arrive back at his home without any additional problems," Todd answered as professionally as he could. For the hundredth time today he wished he had never taken the prowler call that started all this. Getting yelled and cussed at was one thing, but this guy's calm cutting was just too much to take. This whole case was way over the top.

"Officer," Gabe continued, "please provide your badge number, your immediate supervisor's name, and the phone number of your precinct."

"Now wait a minute, Mr. Green. None of this is my fault. I am not responsible for your daughter's condition. And I did *not* cause your grandson to take off like a scalded cat. I will attempt to help you in any way that I can, but I do not intend to tolerate your insinuation that I have been incompetent, nor do I appreciate your thinly veiled threats."

It was Gabe's turn to be contrite. "I'm sorry, officer, I didn't intend to insinuate or threaten, I'm just a bit, you know, undone by all of this. But I would appreciate it if you would give me the phone number of the precinct."

Throughout the entire exchange, Meg continued to cry quietly. Once Gabe was off the phone, Meg's cries increased in volume. He joined her in her crying. They held each other in an awkward embrace and mixed their tears for five or ten minutes and as their crying began to subside their sobs of distress began to change to cries to their heavenly father; pleadings for strength and wisdom. In a few more minutes, they were able to resume the drive. As they drove, it was with renewed purpose. Now they were on a mission to find Zach and be of comfort to him. The biggest frustration was that they were still about ten hours away. But there was consolation in having to focus attention on him, and his situation, and thereby avoid thinking about the decision that was going to need to be made about their daughter.

Zach hadn't planned to run, but the blast of heat that struck him when he went out the doors of the hospital brought with it a compulsion to be alone. Without understanding why, he started running. Away from the hospital; away from the horror of knowing his mother was brain dead; away from the shock of seeing his father tased and arrested; away from his own arrest and expulsion from school. He simply wanted away from the past. He would have run from his future too, if he only knew which direction to run.

As he ran, he expected to hear sirens, or at least footsteps, behind him. After seven or eight blocks of sprinting, two things were obvious: It was too hot to run; and, no one was pursuing him anyway. He pulled up in the shade of a building, tried to catch his breath, and contemplated what to do next. Nothing came to mind.

When his breathing had returned to normal, he was shocked to realize that he was hungry and thirsty. It amazed and appalled him that the grief and fear that he thought he should be feeling was supplanted by the crass desire for food and water.

He stood, thoughts bouncing around in his head like a hand full of super balls dropped on uneven pavement, trying to form a plan. He would probably have stood just like that, until a patrol car came and picked him up, had the business owner from the building he was using for shade not come out and asked him if he needed help. He muttered a quick, "No thanks," and started moving again in what he thought was the general direction of his home.

Zach knew that his house was the first place that the police would look for him, but he didn't have any money, or anything else, with him. He didn't have a clue as to where else to go. He just kept walking toward home. Knowing that he was in for a long walk, he thought that he could formulate a plan before he got to the house.

The heat of the morning began to get to him by the time half an hour had passed. His tongue was sticking to the roof of his mouth and the exhaustion of being up all night made his eyelids so heavy that it felt like there were sandbags on them. People he passed were looking at him like he was some sort of stoned-out street kid.

A block off the street that he was walking on he noticed a grove of green shade trees. The grass beneath the trees was lush, inviting, and green. Zach moved that direction without really thinking about what he was doing. When he got closer, he noticed that the sign in front of the freshly painted building said, "Autumn Fields Funeral Chapel." Somehow, it seemed an appropriate place to stop and rest. With no one around, Zach felt safe going to the shaded side of the small building and crawling into the relative cool beneath the shrubs.

The underground sprinkler system had watered at daylight, and the ground was still wet and felt invitingly soft when he lay down. He was asleep within a minute.

Three hours later, he was awakened by fire ants biting his ankle. The stinging pain felt like a red hot poker was being pushed into his leg. He scrambled out of the shade of the shrubs slapping at the insects and scratching their bites. Then the heat hit him. When he stood, the temperature and dehydration combined with the burning bites and sent his head spinning. He staggered for a couple of steps before going to his knees to keep from blacking out.

While Zach fought to keep from passing out, the manager of the funeral home was watching from his office window. He decided that the youngster in the yard was intoxicated and dialed 911.

Five minutes later a cruiser pulled up behind Zach. The boy looked up and saw the officers when he heard the vehicle's tires popping the loose gravel at the edge of the curb. He did not attempt to escape. Then, for the third time in thirty-six hours, Zach found himself in police custody.

*Even when she concentrated with all her strength, Becky couldn't decide whether her eyelids were open or closed. The light was gone, along with the sensation of being pulled toward it. Everything was ink black. Not dark. Black. She reached up and tried to touch her eyelids with her fingers and still could not discern whether her eyes were open. There was no sensation in the nerve endings of her fingers, or her face, or even in her eyes.*

*She extended her arms out to both sides as far as she could reach but didn't come into contact with anything. While she was stretching, and touching nothing, she realized there wasn't anything under her feet.*

*Panic welled up in heart, but she felt no pounding in her chest. There was no sound of blood rushing in her ears. The heat was so intense that she felt she might combust, but there was no blisters rising on her skin, no sweat beading on her forehead.*

*There was...nothing. Nothing but black and heat.*

# 16

One Month Later

As Gabe and Meg packed to return to their home, Gabe said, "Well, we didn't need to worry about whether or not the doctors should disconnect Becky from life support."

"I understand that, legally, as Becky's husband, the decision is David's to make. But, it would've been nice if he had at least asked for our opinion. I'm still surprised at how adamant he is that she not be unplugged. Why is he insisting, even after test after test has revealed that there is no sign of brain function, and though she can only breathe with the help of a ventilator, that she be kept alive?"

Gabe's voice was tired and defeated when he slumped down onto the bed beside his suitcase and answered, "I don't think it takes a lot of imagination, or intuition, to understand David's motives for insistin' that

**117**

Becky be kept alive. I mean, right now the police are handlin' the case as an attempted murder, not attempted suicide. They haven't charged him, but it's gotta be obvious, even to him, that they are treating him as the person responsible for Becky's condition. He wants her kept alive so the charges aren't changed from *attempted* murder to murder."

"I guess, but it is pure torture to go to the hospital day after day, and sit by her bed, and listen to those machines keeping her body alive." Meg was crying as she continued, "It's obvious that she's was no longer in that shell. Zach couldn't stand to even go back and see her after his second visit. Remember how he insisted that she was not his mother?"

Gabe got back on his feet and paced as he said, "David hasn't visited her once. He has no clue what's goin' on in that hospital, and he doesn't care. That snake is only interested in savin' his own worthless hide. He's so stinkin' gutless that he even sends his lawyers to make certain that Becky is kept on the life support. He can't even bring himself to go into her room for that."

Meg stepped in front of her husband to stop his pacing and put her hands on his shoulders and said, "Hey, we've gotta quit being so negative about David. We can't be talking bad about him in front of Zach. And since Zach is coming to Oregon with us, we better start practicing."

Gabe let out a big sigh and said, "You're right. But it's so stinkin' hard to leave Becky in that hospital bed while David and the hospital are locked in this ridiculous legal battle. It might not be so bad if our feelin's were ever considered."

"I know. But, what *I* wish is that they would take Zach's feelings into consideration. I tried to call David again this morning so I could ask him to talk to Zach before we left but, as usual, he didn't answer."

Habits

"It's sure good to be in our own home," Meg told Gabe the day after they had completed the marathon drive back to Oregon.

"That is for sure," Gabe replied. "But, havin' Zach around is gonna take some adjustin'."

"It's not like this is the first time he's stayed we us."

"'At's true, but Zach ain't exactly the same kid he was prior to bein' arrested and expelled from school. And those are minor issues compared to the baggage that boy is draggin' behind him concernin' Becky's condition."

Meg nodded in agreement and added, "Then there's all the emotional chaos of knowing that his dad is being investigated for the attempted murder of his mother. But he's still our grandson, and we're here to help him work through all this."

"Yeah, I know you're right. But to really be the help he needs is gonna take the wisdom of King Solomon."

"Which God will make available to us if we keep praying and asking for it."

"You're right, again.

"By the way, where is Zach?"

"He took the dogs for a walk. If nothing else, at least he really seems to enjoy spending time with those mutts."

Zach, Meg, and Gabe were at the breakfast table three weeks after arriving in Oregon when Gabe said, "Ya know Zach, I don't think I'd ever have got this yard whipped back into shape after bein' gone for so long if you weren't helpin' me. Just rakin' up all the ponderosa needles would have killed me off. You have been a huge help."

Zach was already blushing when Meg joined in and said, "The dogs are loving you taking them on their morning walks, too. They had gotten pretty fat while we were

119

gone, but you are getting them back into shape in a hurry."

The boy answered while he took his breakfast dishes from the dining room table to the kitchen. "Thanks. I love taking them for their walks. It is really fun to watch them tear through the brush after chipmunks and golden mantles. I wonder what they would do if they ever caught anything."

Gabe laughed and said, "I don't think there's much danger of that. Those mutts are too clumsy to actually catch anythin'."

"Well, I think I'll take them out right now and give them another chance. The great thing is that they never seem to get discouraged," Zach said, smiling.

Meg and Gabe watched out the window as Zach and the two Labrador Retrievers headed into the pine forest. The dogs were running in circles around the boy and grabbing each other by their collars. Dust was rolling up around them like smoke. When he was out of sight, Meg said, "Yesterday afternoon, when I got off the phone with Becky's caregiver, I tried to give Zach an update on her condition. He became really agitated and told me he didn't want to hear about it."

"That doesn't surprise me," Gabe answered. It's like he's purposely closing off that part of his life. I tried to talk to him about what we're gonna do about getting' 'im into school in the fall and he wouldn't talk about that either."

"Is that healthy?"

"I'm sure no psychologist, but I don't think so."

"So what are we going to do to help him through this? I mean, we can't just let him avoid talking about anything that is painful to think about."

"I was awake half the night thinkin' and prayin' about that. I think I may have an idea that might just begin to bridge the communication gap."

"Yeah, what's that?"

"You know how much he loves classical music – I'm gonna offer him a deal. I'm gonna tell him that I'll listen to ten minutes of music with him each day if he will read the Bible for five minutes a day with me."

"Gabe, studying the Bible with you will be like watching grass grow to him. He'll be bored to tears."

"I don't think so. I'm gonna 'story tell' some of the Old Testament sections. You know, the real bloody, excitin' parts."

"Do you think that all that violence is what he needs right now?"

"It'll show him that he's not the only one that ever went through stuff like this. And that God is still at work when ever' thin' seems to be comin' apart at the hindges."

"Okay, but how is that going to help him come out from behind the wall that he is building?"

"Well, I'm plannin' on askin' him to explain the music to me and then I'm gonna ask him to discuss the Bible with me. I don't *know* if it'll work, but I'm hopin' that talkin' about the things we are passionate about will be the catalyst for some meaningful discussions."

Meg nodded and said, "It just might work, except for one small thing. How in the world are you going to stand listening to classical music for fifteen minutes a day?"

"I said *ten* minutes!"

"Okay, ten minutes. You can't stand to listen to music. What makes you think that you can pull that off? And how are you going to discuss it. You don't know anything about music!"

"I'm not sure I can, but I'm sure gonna try. I've gotta do something!

"As for not understandin' the music, that's part of the plan. He'll be the authority and he'll be teachin' me about somethin' that I know absolutely nothin' about. I hopin' that that will open him up. "

"I guess it's worth a try. You are right about having to do something. But I think we better cover this whole plan in a whole pile of prayer."

*Becky had been in darkness and heat for what seemed an eternity. She oscillated between struggling to feel something, attempting to scream, and submissively shuddering in complete terror.*

*During one of the shuddering sessions a portal popped open in front of her. Light poured through the oval opening, but it did not blind Becky. That oddity did not occur to her, though. Instead, she was transfixed on the scene visible through the window.*

*She could see Zach! There was no question that he was unaware of her, but she had an unobstructed view of him. He was walking. The setting was lost on her because the background was blurry. It was like looking at a distant scene through a powerful lens. Suddenly her view included a man who appeared to be stalking Zach. The man was wearing a black baseball cap and jumpsuit.*

*As Becky watched, the sinister figure pulled a long knife with a curved blade from a scabbard that she hadn't noticed before. Raising the wicked weapon above his head, the man quickly closed the gap between himself and the boy.*

*Becky attempted to scream out a warning to her son. The sound did not reach her ears, and certainly didn't make it to Zach's.*

*The portal snapped closed in the same way that it had opened and Becky was left to panic, surrounded by darkness, heat, and her own silent screaming. "Please protect him, Lord. Please don't send him here," she pleaded soundlessly into the darkness.*

# 17

One morning, while Zach was walking the dogs, Meg and Gabe used their time alone to discuss the merits of Gabe and Zach heading out on a camping trip. "How long are you planning to be gone?" Meg asked.

"That depends on how it goes. No longer than five or six days. We'll take the tent and a bunch of great tastin', but unhealthy, food and our fishin' poles. And we'll just play it by ear. I've gotta be back to teach on Sunday so we won't be gone past Saturday."

"What if Zach doesn't like camping?"

"Oh course he'll like campin'. What boy doesn't like campin'? We'll have a blast! And it'll get me away from that stinkin' music!"

"So that music thing isn't working so well for you then?"

"Honestly, no it isn't. Not that I'm ain't tryin', but I just don't get how it works. He'll tell me to listen to this or that and I don't hear anythin' but the melody. I don't know who it's frustrin' more, me or him."

"How is he doing with studying the Bible?"

"A whole bunch better than I'm doin' with the music, and that's a fact!"

"I hate to break it to you, Gabe, but I think Zach will take the music with him if he does want to go into the woods."

Gabe sighed and said, "Yeah, I'm sure he will."

"Well, anyway, let's ask Zach what he thinks about the camping trip idea, and leave it up to him. If he wants to go I'll stir up a double batch of chocolate chip cookies to keep you guys from starving to death while trying to survive on your own cooking."

"Ah, we won't starve; we're gonna live off the land. But we'll take the cookies just the same. And as much other junk food as I can talk you into givin' us."

Zach didn't show much enthusiasm when his grandfather shared the plan with him, but he didn't object either. So Gabe made a list and started gathering the gear and tack that they'd need for a stay in the wilds.

What Zach lacked in excitement, Gabe provided. Meg hadn't seen her husband so animated in quite awhile. Maybe the fishing trip was a good idea, she thought. It might not be therapeutic for Zach, but it looked like it was going to be great for Gabe.

She was dreading the time alone, but not enough to want to tag along. She'd lost interest in tent camping years ago; she missed the conveniences of home—like running water for instance.

By the time everything was loaded, Zach was beginning to warm up to the idea of the trip, which might have been because he loved chocolate chip cookies. He tried not to show it, but helping to arrange the camping gear in the pickup and listening to his grandfather's running commentary on what the items were for began to infect him with excitement, too. Watching the dogs rip around, somehow knowing that they were going to be included in the outing, also helped.

The next morning it was still pitch dark when they set out. Gabe stopped the pickup when they reached the end of the driveway, and Zach thought he must have forgotten something. Instead of going back, Gabe sat with the pickup idling looking up at the cream colored full moon, hung low in the western star-filled sky.

When his grandfather started talking, Zach naturally thought he was talking to him, but it became obvious that he was praying, when he said, "Lord, thank you for this opportunity to go out and enjoy a little corner of your creation. It' just amazing to look up and see the beauty of just a little bitty speck of your handiwork we call the moon. And God, we're here askin' that you give us safety on the road and blessin's as we go. Oh, and Lord, thank you for lettin' Zach stay with us for awhile. Having him here is a true blessin'. And Lord, please be with Becky. I don't know what's goin' on with that girl; she might already be with you. But if she isn't, please relieve her of any pain and sufferin' she might be feelin'."

The prayer made Zach uncomfortable and he was glad when they started moving down the road. That part about him being a blessing did make him feel good though.

When they hit Highway 31 and started south, the moon lit the eastern landscape, a scene that was dominated by Paulina Peak. The mountain was silver against the black shadows cast by straggled-limbed pines. The remnants of the winter's snow pack holding on at the boulder-strewn peak glistened as if a spotlight were shining on it.

"Wow, Paulina Peak is beautiful, with the moon shinin' on it like that," Gabe commented.

For a second, Zach thought his grandfather was starting to pray again; then, when he realized that Gabe was talking to him, he asked, "Why is it called Paulina Peak?"

"I guess it was named for Chief Paulina. He and his tribe spent time around here."

"What was so special about him that he got a mountain named after him?"

"Like most historical figures, the character changes with the political leaning of whatever historian recorded the story. In fact, historians can't agree on Paulina's tribal affiliation. But everyone agrees that the Chief was a fierce warrior who put fear into the hearts of the settlers, and the other tribes, that were tryin' to co-inhabit the greater central Oregon area. He led a group of ferocious warriors that didn't see the advantages of 'civilization'. They roamed the area and pretty much dominated everyone in these parts through fear and violence until sometime in the mid-1860s."

"What happened to him?"

"Well, like most of history's violent characters, he came to a violent end."

"Did the army get him?"

"If I recollect my history correctly, the army captured the band's women and children while the warriors were away from the village and then used them as hostages to negotiate a treaty that put Paulina and his braves on a reservation down by Klamath Falls."

"So that was the end of him? He died on a reservation?"

"Actually, no. He and some of his braves didn't adjust too well to the new lifestyle and went back to roamin' and raidin'. A group of militia, led by a couple of settlers by the names of Lewis and Maupin, are credited with killing Paulina and most of his men in a skirmish."

126

Habits

Zach rode along in silence, staring out the truck window, for several minutes before asking, "So, this beautiful mountain is named after a guy who got famous by basically being a bully and was killed because of it? I don't get it."

"Huh! I never thought of it just like that before. Does seem kinda silly doesn't it? But the thing is, men write history and we aren't really all that great at choosing the right heroes."

More silence followed as the sun painted the edges of the eastern horizon golden. A few minutes later, the thin layer of stratus clouds floating in the southwest were torched scarlet as the sun continued to advance the dawn against the darkness of night. The moon, which had seemed so bright, now appeared bleached as it slid down behind the Cascade Mountains.

Zach's next question took his grandfather by surprise. "Who are your heroes, Grumpa?"

The question set Gabe back for a minute. He couldn't remember ever contemplating the idea. Finally, he responded, "Hmmm, I guess my dad—that's your great-grandfather—has always been one of my heroes. When I was a kid he was so strong and so good at huntin' and fishin' that I wanted to be just like him.

"Then, when I got into junior high and high school and was playin' football, Dick Butkus was my hero for awhile. He was an absolute animal of a middle linebacker who played for the Chicago Bears. He was way violent and a really good player. I thought he was the best and I wished that I could play football as good as he could. He just tore people up and I thought that was cool.

"Now my hero has to be Jesus. He gave up being the absolute ruler of the universe to come down to this puny little world so that he could suffer and die, just because he loved you and me.

"Who's your hero, Zach?"

Zach just responded by shrugging his thin shoulders and mumbling sadly, "I guess I really don't have a hero."

They rode on in silence, both on the edge of tears, with big lumps in their throats.

To help both of them regain their composure, Gabe said, "Hey, you got any of that classical music with you?"

"I have the latest CD you bought me in the pocket of my duffel bag."

"Pop it in the player and let's listen to some of it."

As it played, Gabe thought maybe he could get used to this stuff, given time. It was pretty, but he wasn't ready to admit it yet.

# 18

By the time that they were out of the forest and cruising through rolling hills that were covered with sagebrush, the sun had finished chinning itself on the eastern horizon, illuminating the usually bleak landscape with a golden glow; Gabe saw a pair of ravens swoop down near the roadside about a quarter-mile ahead. Probably a road-kill deer, he thought, and started slowing down in hope that a coyote or eagle may have been feeding with the ravens. Rolling to a near stop beside the focus of the birds, Gabe and Zach saw a dozen shiny black ravens lined up on the posts of the rusty barbed wire fence that paralleled the highway.

Magpies hopped from sagebrush to sagebrush, anxious to get started on their breakfast: a cow's carcass. It was victim of a driver that failed to see, or didn't understand, the "open range" warning signs posted on the roadside. A puddle of green liquid glistening on the pavement and scattered glass and plastic along the roadside were all that was left on the scene of the unfortunate vehicle that was responsible for the cow's demise.

There hadn't been any winners in this collision.

"Grumpa," Zach asked, "why don't the birds get sick from eating rotten meat?"

"What'd ya mean? Why would they get sick?"

"Well, if we ate meat that was as ripe as that cow, and raw besides, we'd get some kind of stomach trouble, wouldn't we?"

"Yeah, we would, but God made carrion eaters different than us. They're made to eat well aged groceries. The riper the entre' the better those guys like it."

"Are you sure that the buzzards didn't just evolve that way?"

Gabe's voice went an octave lower and the cadence of his speech slowed down when he responded to the question. "Well, Zach, I know I'm old, but I really wasn't there to witness the creation of the world. So, if I say that I'm sure that God created the universe and everythin' in it, I can't prove it. I admit, believing in a divine creator is a faith thing. The funny thin' is, the people who believe in the big bang and evolution weren't around for the beginnin' either. There is a requirement of a different kind of faith at the core of those beliefs."

"But there is tons of scientific evidence that prove that things evolved. Christians just refuse to look at that evidence logically."

"I don't think it is quite that simple, Zach. There are a lot of very good scientists, many of whom are not Christians, who believe that there is something called intelligent design. They look at the universe and conclude that it is far too complex, and well organized, to be a product of pure chance. The conclusions that come from the examination of the evidence that you mentioned are largely dependent on the attitude of the people who are examinin' the evidence."

Zach looked out the truck window in silence for awhile before responding. "Okay, but I don't understand how anyone can believe that the earth is only seven or eight thousand years old when the geological evidence makes it so obvious that it is millions and millions of years old. I mean, look out the window. Those rock cliffs over there," Zach pointed at the basalt upheavals that paralleled the highway on the east, "can you really think that those formations are less than millions of years old?"

"I dunno, Zach. There is really no way to prove it one way or the other. The age of these formations, and how long they took to develop, is all guess and speculation. But think about something for me: If you were transported back in time to day seven of the creation account found in the Genesis, and you met Adam, how old would you guess that he was?"

"I don't know what you mean."

"I mean, say you landed in the Garden of Eden right after God had finished his creation and was resting on that seventh day. You look over at Adam as he was tending his vegetable garden, or scratching the chin of a buffalo or something, and you are gonna write your observations in your journal, how old would you say that Adam was? Would you write down that he was one day old?"

"Okay, I get it. If I didn't know the story and looked at this full grown man, I'd think, well, hey, he must be like thirty or something."

"Yeah, and then you look around and you see a beautiful redwood tree. That sucker is three-hundred and fifty feet tall. How old would you guess that the tree was? And if you cut it down, would it have rings in the wood? How many rings would there be?"

"I suppose I would think that the tree was hundreds of years old. And I'd expect it to have hundreds of rings."

"Oh, and you stub your toe on a rock that is lying there, how old does the rock look to be?"

Zach sighed and said, "I think I get what you're saying. God could have made things with apparent age built right into them. The tree thing is really amazing. If creation is true, how many rings would it have?"

"I don't have the answers, Zach. All I know is that, if a person is open minded, there is room to believe that creation could have taken place in a literal week. But a lot of Christians believe that the earth is millions of years old themselves. I personally have some doubts about that, but it's not worth arguing about. The main thing is to believe that God is the creator. When I get to heaven I can check with him on how he did it."

"Why do you think it is so important to believe that there is a God and that he created us?"

"Well, for one thing, the Bible tells us that he did, and the Bible is the absolute foundation of everything that I believe."

"That's just the thing, Grumpa. Why is it so important to believe the stuff in the Bible? A lot of people think that it's just some well-written fables and poetry."

"Yeah, well, people'll think what they wanna think. But did ya know that the Bible was written over a period of time of better than fifteen hundred years, by forty different writers, and is totally consistent from start to finish. *And*, there are predictions made in the Old Testament that were perfectly fulfilled hundreds of years later."

"I guess that those things are easy to believe for those who are believers, but, if it's so clear, why are there so many people who don't agree that what you're saying is true? I mean, there are a lot of really smart people who argue against everything you're saying."

"Yeah, Zach, I know. I'm not sayin' I'm smarter than they are or anythin' like that. In fact there was a time when I would have agreed with them completely. And I know it is considered bad form to use a resource as a proof of itself, but remember, the Bible is my complete foundation. In I Corinthians, God, through the Apostle Paul, explained that the only people that understand are those whose eyes God has opened."

"See, Grumps, there something I just don't get. If the only people who believe the Bible are the ones that God has chosen to reveal the truth to, why doesn't he just open everyone's eyes?"

"Honestly, Zach, I can't answer that. It is somethin' I wrestle with ever' once in awhile. But God is God and I'm not. That's another one of the things on my list to ask when I get to heaven."

Grandfather and grandson both grew quiet as they sped through the desert. A mountain bluebird took off from his perch on the top strand of the barbed wire fence and the sunlight hit his back and ignited the rich blue of his mating colors. The old man saw the bird as an example of the creator's handiwork. The boy saw it as the product of years of evolution. Though neither pointed the bird out as an illustration of their beliefs, both tucked the image away in their minds as support for their position. Neither of them paused to reflect on the fact that what they believed changed the color of the bird not a bit.

When Gabe switched off the pickup's engine they were parked at the same spot they had been at a couple of months, and in many ways, a life-time, earlier. The dogs were ecstatic to get out of the rig and they went ripping through the surrounding brush when Gabe dropped the truck's tailgate. Chipmunks scattered and songbirds took off for quieter spots.

"You know where you are, Zach?"

"Sure. Are we going back to the place where I took my little unplanned bath?"

"We are. I wanna see if those trout still remember how funny we looked when we were flailin' around in the water."

"Have you fished here since that trip?"

"Nope. And I hope nobody else has either."

"Yeah, Grumps, like somebody else might come all the way up here to fish."

"Oh, I'm not the only crazy old owlhoot that haunts these streams. There are a lot of people who have a hankerin' for pan-fried brook trout."

"How would anyone else even find this stream?"

"Oh, the same way I did, I suppose. By accident. Woodcutters and hunters are always traipsin' around through these woods. And loggers file information about these cricks away in their minds, too."

"It seems like a long way to come for some little fish."

"Yeah, I suppose it is. But for a lot of folks, it is about a lot more than the fish; it's about bein' out in the woods, away from all the noise and confusion."

"Like you have a lot of noise and confusion in Rosland!"

Gabe chuckled. "Well, I know it don't seem like much compared to the big city racket of Phoenix, but Rosland seems plenty loud and confusin' to me at times. But enough of this jawin'; let's get goin'."

"Aren't we going to set up our camp?"

134

"Let's see how well the fish are bitin' first. If they are real cooperative we'll pitch the tent somewhere close to here; but, if they're bein' stubborn, we'll keep tryin' streams until we find a place where the bite is on. That'll help us figure out where we want to set up."

Once the dogs were tethered in a nice shady spot, Gabe and Zach pulled their fly rods out of the truck's toolbox and fastened their tackle bags around their waists.

"Why do the dogs have to stay here?" Zach asked.

"You can't fish with a dog around. They're in and out of the water, tearin' all over the place and scarin' every fish for three miles in ever' direction. They'll be fine waitin' for us here."

Zach looked puzzled when his grandfather stood there looking up at cloudless blue sky instead of heading for the stream. After several minutes, the boy couldn't stand it any longer and said, "What are we waiting for? I thought you were in a big hurry to get fishing."

"Oh, I wanna go fishin' right enough, but I'm sorta waitin' on you to lead the way. What say we see if you can find the crick?"

Gabe was both pleased and proud when Zach hesitated only briefly before he started down the old logging skid that had taken them to the stream a couple of long months earlier.

What he didn't find pleasing was the way he was having to huff to keep up with his grandson after they hit the bottom of the slope and started up the other side. Gabe had always prided himself on being able to keep up a pretty good pace while walking through the woods; but, it quickly became obvious that he would be in trouble if this hike covered more than a mile of two at the pace that Zach was setting. "Hey, son, what's the hurry? We got all day to fish. No sense in takin' off like we're in a race."

Zach stopped and turned around before answering. "Oh, I'm sorry. I know we're not racing, but I thought you wanted to get started fishing."

"Yeah, I do, but ya know, half the fun of bein' out here in the hinterlands is lookin' around at the plants and critters. We ain't apt to see much of interest if we're cut-tin' through the brush like our shirt-tails was afire."

"Okay, I'm sorry. Maybe you should go first. That way you can set the pace."

"Naw. You're doin' fine. And I still wanna see if you can find your way to the crick. Just slow down a mite, that's all."

Zach set a slower pace when they started moving again.

"See that bird up there?" he asked, pointed to the medium sized bird that was flying in erratic loops above them. "'At's a bullbat. He's the guy makin' that funny 'peent' noise we been hearin'. I bet there's a momma bird on a nest somewhere close by."

"That doesn't look like a bat to me," Zach responded.

"Oh, bullbats aren't bats. They're birds. And 'bullbat' is just their nickname. Their real name is 'nighthawk'. I just like the sound of 'bullbat' better I guess."

"How do you know he is a he?"

"See the white stripe across the bottom of his tail? Hens don't have that. And those white patches on his wings? The ones on the female are about half that size. That can be deceiving though, 'cause when the young ones start flyin' around their wing patches are all small."

"When do the patches on the young males get bigger?"

"Hmm. That's a good question. They spend winters down in Mexico or South America or somewhere, I sup-pose they molt down there and when the new feath-ers come in I guess the white patches must be bigger. I don't know for sure."

"What does 'molt' mean?"

"Birds lose all their feathers at certain times and grow new ones.

"Man, they must look really weird without any feathers!"

"Ah, it doesn't work exactly like that. They ain't runnin' around nekid or anythin'. The new feathers are coming in at the same time that the old feathers are comin' out. But during the transition they don't fly so good."

"Why is he flying so funny now?"

"I think it's partly because he enjoys flyin'. But he's huntin', too. They eat mosquitoes and gnats and stuff like that. They fly around pluckin' bugs right outta the air."

"Well, he can have all of those he wants as far as I'm concerned. Hey, how do you know so much about this stuff?"

"Oh, I just like to study up on this kinda thing. But, hey, let's get movin'. Do ya know where to go from here?"

Zach turned around and started hiking again. "I think we just go on up this hill, then down the other side to get to the stream."

"That's right, Zach," Gabe replied. "You're doin' really well. And you seem way more comfortable than you did last time we were here. What happened? Aren't you afraid of getting' lost, or attacked by an elk, or et by a bear or cougar, anymore?"

Zach didn't say anything for awhile, covering at least fifty yards before responding. When he did reply his voice had taken on a serious tone. "I guess Mom's dying did something in my head. I just don't find myself thinking about that stuff like I used to. And if something does happen to me, who will care?"

"Zach! First, your mom ain't dead. And, I'm glad you're not scared all the time anymore, but you gotta know that your grandmother and I love ya to pieces. I don't know what we'd do if anything happened to you! And I'm sure your dad feels the same way."

"Yeah, right; she might as well be dead. She's never going to recover. And, if Dad is so concerned about me, why hasn't he called or anything?"

Gabe chose not to address the subject of Becky because he knew that Zach was right. And he had suspected that the question about Zach's dad was bound to come up sooner or later, but was still not prepared with a good answer. "Well, ya gotta remember that your dad has a lot goin' on right now."

"I sure don't know what he is so busy doing. He's out of jail on bail. They won't let him see patients until the charges against him are settled. So what is he so busy doing that he can't even call?"

"I'm sure he is all tangled up in all kinda legal stuff, and he's probably havin' a hard time dealin' with what has happened to your mom." Gabe abruptly said, "Come on, let's get fishin'."

Zach seemed relieved to let the subject drop. He was quiet as led his grandfather across the clear, cut down the game trail, through the timber, and right to the stream, without any help from Gabe. Once at the water, he baited his hook and started fishing.

Watching the boy's growing independence made Gabe proud, but, at the same time, a little sad.

The water level was considerably lower than when they had fished this stretch of water in the spring. At the spot where they first hit the stream, the water was only an inch or two deep. The fish were going to be holding in the deeper pools and holes in water this low. They moved downstream to the spot where Zach had done so well on their previous trip but were disappointed when they caught only a couple of small fish. The hole where

Zach had taken his impromptu bath was a disappointment, too. Between them they caught only about a half dozen fish, and none of them were more than eight inches long.

Gabe reeled in his line and said, "This is why we didn't set up camp before we tested the fishin'. Let's head back to the rig and see if we can't find some water where the fish are a little more cooperative."

Zach responded with, "Okay. But what do you suppose is wrong? Where did all the fish that were here last time go?"

"I dunno. Maybe a couple of otters have moved into this stretch of water and are cleanin' them out. Or maybe another hungry fisherman has been here recently, though I didn't see any tracks. Whatever, I know we can find a spot that is more productive than this."

They were headed back up the creek when Zach stopped to examine a clump of willows. He pushed the grass growing among the willow branches aside. "Hey, come and take a look at this."

Gabe had forgotten the mallard hen until he looked down into the spot that Zach was pointing out and saw the remains of about a dozen duck eggs among a litter of feathers.

"Did something get the duck and her eggs?" Zach asked.

"Naw," Gabe answered, "it looks like they hatched just fine."

"Where are they?"

"Oh, ducklings don't hang around their nests once they hatch. They could be miles from here by now. They can swim almost as soon as they come outta the shell. And they can fly within a couple of weeks. They gotta get goin' fast. A lot of critters are around that would like to turn 'em into breakfast and by fall they hav'ta be able to fly all the way to Mexico."

"They don't have much time to be kids, I guess," Zach commented as they started back on their way to the truck.

"Most animals don't," Gabe answered. "Life is a constant struggle start to finish for most everything."

"I know," Zach answered under his breath.

*Becky waited, frustrated and impatient. She begged for the portal to re-open and allow her a glimpse of her son and his stalker. Not knowing the outcome of their encounter only added to her intense misery. But the window remained closed and the blackness continued to be absolute.*

*Then, in the darkness, she perceived a presence.*

*She didn't understand how, but she knew that a powerful presence had entered her sphere of consciousness. She had no sense of whether this being was benevolent or evil, only that it was.*

*Her words were silent except in the realm of her mind, none-the-less, she pleaded to this presence, asking that they go and rescue her son.*

# 19

At the truck, Zach asked, "Do you know another spot where the fishing will be better?"

"Oh, I know a lot of spots, but I can't guarantee that any of 'em will be good fishin'. But I hope so."

"How did you find all these places?"

"Well, Zach, I've spent years pokin' around through these hills. And I'm always on the lookout for likely lookin' fishin' holes."

"Do you ever bring anybody but me with you?"

"Usually not. I don't wanna come all the way out here and find someone fishin' where I wanna fish. That's how it works ya know: You show someone your secret spot and they teach someone, who teaches someone, and pretty soon, there's no room for you. I use to try to get your mom to come out here with me, when she was your age, but she never liked bein' in the woods much. She always complained about the bugs. Once in awhile your grandmother will come along, but that's rare. So mostly it's just me and the dogs."

"Mom didn't like coming out here?"

"Naw. She said it was boring and too dirty. And she absolutely hated the bugs. She never was much of an outdoors girl."

"Well, I like it out here. I'm glad you bring me."

"And I'm really glad you wanna come. It'd kinda be sad to think that all the 'secrets' that I've spent years learnin' were gonna die with me."

"Who taught you this stuff?"

"My dad mostly. I sure wish you could have known him. He'd pretty much grown up livin' off the land. He knew how to put meat on the table."

They were driving through a stand of old second growth pine and rounding a sweeping turn when Gabe made the meat comment. Just then, a big old cow elk jumped into the road. Gabe jammed on the brakes to avoid the big animal, and the truck slid sideways on the gravel. They came to a stop in a cloud of dust and a spray of gravel.

"Wow! Look at that!" Gabe said. At least thirty head of the long legged animals were milling around on both sides of the pickup; the herd was made up of cows and calves and a couple of spike bulls. The calves hadn't lost their spots and the spike's antlers were still in the velvet.

The dogs went crazy, barking and posturing. The adult rocky mountain elk averaged about five hundred pounds each and were used to having coyotes harass them. They were not too impressed by the two dogs. And the dogs had the good sense to stay in the bed of the pickup.

In the truck's cab, Gabe and Zach sat and watched as the big chocolate-on-tan animals paraded past the rig. The magnificent animals 'poinged' and chirped in a strange communication that seemed more suited for birds than for animals so large. It took about a minute for the herd to drift into the timber, blend into the under-brush, and disappear into the landscape.

"Man!! Those things are huge," Zach said when the last of the elk was out of sight.

"Yeah, aren't they great? That was a treat, wasn't it? But I don't think that Nute and Ace enjoyed the elk too much. They tried to sound tough, even though they were scared to death. In fact, if I let 'em out of the back right now, I'd bet they wouldn't even try to give chase. They'd run around on the road all stiff-legged and woof."

"Grumpa," Zach said slowly, "I thought you said that elk were afraid of people. Those guys didn't look very afraid to me."

"Well, they didn't come in the cab and try to steal our tater chips, did they?"

"No, but they didn't run off like rabbits either."

"They'd have stampeded if one of us would have gotten out of the truck."

"Well, I wasn't going to get out, and I didn't see you hopping out either."

"Zach, I'm tellin' ya, if we'd been huntin' I'd have bounced outta here alright. And those bruisers woulda taken off like a flock of quail. An elk hasn't attacked a person in Oregon in my lifetime. Anyway, they're gone now, so we don't hav'ta worry about it."

"Not until a herd like that catches us when we're out there with nothing but our fishing poles."

Gabe put his head on the top of the steering wheel and started laughing. "Ya don't give up on a thought easy, do ya, Zach?! I gotta tell you, I like that, even if you are wrong."

Half an hour later, they were driving down what was once a logging spur road. Actually, driving may not have been the best description; bouncing may have been more accurate. What once had been a road had been reduced to a poor excuse for a cow path by erosion during spring runoff. It was on a steep downhill grade that snaked around some house-sized boulders and through some old growth lodge pole pines.

It made for rough going and once when they bounced so hard that Zach's head hit the top of the cab, he asked, "Are we lost? You can't be driving through here on purpose, are you?"

"This is the only way to get within easy walking distance of the crick that I want to try next. This road wasn't so rough last time I came down here. But that was a couple of years back. One thing about it, though, I doubt if anyone else has been down here in awhile and that should mean that the fishin' 'ill be good."

"Fishing would have to be excellent to make this ride worth taking. How much longer are we going to have our livers shaken out?"

"We're just about as far as this road 'ill take us."

"How we going to know the difference?" Zach quipped.

They came to a stop on the edge of a meadow. There was an old, broken down, corral under a stand of large lodge poles. The trees were dead, needles still hanging on the branches. A rotting forest service picnic table stood beside a rock-ringed fire pit. Three meat poles hung in strategic trees. It was obvious that there was a time when this was a popular camping spot for big game hunters, but the deterioration of everything made it just as obvious that it hadn't been used in years.

The grass-filled meadow was over half a mile wide and nearly a mile long. A crooked line of willows marked the course of the stream that meandered its way through the field. White, pink and yellow flowers accented the dark green grass that blanketed the meadow; purple lupine blossoms and the blazing red of Indian's paint brush added variety.

A large red-tailed hawk circled high above the grass. Gabe thought it odd that a red-tail had chosen this spot high in the timber since they were a bird normally associated with grasslands. Apparently this three or four-hundred acre meadow was enough grassland for this particular hawk.

The pair of fishermen sat in the pickup and looked out across the clearing. Though Gabe had been here a few times before, he was still struck by the spot's remarkable beauty. The impact of the view was enhanced by the fact that it was so unexpected in this area that was dominated by mile after mile of pine trees.

Checking his watch, Gabe saw that it was almost noon, and said to Zach, "Hey, let's chow down on the lunch that your grandmother packed for us. Then we'll see if the trout in this crick are any friendlier than the ones in the Chewacan were."

"Sure, that sounds good. This is a cool spot. Could we make camp here?"

"Let's see how cooperative the fish are before we decide, but, yeah it is a neat place; if the fish are bitin' it would be a great place to pitch the tent. And I don't think we have to worry about anybody else hornin' in on us here. We should have the place to ourselves."

"For sure. I don't think anybody else would be crazy enough to try to drive down here!"

"So, I'm crazy now, am I?" Gabe laughed. "That comment would've cut me straight to the core if it t'weren't true.

When given the go-ahead to unload, the two labs raced through the surrounding timber until they realized that the cooler had been opened. Then, they came and sat side by side, watching every movement that Zach and Gabe made, as the men straddled the benches on opposite sides of the decaying picnic table and ate their lunch. The canines made it no secret that they were hoping that a spare bite might be flipped their direction.

The fishermen faced east across the meadow. On the far side of the grass a ridge dominated the horizon, but, instead of the green pines that were so prevalent in the area, the trees that covered the ridge were almost all reddish brown. "Why are those trees over there all brown?" Zach asked between bites.

"The same reason that several of the trees right here are brown," Gabe explained, "they're dead. The trees have been attacked by a little guy called the mountain pine beetle. The bug is only about the size of a grain of rice, but if enough of 'em get in a tree, the big old tree is a goner."

Gabe walked to a nearby tree and pointed. "See these little white bumps on the bark of this tree? Every one of those pitch bumps mark where a beetle has bored into the tree."

Zach looked up and down the tree. There were dozens of the deposits of resin. "Do the beetles make the pitch?"

"Sort of. That pitch is the tree's attempt at drowning whatever is attacking it. When the beetle bores in, the tree releases the pitch to cover the wound and drive out the attacker. As you can see, the tactic isn't too effective."

"You mean that all of those trees were killed by a tiny bug? There are thousands of dead trees over there!"

"All the trees that are that reddish brown color are dead. The beetle usually doesn't get in the smaller ones, and it tends to stay away from ponderosas, but, yeah, almost all the trees on that hillside are dead. And there are miles and miles of forest just like that. Millions and millions of acres of trees, stretching from Mexico clear up into Canada; have been killed by little bugs."

"That's terrible. Are there going to be any trees left? Can't something be done to stop the beetles?"

"Oh, there are sprays that can kill 'em, I'm sure. But how much would it cost to spray the whole infected area, and what repercussion would that kind of spraying program cause? Prescribed burns have been used to control the spread of the bugs in some places, but, with this large an area being infected, burns wouldn't be practical. All the trees won't die, anyway. Like I said, the beetles don't seem to be inclined to attack small trees and a few of the healthiest big trees can fight 'em off, so there will be enough survivors to re-seed the area."

"It'll sure make the area ugly for awhile though, won't it?"

"Ugly and more," Gabe answered. "In the short run, the forest fire danger, in an area with this much fuel is going to be extreme all summer. Then, problems with things like erosion will make things interestin' for a long time to come. And that's not to even mention the economic impact that the loss of this much timber will have."

"So, Grumps," Zach said with a smirk that he hoped was hidden, "why did your God create a critter that causes as many problems as this little beetle?"

"Ya know, Zach, I've been asked that about yellow jackets, mosquitoes, ticks, and even skunks. Those things weren't created to be the problems that they are now. Originally, they had good, useful, purposes, but when Adam and Eve fell to that original sin, every part of earth's creation was affected. The Bible says that 'all creation groans' as it waits for God to bring in the new earth. With that new earth, everythin' will be put back to perfect. Then those pests will go back to doin' what God originally intended for them to do."

"You mean God is making us all pay for the mistakes that Adam and Eve made?"

"I don't see it quite like that, Zach. The way I see it, it's God's mercy and love that allows things like weeds and hornets and skunks and even these stinkin' pine beetles."

"How can those things come out of mercy and love?"

"The bad things are designed to drive us to God. If things were all enjoyable, we wouldn't be very inclined to seek a relationship with him."

"Well, I need to tell you Grumpa, the plan isn't working for me. If God is trying to get my attention by allowing bad stuff to happen, he's going to be disappointed."

"Funny thing about that Zach, God is never disappointed. He knows everythin' from beginning to end."

"If believing that stuff is a comfort to you, I'm glad for you, but I just don't see it."

"That's alright, Zach. I'll just keep prayin' that you do."

"See, there it is again. If God knows everything, beginning to end, how could prayer possibly change anything?"

"You can't get there by logic, son. God, and his ways, is just too big to figure out through our puny thought process."

At that, the pair sat quietly and finished their lunch while they looked out at the view. Once the dogs realized that the food was gone they started casting about for interesting scents. Gabe let them run for about ten minutes and then called them back and hooked them to their tethers. "You two knot heads stay here and rest," he said to the dogs. "We're goin' fishin'!"

Turning to Zach, he said, "You comin'?"

"You know I am," Zach replied.

The seriousness of their conversation was pushed to the subconscious levels of their minds as the pair moved to the stream, fly rods in hand. Gabe stood to the side and let his grandson flip a baited hook into the water first. He watched with interest as the bait drifted down toward the hole. The worm wasn't out of sight; in fact, the bait was no more than a foot into the water, when a nice brookie swam up and sucked the hook, and the worm covering it, into its mouth. Zach played it perfectly and put it into his tote.

Since brook trout do not generally bite aggressively, Gabe knew from the response on that first cast that this stream was full of fish that were competitive and hungry. That was a great combination for the fisherman.

"Zach, one thing to remember here, we're not goin' home for a few days, so we can only keep as many fish as we can eat for dinner. The day we're going to leave we'll stock up on the smoker fodder, but un- til then everythin'we aren't gonna eat will have to be thrown back. The best thing to do is throw back any fish that isn't hurt. The ones that are bleeding or look hurt we'll eat."

"Okay."

They fished for thirty or forty minutes, and fish were af- ter their hooks the entire time. "Well," Gabe said, "it's ob- vious that no one has fished this stretch of crick all sum- mer. I don't think I've ever seen brookies that were more eager to grab a fly. But we better quit for today. I've got as many as I'll be able to eat for dinner, how 'bout you, Zach?"

"Yeah, I'm sure I do. But, man, I hate to quit. This is a blast!"

"It's fun alright, but we don't wanna get 'em all sore- mouthed today. We'll give 'em another go tomorrow."

On the way back to the campsite, Gabe walked slowly and pointed out animal tracks to Zach. Game trails crisscrossed the meadow and they found deer, elk, coyote, and raccoon tracks in the dust and mud of those animal highways. Within half an hour, Zach was able to correctly identify each type of track. Gabe also had the boy compare the tracks they had made when they first arrived to the ones they were making right then to show how a little time changes the look of a track.

When they were almost back to the pickup Gabe said, "Maybe tomorrow we can go up on a ridge that I know about to the south of here and find some cougar or bear tracks."

Zach answered, "Wow, that'd be awesome. Do you think we might find some?"

"Yeah, I think there's a pretty good chance. There are quite a few bear in this region, and there are more and more cougar every year. But right now let's go clean the fish we have and then we can do a little target practice with the .22 rifle."

"Great! What are we going to shoot?"

"Oh, we'll find some cans or something lying around. We'd better set up camp first, though. I don't think we're gonna find better fishin' than we've got right here. I just hope the skitters don't get too thick once the sun starts goin' down."

When they started to clean the fish, Gabe pulled a Buck knife out of his pocket and handed it to Zach. It was identical to the one that the school had confiscated. "Here. You ain't gonna get out of cleanin' fish just 'cause you don't have a knife. But see if you can manage to hold on to this one a little longer, will ya?"

"Thanks, Grumpa. I can't believe that you trust me with another knife after what I did with the last one!"

"Ah Zach, everyone makes mistakes. That's why I believe in second chances. God has sure enough given me a truck load of 'em."

# 20

The dozen fish that they had kept for their dinner were cleaned in a few minutes. Camp didn't take long to set up either, so they were ready to do some plinking within an hour of putting their fishing poles away. For targets they scrounged up some old beer cans that an inconsiderate camper had left behind. They filled the few cans they found, that hadn't already been used for target practice, with water and set them against an old cut bank so they wouldn't have to wonder where the shots were ending up. A few ponderosa pine cones were interspersed among the cans for variety.

Gabe retrieved the rifle, ammunition, and clips from the pickup and stepped off fifty paces from the targets. "Okay Zach," Gabe began, "this is the same rifle you used before. Do you remember what it is?"

"A Ruger 10/.22."

"Why'd they name it a 10/.22?"

"Well, it's a .22 caliber and the factory clip holds ten bullets."

"Right. Do you remember how to put the shells in the clip?"

"I think so. Don't you just line them up with the opening and push down with your thumb?"

"Hey, you remember this stuff pretty good. So, do you remember the number one rule about handling firearms?"

"Treat every gun as if it were loaded. And never, ever, point a gun at anything that you wouldn't want to shoot."

Gabe smiled and said, "Man, I must be a really good teacher. You've got the answers down pat."

Gabe handed the rifle to Zach, the barrel pointed in the air. "Okay, here you go. What's the first thing you're gonna check?"

Zach took the rifle and was careful to keep the barrel pointed up. He worked the bolt, saying, "I can look in here to make sure that there isn't a round in the chamber."

"Good job," Gabe said and handed Zach a loaded clip. "You remember how to put this in?"

Zach took the clip and snapped it into place. Then he worked the bolt, bringing one of the shells into the rifle's chamber. He turned to take aim on the targets, but his grandfather stopped him. "Whoa. Wait a minute. What'd you forget?"

Zach looked puzzled and said, "I don't think I forgot anything."

"How 'bout snapping on the safety? That's the one thing I don't like about these Rugers. You can't activate the safety until a round is in the chamber."

"I'm sorry. I knew that, but I forgot."

"'At's alright. It's been awhile since you shot. That's why I'm walkin' you through this nice and slow. Now, are you gonna shoot off-hand or do you wanna take a rest on somethin'?"

"I want to give it a try without a rest to start with. We're pretty close to the targets."

"Okay, go ahead and blast away. Let's see if you can hit the can on the far right first, then work your way to the left."

It took Zach three shots to hit the first can, but then he made direct hits on the next two. When the ten round rotary magazine was empty, he had scored five hits and five misses.

"Not bad. Not bad at all," Gabe said. "With a little practice you're gonna be a real fine marksman."

"Thanks. I like to shoot."

"Yeah, me, too. I don't know why, but it just feels good, doesn't it. And the smell of burnt gun powder always smells good to me. I suppose I'm more than a little bit goofy."

They spent the next hour and a half taking turns shooting. The targets kept getting smaller and farther away. Toward the end of the session they were shooting at bottle caps from seventy-five yards, and hitting them once in a while.

Gabe was more than a little pleased with the boys shooting prowess; and he was even more proud of the way that Zach handled the firearm in a safe manner. "Hey, you remember a while back when you told me you weren't good at anything? Well, I kinda think you found somethin' that you're good at now. That was some fine shootin', son."

"Thanks, Grumpa. But I don't think I'll have much opportunity to show that talent off. There aren't exactly a lot of shooting contests in Phoenix."

"You can't tell when it might come in handy. Besides, being able to shoot a rifle as well as you've been shooting means that you have a steady hand and a good eye. Those are things that are important in a lot of ways."

"I guess, but I haven't found any of them yet. Just ask my dad."

Gabe wasn't sure how to respond to that comment, so he just took the rifle from Zach and said, "Come on, let's go wipe the gun down so it doesn't rust from our fingerprints; then, we'll cook us up some vittles. How do fried spuds and fried trout sound to ya?"

"It sounds good to me. My mom doesn't ever…didn't ever…" Zach couldn't finish the sentence because he was suddenly on the verge of crying.

Gabe spoke softly, "She probably said that fried food wasn't healthy, didn't she? Well, I suppose she was right about that. But it sure tastes almighty good from time to time. And camping food doesn't count for calories or cholesterol or any of that anyway.

"You really miss her, don't cha? Yeah, well, so do I."

"Why'd she have to end up like she is?" Zach said as he wiped tears from his eyes with short angry strokes. "If your God is so great, why is Mom in a coma?"

With water welling up in his eyes, Gabe stepped over to his grandson and hugged the boy. The two stood crying quietly for a long time before Gabe answered, "I gotta be honest, Zach. I don't know. But, there are lots of thin's that I don't understand. That's why I'm glad that God is in control of all this and not me."

Zach blew his nose and replied, "It doesn't look like anyone is in charge to me!"

"Oh, he's in charge right enough. Someday you'll understand. Come on, let's go make some dinner. Can I get you to peel some spuds while I get the stove all hooked up and ready to go?"

It didn't take long for them to have a good mess of spuds and trout fried to a golden brown. As quick as they had been at getting the meal prepared, they were even quicker at getting it eaten. The dogs noisily cleaned up the leftovers that Gabe scraped off the plates onto a couple of pieces of wood. When the meal was finished and the dishes cleaned, Gabe and Zach sat on blocks of wood and looked at the view. A flock of camp robber jays had moved in while the men had been eating and Zach was using some bread to coax one of the gray-backed thieves in close enough to pet. Within a few minutes, there were two of the noisy birds that would land on his hand to grab a bite of bread. The dogs were interested in the birds and whined and wiggled as they tried to get to the bread the birds were enjoying.

"Those are some strange little pests," Gabe said. "They like people good enough to take food right out of your hand out here in the woods, but you never see one of 'em in town where they could get a handout anytime they wanted. They're smart, too. Not too many birds know enough to stash food, but these varmints make a kinda paste out of excess vittles and glue the balls of the junk on trees, for later. I don't know if they ever remember to come back to their stash, but they must, if they go to all that trouble."

When the bread was gone, the birds disappeared as quickly as they had arrived. "Where'd they go?" Zach asked.

"Off to find some more food, I guess. But don't worry, those rascals 'ill be back in the mornin' in time for breakfast."

"How do they know when we're eating?"

"I have no idea. They must smell the food or somethin'. All I know is that anytime you start cookin' or eatin' out here in the woods, a flock of those little crows shows up to give you some help cleanin' up the vittles."

"Those little birds aren't really crows are they?"

"They're related to crows and jays, I think."

"If they're related to crows, do you think you might be able to teach one to talk. There's a pet store in Phoenix that has a talking crow. It's really cool."

"I've never heard of a talkin' camp robber, but I wouldn't be surprised. They mimic all kind of other bird calls, I know that. But don't get any ideas, there's no way that your grandmother would let you bring one a those guys in the house."

"Why not, they're not very big, and even if they are gluttons, they couldn't eat much."

"It's not how much they'd eat that'd be the problem, it's the dirt."

"What do you mean dirt?"

"Birds are dirty. I've never seen one that was house-trained. And they are always dropping feathers and dander."

"I could keep him in the shop. Your shop is dirty enough that a little bird couldn't make much difference."

"Yeah, you have a point there. But I don't think you'd wanna have one a those whiskey jacks as a pet any-way. Like I said, they don't like people in more'n very small doses. But hey, changin' the subject here, it's star-tin' to cool down, what say we gather up some wood and get us a fire goin'?"

"That sounds good. Do we get to have s'mores?"

"It just so happens that I have some marshmallows, graham crackers, and chocolate bars, so I think s'mores could be a very good possibility. Let's grab some limb-wood. We don't need a very big fire only one that's big enough to take the chill off, and provide some roastin' coals, of course. And a small fire will be easier to douse when we get ready to go to bed."

Tall piles of white clouds with dark grey edges built in the western sky. The sun went down in a horizon washed in pinks and reds as evening gave way to twilight. Grandson and grandfather sat beside a small pile of glowing embers. Their fingers were sticky with the residue of roasted marshmallows. A patch of stringy white decorated Gabe's rust and gray mustache.

The pair stared at the coals and thought.

If organizers of Washington think-tanks knew the effects and advantages of thinking while looking into a pile of hot coals, there would be working fireplaces in every meeting room.

Bats flew between the trees and darted and rolled. To the east, a coyote howled. Seconds later, what sounded like an answer echoed in the west. The sky darkened and stars appeared one by one, between the building clouds, until there were thousands of jewels sparkling like polished diamonds against a jeweler's black velvet cloth. A breeze caressed the tops of the trees, lending harmony to the bass notes of a great horned owl. These were the sights and sounds that defined a high desert night in Gabe's mind and he was delighted to be sharing the show with his grandson.

"What do you think, Zach?" Gabe asked. "Can there be anywhere that is better than this?" A meteor blazed a brilliant trail across the sky at that very second as if to underscore the question.

"Oh, it is pretty and the sounds are interesting, but I'm not sure that I really like it. In fact, to be honest, it's kind of spooky."

Gabe pointed to Nute and Ace, who were laying one on either side of him, as close to him as they could get, and said, "I think these big mutts agree with you. Look at these brutes, they act like they are afraid that some ornery critter is gonna come and gobble 'em up. But there isn't anythin' 'round here that is apt to hurt them, or us."

As if on cue, Ace lifted his head off his paws and sniffed the night air. Then, he jumped up, the hair across his back stood on end, and a low, vicious growl came from his throat. Not to be outdone, Nute was instantly up, and he lunged, barking, in the direction that Ace was facing.

"Knock it off, you two knuckleheads; you know there ain't nothin' out there!" Gabe scolded. The dogs weren't convinced, and it took several minutes for them to settle down.

"What was that all about?" Zach asked.

"I dunno. I suppose a mouse sneezed or a toad tooted. These big oafs are afraid of their own shadows sometimes."

"But how do you know there isn't something like a bear or cougar out there."

"Maybe there is. But if there is, they aren't gonna hurt us. Like I keep tryin' to explain, those varmints are way more afraid of us than we are of them."

"Well, I have to tell you, they must be pretty darn scared then," Zach replied. "If some big hairy beast came busting in here right now, it wouldn't have a chance of eating me alive because it would instantly scare me to death."

"Oh, come on, I thought you told me that you were over all that bein' afraid stuff."

"That was in the daylight. Now, in the dark, the fear factor is alive and well."

"Ah, after you've spent some time out here, you'll get so you don't even think about anythin' gettin' you. You'll just soak it all in and enjoy it."

"You really do love it out here don't you?"

"You bet I do! Bein' around a bunch of people is what gives *me* the heebie jeebies."

Zach thought about that for a few minutes and said, "Then how come you like going to church so much. There's a bunch of people there."

"Ya know, that's a really good question, Zach. It used to bug me a lot, especially if I couldn't sit in the very back row. Having people behind me like that would almost make my hair stand on end—back when I had hair. But, somehow, God over the years has taught me that celebrating him and his goodness, with other people that love him is too special for me to allow it to be polluted by my phobias."

"There you go with all that God stuff again."

"Yeah, well, you asked, and I can't help talkin' about him since God is the most important thing in the world to me. I don't know how people can cope with life without him."

"So it's like Dad said, you use God as a crutch?"

"Oh, he's more than a crutch. Crutches don't do dead people any good. And that's what I am outside of Jesus Christ, just a dead man.

"But speakin' of your dad, when he and your mom first started dating, he claimed to be a Christian. It'd be interestin' to know what happened with that. By the way, do you miss him?"

"Nah, I never saw him much anyway. And whenever I did it seemed like all we ever did was fight and argue. Do you think he poisoned Mom?"

"I don't know what to think about that. I don't know why he would, but the police seem to think he might be to blame."

"What do you think about the rope on my bedroom door? Why would anyone do that?"

"To keep you in your room I guess. So you wouldn't find your mom and try to rescue her? If your dad was trying to kill her, he might have done it, but, on the other hand, if your mom was tryin' to kill herself, she may have done it. The whole deal has me all kinds of confused. I don't know why he'd try to kill her or why she'd try to kill herself."

"I think it was because of me. They were really upset at me about that deal at school."

"Zach," Gabe said sternly, "quit thinking like that. What happened to your mom is not your fault."

"Then why did this happen the same day that I got arrested at school?"

"I dunno, but things like what happened to your mom don't happen just because a kid gets in trouble at school. There was way bigger stuff involved with your mom than your little mishap."

# 21

Officers Todd Evans and Buck Rivera were in a conference room with Phoenix detectives Bruce Schiller and Randy Mack. Todd and Buck had just finished going over all the facts of the case.

Schiller was a medium sized guy. He remained standing though the other three men were seated. The two oversized patrolmen irritated Schiller, and he didn't even know why.

"What'da ya mean, you were thinkin' suicide all the way when you found her? Ya think nobody ever staged a suicide when they offed their old lady?" Schiller asked in an irritated tone.

Buck was too steamed to answer the question, so he just sat and tried to keep from jumping up and putting a choke hold on this idiot. Todd was slightly more controlled and was able to field the question calmly, though with a sarcastic tone, clicking the points off on his big meaty fingers. "Well, let's see. The address had a history of attempted suicide. There was an empty pill bottle on the counter. Nothing in the part of the house where we'd been suggested a struggle. Yeah, Mr. Smart guy De Tec Tive, I guess it does sound like we should have ruled out suicide right away. What'd ya expect us to think? And, oh, our Sergeant had just told us to be careful because the owner of the house was a personal friend of the Mayor. So lose your attitude, ya little jerk, before I let Buck here eat ya for breakfast and pick his teeth with one of your leg bones."

At that last comment Schiller had yelled, "Come ahead." The older, larger, calmer detective grabbed his partner.

"Come on, Bruce. Calm down," Mack told Schiller. "These guys are on our side. I think."

Now Buck was on his feet, too, and was more than a little bit sorry that Schiller hadn't come across the table. When he spoke his voice was an icy whisper, "Anytime you think you've grown up enough to have a piece of me, Schiller, you just let me know. I'll wad you up like a used napkin and stuff you in a half-gallon trash can."

Now it was Todd's turn to try to calm his partner. He said, "Okay Buck, sit down. This guy might not appear to be too smart, but he's gotta be bright enough to know that if he's gonna fight you he needs to practice fallin' down and learn how to eat mashed taters." That last comment cut through some of the tension and even had caused Mack to smile.

When everyone had more or less regained their composure and were re-seated, Mack tried to start over. "So, did you guys see the rope on the door handles?" He flipped a photo of the rope onto the table.

"Yeah," Todd answered. "We saw it. In fact, I took that picture, but not until Sarge told us about it and had us go look."

162

"Did you notice anything about the knots?"

Buck took this question and answered, "I did. The knots were neat. The one on the boy's doorknob was a simple bowline. But on the other door was a sweet knot. I don't know what it's called but it was a loop in the middle of the line and the excess line was coiled on the floor, not just thrown in a heap like you'd expect someone to do. Whoever tied those doors together had built knots and handled line before."

Buck had caught Mack's attention. "You said 'line' while most people would say rope. Why is that?"

"I dunno. Some folks say rope, some say line. I guess it depends what you're doin' with it. Like when you use a block with it, all of a sudden your 'line' becomes 'tackle'."

"Hmm. I guess that doesn't help, but it's interesting. You think this person who tied these knots knew what they were doing, though."

"Oh yeah, they knew their way around knots alright. Ask your average guy off the street to tie two doorknobs together with a long line and you'll end up with a tangle that looks like a giant spider on crack had been there. And when they get done, they'll leave the excess in a mess of a pile. The guy who tied these knots knew his way around alright."

"Hey, Bruce, do we know if Mr. Mertz had any reason to have experience with knots. Was he a boy scout, or sailor, or anything?"

"I don't know," Bruce answered, "but you can bet I'll be finding out."

This whole knot business had captured everyone's attention and Todd weighed in with a question of his own. "Buck, you said 'guy'. Is there any reason that it couldn't have been a woman who made those knots?"

"Not that I know of," Buck replied.

"Then I guess we better check Ms. Mertz's back-ground for rope tying experience, too," Bruce added. "But I still like him for this."

"I don't get this," Todd said. "What's wrong with this being a simple suicide attempt?"

"Well, I might be more inclined to go along with you on that except for some of the dirt we came up with on Dr. Mertz."

"What kind of dirt?" Buck wanted to know.

"Well, it seems that our pal Dave Mertz was having considerably more than a professional relationship with a certain female doctor who was a colleague of his. In fact, she had already left her husband and claims that David was planning to leave Ms. Mertz and move into a well furnished condominium that the two of them were renting together. Ms. Mertz's untimely demise would certainly cost him a lot less than a divorce settlement.

"Then, there was some interesting information that the boy gave us when we interviewed him. Zach Mertz claims that during the last conversation that he had with his mother, she had been making plans to take him and leave for Oregon. If Mr. Mertz had gotten wind of that it may have increased his fears of a costly separation."

"Okay, enough of this speculation. Is there anything else from the scene that might help us out here?"

"Not from the scene, but from the hospital. I don't know if it's even worth bringin' up, but when I was baby-sitting the kid, I had to leave him for a minute to go the john; when I got back, the kid was gone. I found him hiding in the x-ray waiting area, and he gave me this crazy story about some guy all dressed in black. He claimed that the guy had been in his yard the night before and that he had seen him previous to that up in Oregon."

Schiller's banty-rooster posturing started again while Todd was talking and he said, "I didn't read anything

164

about that in your report. Didn't you think that this guy might be a witness, or maybe even a suspect?"

"Settle down, big guy. The kid claimed that the guy was dressed in a jumpsuit, baseball cap, and boots, all black. Since it was hotter than Hades, I kind of doubted the story. I mean, who goes around dressed like that when the temperature is over the century mark? And nobody else saw the guy. Not the neighbor who originally called us to the Mertz home because Zach looked like a burglar, not the receptionist at the hospital, and not me."

Schiller just shook his head and looked peeved.

Mack said, "Okay, I think we better get hold of the kid and find out what else he remembers about the mystery man.

"That's it then," Mack concluded. "Let us know if you think of anything else."

# 22

By the time the embers of Zach and Gabe's fire had burned down to grey powder, nothing was calling but the crickets. Gabe poured a bucket of water into the ashes and stirred them with a stick as he said, "Hey, let's climb into our sleepin' bags and get some rest so's we can handle them big trout that we'll be doin' battle with tomorrow."

They crawled into the three-man dome tent and wiggled into their sleeping bags. The combination of the emotional discussion and the fresh air and exercise had them both asleep within minutes.

Three hours later, they were both wide awake. The roar of the wind through the trees sounded like there was a jet airplane taking off less than a hundred yards away. The little nylon tent was shaking and whipping until it seemed it would have to come apart at the seams.

"What's going on, Grumpa?" Zach wanted to know.

Gabe had to shout to be heard over the roar of the wind through the trees, "We're right in the middle of a big old thunderstorm son. I just hope it doesn't bring any hail with it. A good sized hail storm 'ill cut our little tent to pieces and beat us up real good in the process."

Zach's breath was coming fast as he lay listening to the storm. "Are we going to be alright?" he yelled against the storm.

Gabe didn't answer, but Zach could hear him praying: "God, we're stuck in a storm here. I know that you know it. I don't wanna be like Peter and them when they were out on the sea in that storm, but I gotta tell ya, I'm a little scared. Please give us the faith to believe that whatever is gonna happen is what you want to happen."

Flashes of lightning were bright enough to illuminate the inside of the tent, and the peals of thunder followed the flashes within seconds. Tree branches were banging together above them and cones and needles were pelting the tent. The whoosh and crash of a tree falling, punctuated by ground shaking from the impact, got Gabe moving. He remembered the dead trees that they were camped among and shouted, "Come on, we've gotta get out of here before one of those trees lands on us!"

While they were scrambling into their clothes, Zach asked, "Where are we going to go?"

"We'll jump into the truck and drive down the road a ways. We'll be a lot safer in a stand of smaller timber that doesn't have so much dead stuff in it. We could drive out into the clearing, but I'm afraid that we might get struck by lightning out there."

As Gabe crawled out of the tent, the dogs came out from their shelter under the picnic table and both of them tried to lick his face. He swatted them away and headed for the truck with the sleeping bags—he wanted to keep them dry if possible. By the time he had thrown the bags into the extended cab of the pickup, Zach had started out of the tent and Gabe yelled, "Hang onto the tent, Zach, or it'll blow away."

Zach was trying his hardest to comply with his grand-father's instruction, but an especially strong gust of wind grabbed the tent and blew the boy and the tent end over end. When they hit, Zach let go of the nylon kite, and it went rolling across the meadow like a lopsided beach ball. The boy started after it but stopped when Gabe yelled, "No, Zach, let it go. We'll get it tomorrow. Come on, we've gotta get out of here."

To emphasize the point, another tree boomed down nearby. Zach jumped into the pickup and struggled to get the door closed. Gabe used the sides of the truck to keep from being knocked down as he went to the back of the truck to open the tailgate so the dogs could load. Nute jumped in, but Ace crawled under the truck just as the rain hit like an ocean wave. Gabe was soaked to the skin before ten seconds had passed.

He had his head under the tailgate, trying to coax the dog out from beneath the truck when the tree hit. It was a dead lodge pole pine, more than twenty inches in diameter at the stump, and it hit full force across the bed of the pickup. There was a squeal from Nute amongst the crashing of the dry limbs breaking and the screech of the truck's steel being smashed, but Gabe didn't hear any of it. The force of the blow of the tree on the truck had sent the tailgate into the back of his head and knocked him out. He landed face first in the rivulets of rain water that were already running down the hill and under the truck.

Inside the cab, the impact was so violent that Zach was bounced off the seat and the top of his head banged against the truck's roof hard enough to crack his teeth together. Momentarily dazed, Zach sat looking at the raindrops bouncing off the windshield.

An exceptionally bright flash of lightning lit the landscape and illuminated *him*. He was right in front of the truck, the man in the jumpsuit and hat. The boy's involuntary scream was drowned out by the boom of thunder, as the scene went back to black on black. Zach found little comfort when the next bolt revealed only a wet windswept field and no sign of the man.

Gabe's return to consciousness was accompanied by a roaring headache. He spit out a mouth full of mud, shook his head in an attempt to focus, and tried to get up. The movement caught Ace's attention, and the dog wriggled over to lick Gabe's face. This overt show of affection didn't do much to lighten the man's disposition, nor did the fact that he couldn't move his left leg. A little frantic investigation revealed that one of the lower limbs of the fallen tree, a piece of timber in its own right, had hit Gabe just above his knee. The jagged end of the branch was pinning his jeans to the ground. Assessing the odd angle of his leg led Gabe to the conclusion that the leg was broken.

As Gabe's thinking began to clear, he realized that he didn't know if Zach had been hurt by the falling tree. "Zach," he called, "hey, Zach, can you hear me?" Though he was yelling at the top of his lungs, the force of the wind was whipping the sound away and there was no answer.

He had to get loose from this tree and find out if the boy was alright. Trying to pull the limb off his Levis proved futile. The branch was still firmly connected to the tree, and moving that tree was not going to happen. Next, he tried getting his hand into his pocket to extract his knife, but getting his big old hands into a soaking wet pocket while he laying on his belly in the mud proved to be a difficult chore. Finally, though, he managed to get the knife out and it only took a few minutes to saw through enough of the denim to free his leg.

He crawled out from under the truck and a flash of lightning provided enough light for him to see what he wished he hadn't. Nute had been hit by the tree. The pickup's side rails had taken the main force of the blow but the broken end of a huge limb had hit squarely on the big dog's back. The twisted position of the labs body left no need to check for signs of life. Tears mixed with the rain water running down Gabe's face as he stood and tried to swallow the big lump in his throat. Images of Nute's bright eyes, as he retrieved a mallard drake from the muddy water of Summer Lake, raced through Gabe's memory.

Forcing himself back to the present, Gabe took a step toward the cab to check on Zach; when he put his weight on his left leg he went back down in the mud. Though there wasn't a lot of pain, it was obvious that something was wrong. He investigated with his fingers and found that the pant leg, despite the hole he had sawed in it with his knife, was as tight as an overstuffed sausage. Swelling had already brought the leg to half-again its normal size. Gabe was somewhat relieved to find that he couldn't feel any open wound or jagged bones, so apparently it was not a compound fracture, at least.

He pulled himself up with the side of the pickup and carefully started for the cab again, this time without putting any appreciable weight on the injured leg. It just took a couple of hops to get him to where he could reach the door handle, but when he pulled up on it, he found it was locked. The windows were all fogged up, making it impossible to see into the cab. Frustrated and frightened, he banged on the window with the palm of his hand and yelled, "Zach, are you in there? Open the door."

The passenger side window rolled down a crack and Gabe heard Zach shout, "Is he still out there?"

"Is who out here? Are you hurt?"

"I'm okay, but is that guy still out there?"

"I don't know who besides me you think might be out here, Zach, but I need for you to open the door so I can get out of this rain and off my broken leg."

The door came open, and Zach crawled over the console into the driver's seat so that Gabe could sit in the passenger's seat. He had to use his hands to pick his leg up and swing it into the cab.

Once he was inside, he asked Zach again, "Are you hurt?"

"No, I just have a knot on my head from bouncing it off the roof of the truck. Other than that I'm okay. But what's wrong with your leg? Is it really broken?"

"Yeah, I think it's busted alright. It's swelling like crazy, and I can't put any weight on it."

"Can you drive?"

"I don't think it matters much whether I can drive or not. This little rig isn't goin' anywhere with that big stinkin' tree laying on it. Fact is I don't know if it will go at all after taking the hit it took. Are you sure you're okay."

"Yeah, but what are we going to do to get out of here?"

"I dunno. We'll try to figure somethin' out when it gets light. But why did you have the truck locked?"

"That guy was out there looking in the window—the guy in the black hat and jumpsuit."

"That's impossible, Zach," Gabe said. "There is no way that anybody is wanderin' around out there in this storm."

"Well, I saw him. He was standing right in front of the truck, looking straight in the windshield. I don't know why, but I think he's after me."

Gabe sat awhile before asking, "You don't know why he's after you, or you don't know why you *think* he's after you?"

172

"I don't know. Both I guess. But what I do know is that he's freaking me out. What does he want?"

Again, Gabe didn't answer for awhile. He rubbed the back of his head and fingered the big goose-egg that had formed beneath a four inch split in his scalp; blood had run down his neck and mixed with the water from the rain. Finally, he said, "Zach, I don't know what you saw, but my head is busted open and I've got a doozey of a headache that is makin' me as dizzy as a dodo bird. My leg is busted, and my pickup is smashed. If all that ain't enough, we're forty miles from the nearest cell phone reception and one of my dogs is squashed to death in the back of my truck. I've got absolutely no idea how we're gonna get out of here.

"So, I've gotta tell ya, I've also got no earthly idea of what you're talkin' about with this guy in the black clothes thing. Son, there is no way under heaven that there is anybody way out here in the middle of nowhere, on this night, in this storm. And even if there was, he'd be huntin' for a hole to crawl into, not standing around lookin' into our windshield."

It was Zach's turn to be quiet. The pair sat listening to the wind and the thunder and watching the lightning striking in every direction around them. Huge raindrops were splashing out a rhythm on the glass. Then, as the time between strikes got longer and the gusts of wind were losing their strength, Zach quietly said, "I am not making this stuff up."

"I didn't say that I thought you were lying," Gabe said with a slur.

"What then, you think I'm nuts?"

When no answer came from across the dark of the pickup cab, Zach sat thinking that his grandfather did indeed think he was crazy. For the first thirty seconds, that thought made him angry, and he started formulating words that would convey his rage. But, as he mentally concocted an appropriate reply, fear set in. What if he was crazy? His mother must have been, to take all those pills. Maybe insanity was hereditary.

But he had seen that guy. He knew he had.

Zach oscillated between anger and fear, with tears running down his cheeks, waiting for any comment from Gabe. Finally, the anger got the upper hand and he flung the pickup door open and lurched out of the truck into the wind and rain. He started quickly downhill, with no clue of where he was headed—besides away. Three long strides from the truck he slipped on the rain saturated ground and went down hard on his backside. He got up, soaked and muddy and mad. Then, he remembered the lunatic that was out in this storm. He stumbled through the dark, back to the pickup and jerked open the passenger side door prepared to unleash his emotions on his grandfather. That anger was multiplied by two when Zach saw that the old man had fallen asleep!

Zach was a dozen angry words into a full tirade when he realized that the eyes of the man he was verbally assaulting were twitching. The realization that his grandfather was unconscious, not asleep, didn't snap into place until several more venomous words had spewed out.

As Zach stood in the dark, rain was hitting the exposed skin on his neck and the back of his arms so hard that it stung. His stomach ached and it felt like someone had placed a heavy weight on his chest. His anger turned to fear, and the fear morphed into panic, as the ramifications and desperation of his predicament began to sink in. He shouted into the blackness, "What am I supposed to do?"

Unable to formulate a plan, or even a first step, Zach realized that he was starting to hyperventilate. Not knowing what else to do, he shut the passenger door and went back around to the driver's side of the pick-up and crawled back in out of the rain. The dome light automatically stayed on for about ten seconds after the door closed and Zach used that short period of il-lumination to watch his grandfather's ribcage rise and fall, signifying that he was still alive. That, at least, was a relief.

His anger toward his grandfather had completely dis-sipated, and he sat in the dark and began to shiver from being wet to the skin, and from fear. Half an hour later, his teeth were rattling and he was shaking uncontrolla-bly. He reached behind the truck's seat and pulled out his bag and dug out a set of dry clothes. He managed to squirm out of his water soaked clothes and into the dry ones.

Shaking so hard that his teeth were clacking together, he grabbed the sleeping bags that his grandfather had stuffed behind the seat when the storm first started and tucked one of them around Gabe, whose skin felt so cold that, until Zach forced himself to check for a pulse in his grandfather's carotid artery, he was afraid that his grandfather had died. Zach was more relieved than he thought possible when he found a steady thump in the vein. The fact that Grumpa hadn't as much as groaned or twitched during the process didn't provide much encouragement.

Not knowing what else to do to improve their condi-tion, Zach tucked the other sleeping bag around himself settled back in his seat and tried to concentrate on get-ting warm. From the combination of the water in their rain-soaked clothes and their breath, the windows of the truck were completely fogged over. Though he couldn't see out, from the sound, he could tell the big drops of rain were lessening and the wind was dying down. The lightning and thunder had moved on.

Somehow, in spite of the combination of adrenaline that had been pumping through his veins and the cold, Zach fell asleep and began to dream. In the dream were the same warriors that had visited his sleep the night that his mother was taken to the hospital.

Much like in the last dream, the two were circling one another like two boxers. The man in black was the obvious aggressor, continually advancing on the shiny man, who was giving ground and circling to the left. Projectiles were flying from the sinister man's tongue in rapid succession like paintballs from a paint ball gun. The shiny man was again limiting the use of his large sword to shield himself from his adversary's missiles.

Zach wondered why the man didn't use the sword to attack. It appeared that the man in black's sole weapon was his tongue and that he would have no defense against an assault. But, as before, the shiny guy made no attempt to attack.

This battle was taking place in the meadow that Gabe and Zach were camped beside. The sky was blue and the sun was shining brightly on the green grass. There were no birds or animals around, and the scene was as quiet as death.

At each spot where the projectiles that were flying from the man's tongue landed, a puff of smoke rose and the grass was instantly turned brown. Soon, a quarter of the once beautiful area was turned to a withered and smoldering wasteland.

Suddenly the battle dance stopped and both men turned and faced Zach. Though the boy could not see the eyes of either man, he knew that they were looking directly into his as if expecting some response from him.

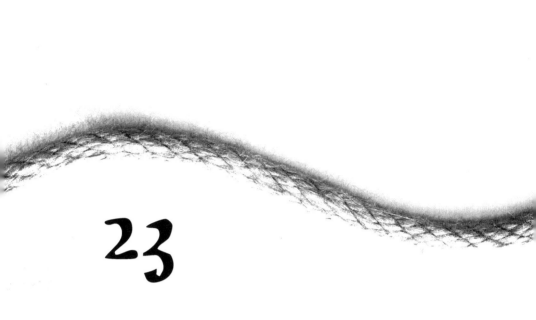

# 23

Zach awoke dazed and confused. It took him a few moments to realize that he wasn't on the edge of the meadow watching a bizarre bit of warfare. He sat behind the pickup's steering wheel. The seat was tipped back as far as it would go, and he lay staring at the truck's ceiling, listening to his grandfather's breathing, and contemplating the strange dream that he had just experienced.

Unable to catch hold of a thought long enough to begin the formulation of a plan, he was slipping back to sleep when something hit the pickup with enough force to rock the truck on its shocks. Zach sat up, trying to see through the foggy glass, straining his eyes. He could make out the shape of someone, or something, on the hood of the truck.

Too frightened to scream, Zach shook while he watched a big finger touch the glass and slowly write,

"I OWN YOUR MOTHER. U R NEXT." Zach closed his eyes, expecting the glass to shatter and the big hand to come through the shards and drag him out into the semi-light of dawn.

Nothing happened for several minutes, and logic began to make progress against the paralyzing fear. Zach began to convince himself that what was taking place on the hood of the pickup was nothing more than an extension of his dream.

It had to be a dream, Zach thought. If someone were writing on the outside of the glass, the letters would be backwards. And the fog was on the inside of the glass, so a writer on the outside would not be able to write in it. Convinced enough to open his eyes, Zach looked at the windshield. The block- letter message was still there. The being on the hood was gone.

When the sun was high enough on the eastern horizon to illuminate the meadow, Zach rolled down the window a crack and looked out at the grass, expecting to see the brown dead spots that marked the dreamland war zone. The meadow was a carpet of rain washed green. The only brown spots in the grass were the products of earthworm-hunting moles. Confused and afraid, the boy sat in the pickup and stared at the message on the glass. Who owned his mom? He wondered. And why would they want him?

As the warmth of the rising sun hit the glass and the open window allowed the humidity to escape the cab of the truck, the windshield began to clear. The message in the fog slowly faded, then disappeared.

The increasing daylight gave Zach enough courage to climb out of the truck, and his first step was to check in front of the truck for tracks. With the tracking lessons that his grandfather had given him the day before, he hoped to be able to tell something about whatever or whoever had been on the hood of the pickup. But the mud created by the downpour of the previous night was as unmarked as the grass of the meadow.

Zach tried to ignore the implications of the unmarred mud by looking around the camping area. He scanned the area for any sign of the man who left the message on the windshield. Despite, or perhaps because of, seeing nothing, the hair on the back of Zach's neck stood on end. He could feel someone watching him. He spun in a circle trying to catch a glimpse of his stalker and then got the .22 rifle from out of the pickup, slipped a loaded clip into it, and racked a round into the chamber. The weight of the gun in his hand lent a little confidence.

He looked around the camping spot and saw that trees were on the ground everywhere. Most of the beetle killed trees had been blown down, along with quite a few green trees. The dead trees and many of the live ones had been uprooted, but a few had broken off, ten or twenty feet in the air. They lay in a jangled tangle all around the camp.

The tree that had struck the truck had been dead long enough to have lost all its needles. Insects and rot had weakened the roots beneath the stump to the point that they had broken off cleanly when the tree fell. The impact of the landing had snapped the trunk off about ten feet the other side of the pickup, leaving about twenty-five feet of tree resting on the rig.

While assessing the tree on the pickup, Zach was shocked to discover Nute's body in the back of the truck. He remembered that his grandfather had said that one of the dogs was dead, but he had been too distraught over the man in black for the fact to register. Now, the sight of the lifeless body breached the dam that was holding back Zach's emotions and he started to sob. He slumped to the muddy ground and cried as memories of the dog overwhelmed him.

When he managed to get his emotions reined in he tried to avoid looking at the gore covered black lump in the back of the truck that had been Nute and started thinking about what he should do next.

To keep busy and to avoid thinking about his predicament or the loss of the dog, Zach searched the area for something to use to pry the section of log off the pickup bed. He had moved about thirty yards from the truck when he heard the hollow thumping of something running toward him. He snapped the rifle's safety to the off position as he spun in a circle trying to see whatever it was that was attacking him.

Fear distorted his vision and hearing, as well as his thought process, and he had the rifle on his shoulder ready to shoot whatever was coming at him, before he realized that it was Ace. The dog raced out of the woods in an excited low-butt run, and the yellow lab ran in circles around Zach, barking and yipping in a frenzied display of delight.

Zach leaned the rifle against a tree and concentrated on giving Ace a serious bit of petting. Dog and boy were relieved to have each other for company. Ace whined, wiggled, and licked Zach's face while Zach hugged the dog's neck and cried.

When the emotion of the strange reunion had run its course, Zach broke loose and renewed his search for something to use as a pry and Ace ran over and put his front feet on the tailgate of the pickup and looked at what had been Nute and barked.

There was no shortage of poles from which to choose a pry pole. He picked out one that was limbless and about fifteen feet long. He dragged it over to the pickup and positioned it under the log, trying to avoid looking at the dead dog. Subconsciously fearing failure, Zach didn't try to move the log that was pinning the pickup. Instead, he went around the truck to check on his grandfather.

Gabe was still in exactly the same position as he had left him when Zach opened the pickup's passenger side door. Zach was again relieved to see the rising and falling of the man's chest and said, "Grumpa, Grumpa, wake up!" Gabe didn't awaken, but he did groan and roll his head to the side. Zach didn't know whether that was a good sign or not.

Not knowing what else to do, the boy shut the pickup door and went back around the bed of the truck. When he got back in the pickup bed, he realized that he needed to do something about Nute's corpse if he was going to be able to work on freeing the truck from the tree. Looking around for something to wrap the dog in, he spotted the tent's rain fly, hung up in the willows about a hundred yards from camp. It had apparently lodged there when the wind sent the tent rolling across the meadow like a tumble weed.

Zach retrieved the piece of nylon material and brought it back to the truck where he rolled Nute onto it and pulled it and the dog out of the truck. It surprised him that he was able to handle the dead animal without being too squeamish, but the hollow sound that the body made when it hit the ground caused Zach to wince. Ace sniffed his life-long companion, licked him once, and then seemed to forget all about him. Zach pulled the tent fly and the dog's corpse out of the way and carefully placed a limb across the nylon to keep the dog covered.

Zach's first attempt at lifting the log raised it an inch or two, but when he let his pry-pole back down, the log settled right back into the indentation that it had made in the sides of the pickup bed when it fell. He needed to figure out some way to move the log enough to get it out of its dent. He looked around, trying to think, but coming up with nothing, he lifted again, with the same result.

Frustrated, he opened the diamond plate tool box that rested across the back of the truck and rummaged around in it looking for something that might be useful. He discovered a tool with a two-foot handle, a spool of steel cable, and a couple of big hooks. It looked like it was built for pulling...if he could just figure out how to operate the device; he thought that it might just work to get the log off of the truck.

After a half-dozen failed attempts, Zach got one end of the tool fastened with one of the loose cables to a live tree behind the truck. Then, he pulled the cable off the spool and fastened it around the log that rested on the pickup. In a few more tries, he figured out how to use the handle and set the ratchet so the gadget would start pulling.

Discovering how to use the tool had been the hard part. Once he got it setup, he had the log off the truck in no time. The only problem was he forgot to close the tailgate before pulling the log off the back of the truck. When the log got to the end of the rails of the pickup bed, it fell off onto the tailgate and put a huge dent in the metal and broke the left hinge. It also bounced up and broke the glass out of the taillight on the driver's side of the rig.

Zach felt dumb for having caused this additional damage to the truck and wondered how he was going to explain it to his grandfather. The feeling of failure and guilt overshadowed whatever feeling of success that he had over getting the log off the truck.

It took some wrestling to get the cable and hook out from under the log, but he freed it and was able to rewind the cable onto the spool and get the tool stowed back into the truck's toolbox.

With the task complete, he went back to check on his grandfather. He was still breathing, but Zach still couldn't get him to respond with anything more than a groan.

Not knowing what to do to help his grandfather, Zach went to work trying to decide what the next step in getting out of here should be. While he was thinking he realized that he was hungry and went to rummage through the food supplies to see if he could find something to eat. Ace was right at his side, expressing with his body language and whining that he was in favor of this activity. Locating a box of breakfast bars, Zach sat on the log that he had just pulled off the pickup and opened one of the foil packets and took a bite of the cinnamon-apple flavored bar.

Ace sat in front of him, head cocked at an angle, and drooled until Zach tossed a piece of the treat into the air. The dog deftly caught it in his mouth and swallowed without chewing. The pair went through four of the bars, one right after the other. The action of eating, and the interaction with the dog, allowed a brief distraction from thinking about his grandfather lying unconscious in the pickup, and the hundreds of downed trees that blocked the road back to civilization. There was no relief from the feeling of being watched, however. Zach constantly scanned the tree line around him for signs of the guy in black.

The morning air was cool. As long as he had been working at getting the tree off the truck, Zach had been warm enough, but the inactivity of the breakfast break allowed a chill to begin slipping down the neck and up the sleeves of his coat. He decided to build a fire.

The wind had left dead limbs everywhere. Gathering an arm load of them was quick and easy. He had noticed some newspaper in the truck's toolbox when he was looking through it, so he got a couple of pieces of it, crumpled it up, and put it in the makeshift fire ring that they had used the day before. Taking a match out of the water-proof container that his grandfather had given him when he had first started taking the dogs for their daily walk, he ignited the newspaper, and then laid a few small limbs on the flames. The flames consumed the paper, but aside from a little smoke, the wood was untouched.

He got more paper and tried again, achieving the same result.

Frustrated and cold, he went back to the pickup and climbed into the driver's seat. Ace tried to climb into the truck with him, but he pushed the dog back out and slammed the door. He sat the rifle beside his right leg, where he could easily grab it if the unwanted visitor should happen to return.

With a chest full of apprehension, Zach checked to make sure that Gabe was still breathing. Once sure that he was, Zach gently shook the older man in an attempt to get him to rouse. There was no response, and Zach's emotions ran from discouraged to terrified. He pulled his sleeping bag over himself and closed his eyes. Fear, cold, exhaustion, and depression comingled to become a drug that put Zach asleep.

# 24

Zach awakened slowly. The sun was shining into the pickup's windows; it had gotten warm inside, and he felt like his head was filled with cotton. He was thirsty and hungry. He looked at his grandfather and was surprised and thrilled to see that his eyes were open. "Grumpa, you're awake."

Gabe slowly turned his head and replied, "Yeah, Zach, I'm awake, but I gotta tell you, I'm not that excited about it."

"What's wrong?"

"Well, for starters, my head feels like it has been used for the ball in a soccer game. My leg is throbbing like crazy. And I am so thirsty that I could drink the crick dry. Other than that, everything is great."

"What are we going to do? Have you seen how many trees fell down across the road leading out of here?"

"Yeah, I've been cogitatin' on that. Even with a good chainsaw, it'd take days to cut your way outta here if there are trees down the whole way like there are here. And I ain't got my chainsaw with me. But I did see that you got the tree off the truck. How'd you do that?"

"I got that thing-a-ma-gig out the toolbox. You know that thing with the green handle and cables."

"That's called a Come-a- Long, or a hand cable winch. But how'd you know how to use it?"

"I didn't. I just kind of figured it out."

"Good job, Zach, that's amazing!"

"You won't think it's so amazing when you look at the back of your truck."

"Why? What happened?"

"Well, I'm sorry, but I forgot to put the tailgate up, so when the tree went off the end of the pickup bed it crashed down on the tailgate and smashed it, then it bounced up and broke out the taillights."

"Don't worry about the damage, it's just a stupid pickup, and we got a lot more things than that to worry about. I'm really proud of you for figuring out how to use the Come-a-Long."

"Mostly, I just wanted to have something to do. I tried to light a fire, too, to warm up. It was cold out there this morning. But I didn't have any luck at that."

Gabe was holding his head and his hair was drenched with sweat, but the bleeding had stopped. He spoke in a calm voice, trying to keep Zach from panicking. "Yeah, the wood would be pretty wet after that downpour last night. What you need is a little pitch, some dry ponderosa pine needles, and some bark that was sheltered from all that rain. Getting the pitch is easy. You can just cut some of the pitch bumps off those trees that the beetles killed. You'll have to search for dry bark, but you should be able to find enough to get you going from the underside of

186

some of the bigger trees. And there are mountains of dry needles around the base of any of the big ponderosas. "

"Okay," Zach said, "but do I need to build a fire now that you're awake? It's plenty warm now, and, I mean, aren't we going to get out of here?"

"Building a fire may *be* the way out of here."

"How's a fire going to help us?"

"The Forest Service will be flyin' over here lookin' for spot fires started by all the lightning last night. If we start a good smoky fire it'll bring the firefighters in like a good set of decoys brings in ducks."

"How will we make a fire big enough for the firefighters to see without catching the woods on fire?"

"Well, first of all, I think the 'we' is you. I don't think that I'm gonna be doin' much of anything with this leg the way it is, even if my head would stop poundin' like a bass drum in at a rock concert. If I could ignore the pain, I'm so stinkin' dizzy I doubt I could stand up without passin' out. But what *you're* gonna do is build the fire out there in the meadow. You remember that spot out there were the crick splits and the two branches go around forming that little island?"

"Yeah, I guess so," Zach answered.

"You're gonna build a fire on that island. That way, the fire won't be too apt to get away from you. The down side of it is that you'll have to pack all the wood for the fire out there."

"That's okay. But why don't I just throw a bunch of limbs and stuff in to the back of the truck and we can drive it out as close as we can get to that little island. That way I don't have to drag it so far?"

Gabe nodded and said, "That's a really good idea. Out there, when a plane flies over, they'll be able to spot the pickup and maybe understand that there's someone down here that needs some help. I wouldn't be surprised to find out that the storm started a whole mess of fires, so when they see one on a island in the middle of a stream, they may make it a pretty low priority."

Zach was eager to get started and said, "Okay, now what kind of wood should I get?"

"Get the ax out of the toolbox and see if you can knock some of the larger dead limbs off of one of the trees that the wind blew down. Once you get a good hot fire goin' with the dead limbs, you can throw some green limbs on top of it. That'll make a big batch of smoke."

Gabe had noticed the rifle beside Zach's leg while he was giving the instructions on how to build the fire. He watched the boy's reaction out of the corner of his eye when he asked, "What's with the gun?"

Zach's ears turned instantly red and he stammered, "Eh, I wanted it close in case anything happened."

"What'd ya think might happen, Zach?"

"I don't know. A bear or cougar or something might come and I just wanted to be ready if they did."

"It's not too likely that a bear or cat is gonna give ya much trouble when you're in the cab of a pickup is it?"

"I don't know. It just seemed like a good idea to be ready in case anything happened, that's all."

"You saw that guy again didn't you? That guy that couldn't possibly be here, but was here, he was back wasn't he?"

Zach silently looked out the window of the pickup. His posture was all the answer Gabe needed to know that the epiphany, or whatever Zach was experiencing, had occurred again.

After several minutes, Zach opened the truck door and said, "I'm going to start gathering wood."

"Hold on, Zach, tell me what you saw."

"Why, so you can call me a liar again? You don't believe that I saw anything so why are you asking me about it?"

"I'm sorry, Zach. I'm just tryin' to figure out what's goin' on that's all."

"I don't know what's going on, okay? I wish I did but ever since I got in the ruckus at school, everything has been all kinds of confused. I guess I really must be going crazy."

"You are not going crazy, Zach. But I don't think that whatever you have been seeing is what you think it is. I think we should spend some time prayin' that God would let us know what's goin' on."

Zach finished climbing out of the truck and was facing away from Gabe when he answered, "You go ahead and pray if you want. I haven't got much confidence in God, if there even is a God."

Zach was sure that the last comment was going to reap some wrath from his grandfather, so he was surprised when Gabe simply asked, "Could you tell me a little bit more about that?"

"I don't know, Gramps. We already talked about Mom's condition, and why a being that is supposed to be in charge of the whole universe would allow that, but it is more than that."

"Like what?"

"Like, if there is a God, why'd he make me so messed up? Like, why was it me that got in trouble back in school instead of that bunch of stupid bullies? Like why, when you prayed and asked him to keep us safe, did he let you get hurt? You are all the time going to church and teaching classes and being all good and everything and zap, God does all this. It just doesn't make sense to me."

"Well, Zach, the deal is, we can't see the big picture. And what you gotta remember is: It's not just about us."

"Oh, fine! What's it about then?"

"It's about God's kingdom."

"Yeah, right, whatever that means. I'm going to go to work on that fire building. You go ahead and do your praying thing, but don't be surprised when I don't join you—or when nothing happens."

Zach was throwing limbs and bark into the back of the pickup with the ferocity of someone killing snakes with a hoe. Gabe sat trying to think of something to say or do to take some of the edge off the boy's anger, but he had the worst headache of his life and his broken leg was throbbing with pain. He was having serious difficulty concentrating. About the only thing he could manage was to pray. So he prayed asking for God to give him wisdom and to soften Zach's heart.

*With no light or external sensation, judging the passing of time was impossible, but Becky felt that she had been in this state of suspended agony for years, at least. Scenes from her life kept playing through her mind. Most of the memories centered on the errors she had made. And many of those involved her interaction with Zach.*

*One particular event kept cycling through her mind. Zach had been in the second grade. She could see it in living color like it was happening right now. He had made an ice-cream stick fort for a social studies project. It was supposed to be a replica of a frontier outpost. The fort was pathetic: out of proportion, sloppy, and crude. Many of the sticks had too little glue and were going to fall off as soon as they were touched. Others had so much glue, big globs of dirty glue, on them that you could hardly see the wood. All in all, it was a mess, but Zach had been extremely proud of it.*

*Zach had led her by the hand into the garage, where the ugly project was littering the work bench. She had taken one look at it and said, "Oh no, you cannot take this mess to school." She had then completely disman-tled the entire project and rebuilt it herself. The end prod-uct was a beautiful disaster.*

*The memory of the look on Zach's face as she was tearing his work apart burned a hole in her mind. At the time she was only concerned with building a product that would be 'acceptable' to the teacher. She gave no thought as to what her reaction was doing to her son. Looking back she was all too aware that she should have been concerned with what she was building into her son. But realizing her error now was valueless. She no longer had any opportunity for influence on him.*

*This truth was the twisting of the knife in her guts that pierced to her soul.*

*Then, her memory brought up the last words that she had with Zach. What had that conversation done to him? She cried out soundlessly in the dark, "Lord, please spare him! Open his eyes."*

*She wanted to feel the tears run down her face and to taste them when they hit her lips, but her sole sensa-tion was the taste of the agony of her emotions, mari-nated in bitter memory.*

# 25

Ace was waiting for his chance and when Zach opened the pickup door the dog leapt into the cab. He was licking Gabe's face and whining before Zach knew what was happening, let alone be able to stop the dog.

"Get off me, you big idgit. What's wrong with you?" Gabe swung his door open as he was laughing and yelling at the dog and pushed the big Labrador out. "I don't know what's gotten into that big oaf," Gabe said to Zach. "He knows he never gets to be in the cab of the truck. I guess he's just nervous about ever'thin' 'at's goin' on. But then, I guess I'm a bit nervous myself."

Zach didn't show any sign of seeing the humor in the dog's antics but simply said, "I think I have enough wood loaded up. Do you think you can drive it across the field so I can get to work on building the fire?"

"I don't know. But we'll give 'er a try, if I can get myself hauled around to the driver's side, that is.

Using the side of the pickup for balance, Gabe hopped around the truck on his good leg. When he flopped down in the driver's seat, his forehead was beaded with sweat and he was completely out of breath. He sat for awhile regaining his composure. When his breathing had returned to something near normal he said, "Man, I didn't realize that I was this out of shape. I gotta start spending more time in the gym!

"Have you got some pitch and needles gathered up?"

"No," Zach answered. "Where did you say I could get the pitch?"

Gabe looked around and pointed to a big lodge pole pine that had fallen. "Ya see those big yellowish-white bumps on the stump end of that tree? Just take the axe and use it to scrape some of them into a sack or something. I think there's a paper sack in the toolbox. Then, go to that big old ponderosa tree over there," he waved at a big tree that was still standing, "grab an armload of needles from right beside it. That should give you enough tinder to get a fire goin'."

Zach set about following his grandfather's directions and Gabe watched from the cab of the pickup wondering if he'd be able to drive with his leg busted up the way it was. For one of the only times in his life, he was wishing that he had a rig with an automatic transmission. He maneuvered himself behind the steering wheel and depressed the clutch pedal with his right leg and flipped on the key. He was relieved and a little surprised when the engine started right up. He shifted the rig into low range four-wheel drive and tried to gently let off the clutch. The truck took a big lunge and died. Operating the clutch with his right leg was going to be challenging, especially since he couldn't give the rig any throttle because his gas pedal foot was operating the clutch. A couple more tries had the same results, and the throbbing left leg was screaming at him for the jouncing it was getting.

When Zach came back with the pitch and needles, Gabe asked, "Hey, have you ever driven a rig with a clutch?"

"I've never driven anything at all, except a go-cart once."

"Well, you ain't gonna learn any younger. I can't seem to be able to operate the clutch and gas both with one foot and my broken leg isn't too enjoyin' the bouncin' around. We're gonna have to give you some on the job training on how to operate this vehicle."

"I don't know about that. Aren't you afraid I'll crash?"

"Look at this rig. Do you really think you can do it much harm? And you won't be goin' fast enough to hurt us."

"Well, at least it's running. I could blow it up or something."

"You don't need to worry about that. I've got it in low range four-wheel-drive, which means it'll only go about as fast as a three-legged turtle, but it'll have plenty of power. Here, let me get back around to the passenger side and you can take a try."

The trip back to the passenger side left Gabe completely exhausted. He didn't say anything to Zach, but he doubted that he would be able to make it around the truck one more time anytime soon.

When Zach was behind the wheel, Gabe asked, "Do you need to move the seat? Here, the lever behind your right heel will let you get a little closer to the steering wheel. Okay, now push in the clutch—that's the pedal on the left. Hold that clear to the floor and turn on the key."

The truck started instantly, but Zach kept turning the key, resulting in a nasty grinding noise from the starter. "Oh," Gabe hollered, "let off the key!"

"See, I told you I couldn't do this!" Zach said with a little panic and a lot of frustration in his voice.

"You're doin' fine. That didn't hurt anything. Just, once it starts, you gotta quit turning the key. Now, the pedal on the right is the throttle. 'At's what makes us go. You gotta be kind of gentle on it. Give it a try and just gently push down on it."

The engine revved up fast and roared. Zach let off the pedal and said, "I don't think I can do this. Are you sure you can't do it?"

"I tried Zach. My broken leg is not gonna let me drive. But I know you can do this. All you have to do is ease out the clutch and give it just a little touch of gas. Try the gas pedal a few more times to get the feel for it. Once you're comfortable with that, I'll have you try the clutch."

It wasn't long before Zach was able to operate the throttle, revving the engine fairly smoothly and Gabe thought it was time to try letting the clutch out. "So, the clutch needs to come out slowly. At first nothin' is gonna happen. Then, when it's almost all the way out the truck's gonna start forward. In first gear and in low range it's not gonna go fast. So go ahead, real gently ease the clutch pedal up."

Zach was gripping the steering wheel so hard that his knuckles were turning white, and he was letting off the clutch so slowly that Gabe wondered if they'd run out of gas before the rig started to move. When the truck finally started rolling, it was with a jerky lurch. Zach panicked and jammed the clutch pedal back to the floor.

"'At's okay," Gabe said, "give 'er another try. You've just about got the hang of it."

Zach didn't respond. His face was contorted into a serious frown as he let the clutch out again. Then they were moving at a slow crawl.

Habits

"There ya go, now just stay a little ways away from the crick and we'll see if we can't just drive to the spot where we wanna build the fire," Gabe instructed.

Ace trotted alongside the pickup; with an occasional bark, he looked worried as they bounced the three hundred yards to the spot where they were going to build the signal fire. Even the dog looked relieved when the truck stopped rolling.

"Great job, Zach! I told you that you could do it."

"Thanks. Now, how do you want me to build the fire?"

"Just take that sack with the pitch in it and fill it up with some of the needles that you got there. Set that down on that little island in the crick and stack the rest of the needles on top of it. Then, take some of the smaller, drier branches and put them on top of that. Then just light the sack on fire. It should take right off. Then add some of the bigger dry limbs and we should have a rip-roarin' fire goin' in nothin' flat."

Zach climbed out of the truck and followed his grandfather's directions. In fifteen minutes, he was placing limbs on a nice blaze. "How's that?" Zach yelled across the stream.

"Perfect. Now, let it get goin' really good; then add some of those green limbs. That'll make a good bunch of smoke. The fire-watch guys should spot it easy enough. While we're waitin' for the cavalry to ride to the rescue, let's drive back over and get the cooler and see if we can scare up a couple of sammitchas. I'm still not feeling too good; in fact, I'm havin' a little trouble getting' my eyes to focus. But you must be so hungry that you're left handed."

"I had some of those breakfast bars this morning while you were unconscious, but I sure wouldn't mind some lunch."

197

Zach started the pickup and drove a wide loop to head back to the camping equipment. He even managed to shift the transmission from first to second and hit five miles an hour on the return. Ace had jumped in the bed of the truck for the return trip. He ran back and forth from one side of the truck to the other, whining his request for more speed.

When they got back to their demolished campsite, Gabe said, "Why don't you grab the ice chest and Coleman stove and throw them in the back. Don't bother to unhook the propane tank from the stove; we'll just set the stove up on what's left of the tailgate and I'll fry a couple of kielbasas so we can have a hot sammitch. That way, we'll be out in the open when the fire plane flies over."

Zach climbed out of the pickup and followed Gabe's instructions. When he got back in the truck, he asked, "Do you think they'll fly over today?"

"I can't guarantee it, especially since they may have already flown over here a couple of times without seeing anythin'. They have a lot of territory to cover, but my guess is they'll make another pass or two over this spot before they're done. There were too many lightning strikes here last night for them to not be pretty interested."

"But what are we going to do if they don't?"

"Let's worry about that when it happens. Right now, let's get ourselves on the outside of some lunch."

Zach drove back to their fire site without any problem with the clutch or gas. Gabe looked at him out of the corner of his eye and was amazed at how calm Zach looked now compared to an hour ago. Young people learned so fast, he thought.

Again, Ace rode in the back of the pickup and whined.

"Could you throw a few more limbs on your fire, Zach? It's already starting to burn down. While you're doin' that, I'll see if I can get some food together," Gabe said.

Gabe got out of the truck and used the side of the truck for support while he hopped to the back of the truck. His head was throbbing, and his broken leg felt like it weighed five hundred pounds and was on fire, but he couldn't stand to watch his grandson do all the work any longer, so he forced himself to keep going.

He sat on the damaged tailgate and got the stove going, split a couple of kielbasas length-ways and put them in the cast iron frying pan. The smell of the spicy meat reminded him of how long it had been since he had eaten. Gabe wasn't the only one that thought the cooking kielbasa smelled good. Ace was sitting as close as he could get watching every move that Gabe made, and Zach wasn't getting far from the aroma either.

"All the wood I gathered is going to be gone in another hour or two. Do you think I should get some more to keep the fire going?" Zach asked after they had wolfed down their hot sandwiches.

"Yeah, and you might want to get something bigger than the limbs, they're burnin' up awful fast. Take the pickup back over to the trees and see what you can do. Grab some more green stuff, too; we need to keep that smoke goin'.

"I'm sorry to dump all the work on you, but I've got to rest for awhile. My head and leg are killin' me."

"It's okay, Grumpa, I like this driving thing." When Zach started the truck, Ace jumped into the back. As they drove away, the lab noticed that Gabe had been left behind, sitting beside the stream. The yellow dog barked, hopped out of the truck, and ran toward his master. Gabe ordered, "Go get 'im, Ace. Go!" and pointed back at the truck.

Ace stopped, looked back at the slow moving pickup, then back at Gabe. Gabe shouted again, "Go," and pointed at the pickup. The dog obeyed, and when he caught up to the moving truck, he jumped in and slid right up to the diamond-plate toolbox.

Gabe lay back in the grass and closed his eyes. He started praying aloud, asking God to send a plane over them soon. He asked God to protect Zach, and to get them out of there. As he cried out he felt the earth spinning beneath him, a long oblong, clockwise spin that landed him in a deep sleep before the second full revolution was complete.

Zach didn't have any trouble finding wood. Within half an hour, he had the pickup bed filled with chunks and pieces that had been left behind by some long-ago wood cutter who apparently hadn't been interested in anything but the best wood. He added a bunch of green limbs to the load and ordered Ace to 'load up.' The dog looked puzzled at the command and jumped up with his front paws on the tailgate and looked at the load in the truck. He looked over his shoulder at Zach and whined.

"Go ahead, load up," Zach encouraged. "You can do it, just climb up there."

Ace whined again, but then scrambled up on top the load and tried to balance on one of the larger pieces of wood.

Trying to judge from the dog's expression, Zach couldn't tell if the mutt was embarrassed by his awkward posture or proud of himself for being so brave, so he said, "Atta boy, Ace, you stay right up there. Good boy!"

Zach drove the pickup back to where he had left his grandfather. It made him nervous that the old guy didn't sit up when the rig pulled up beside him. When Zach shut off the truck motor and climbed out of the cab, Gabe still hadn't stirred. Ace half jumped and half fell off the load of wood and sniffed and nuzzled his owner.

Zach's heart was pounding out a strong cadence that matched the dog's tail when he rushed over and knelt beside his grandfather to say, "Hey, you okay?"

"What? Oh yeah. I'm fine, just really sleepy," Gabe said thickly. Then, clearer and louder, "Ace, get off me, you oaf!" The dog trotted off.

"Isn't it like a really bad sign to be sleepy after a bad blow to the head?"

"Yeah, I suppose, but I think I'm just shot from the pain and from bein' up all night. And I haven't been too sick to my stomach. I think that's the big indicator of a serious concussion."

He looked at the pile in the pickup and said, "Looks like you got some wood that'll hold fire awhile on this load. Better throw some of it on your fire right now; it's pretty much burned itself out. And add a big bunch of those green boughs, too. That should put up a smoke. "

Zach set to work and Gabe tried to get his head to clear. Everything was spinning around and around again, and he couldn't get his eyes to focus. He lay back down on the grass and asked God, again, to get them out of this mess. Everything was fading back to black when Zach came and flopped down beside him and said, "What else should I be doing?"

"Not much to be done now but wait for someone to spot our smoke and come to investigate."

The sun was warming the air and, aside from a few contrails from passing jets, the sky was an endless blue. Birds and squirrels provided a pleasant racket. Under normal conditions, Gabe would have thought this was a piece of heaven. Instead, it felt like a large slice of the alternative.

**201**

To add to the misery of the situation, the rising temperature resurrected swarms of mosquitoes. First, there were just a couple of the little blood-suckers buzzing around. Then, in correlation to the increasing warmth of the air, the numbers rose.

Zach was slapping and swatting and griping about the bugs. He couldn't believe that his grandfather didn't even seem to realize that the pests were biting him. "How can you stand that?" he asked.

"What?"

"There are mosquitoes all over you. They're about to eat you alive!"

"Oh, why don't ya grab that bottle of bug dope out of my fish bag and slather a liberal dose on you, then give it to me.

"Then, if ya want, you can go see about catchin' enough fish for our dinner. That way, if I'm wrong about the Forest Service comin' to our rescue this afternoon, we'll at least have something to eat."

"Okay," Zach replied swatting at a swarm of mosquitoes, "maybe these little pests will be a little less annoying if I'm moving around a little. But, are you going to be alright here by yourself?"

"Sure, I'll be fine. You go on ahead and fetch us some nice fat trout. I'm gonna see if I can get a little more sleep. For some stupid reason, I feel absolutely exhausted. And every time I try to sit up, everything goes black.

"Better tie Ace to the bumper of the truck before you go, though. You won't stand a chance of catchin' any fish if that knucklehead is with you."

"Do you think I should go upstream or downstream, Grumpa?" Zach asked.

"Probably doesn't matter much," Gabe replied. You're gonna catch fish either way. I bet that the downpour last night washed enough worms into the creek to have the fish in a feeding frenzy. But, if it was me, I think I'd go downstream. There are some beautiful holes down there that always hold a bunch of fish."

Zach started off, but when he got about twenty yards from the truck he stopped and turned and called back, "Are you sure you're alright? You're not going to be…unconscious…or something when I get back, are you?"

"I'll be fine. Like I said, I just need to get some sleep. You go on and catch us some supper; but, don't bring back more'n about fifteen fish. Remember, any of 'em that we don't eat now 'ill just rot."

Zach was moving back toward Gabe even while Gabe was answering. His head was down and it was obvious to Gabe from the boy's body language that he wanted to say something else. "Zach, don't worry, I'll be fine. You go ahead."

"Okay. But do you think it'd be alright if I took the .22 with me?"

"Havin' that thing along is gonna be a pain while you're fishin', but I guess it'd be alright for you to take it. Why do you think you want it?"

"I don't know, in case one of those cougars comes along I guess."

"That little pea-shooter wouldn't do you much good against a cougar, but take it if you want. I'll rig you up kind of a sling so you can carry it on your back if you fetch me a length of that braided rope out of the toolbox."

Gabe fought off the dizziness long enough to rig a sling on the little rifle and hung it across Zach's shoulder. Before Zach started out this time, Gabe gave him some instruction. "Leave the gun's chamber empty; you don't want the trigger on this thing catchin' on a willow and goin' off while it's strapped on your back. Just remember, to use it you'll hav'ta cycle the action and get a round in the barrel. Once you do that, it'll be ready to fire. The safety will *not* be on, so be careful."

Ace got aggravated when he saw Zach *and* the rifle leaving without him. The dog whined and yipped. He seemed to be trying to convince the boy that a dog was needed on this adventure. Gabe ordered, "Stop. Lay down." The dog complied, but that didn't keep him from laying, with his muzzle across his paws, staring at Zach's back until the boy disappeared into the willows.

# 26

Schiller and Mack had fielded one case right after another for the past month, and the Becky Mertz file had gotten shuffled to bottom of the pile. It was a surprise to the two that the mayor hadn't been putting any pressure on the department to solve it.

The two detectives had gotten a couple of free hours one afternoon and were using the time to go back over the case. They sat reading through the file trying to see if anything jumped out at them; something that they had missed before. Bruce put the thin file down on his cluttered desk and said, "Ya know, Mack, I think we ought to go out and talk to the doctor about his wife one more time. I don't see anything in these notes to indicate that anyone asked him about his wife's prowess with knots. That whole deal with the kid's door being tied shut just keeps nagging at me."

"Oh, we can go out and talk to that chump again, but I doubt he's gonna be too cooperative."

"His hearing for the assault of that hospital security guard is scheduled for next week. If he were to mistakenly get the impression that cooperation on this case might help in that one, he might sing like a bird."

"I don't think that it's gonna be that easy, but we can give it a try. The way it stands right now we may as well let the c.o.d. be put down as an intentional overdose because with the information we have now, we sure aren't apt to prove anything else."

They drove to the Mertz's home. They weren't surprised to find that no one was there, but they did find it a bit curious that there was a 'for sale' sign in the front yard. They looked in the windows and saw that there wasn't any furniture left inside the house. Nor were there any vehicles in the garage.

"Where to now?" Bruce asked his partner. "It doesn't look like we're gonna find him here."

Randy snagged a brochure from the realty sign and said, "If anyone can tell us how to catch up with this chump, it'll be the realtor. Let's give the agent a call and see if they know where to find him. They'll probably be a little more cooperative than Mertz's bail bondsman."

Within an hour, the two detectives were ringing the bell at the door of the condominium whose address the realtor had provided. They had just about decided that there wasn't going to be an answer when they heard footsteps inside and the door opened. A teenage girl with the ear buds from an ipod draped around her neck said, "Hi," and looked from one detective to the other with a confused look on her face.

"Hello," Mack said, "I'm Detective Mack of the Phoenix Police Department, and this is Detective Schiller. We're looking for Dr. David Mertz. Is he here?'

"No, he's not. When I heard the doorbell I thought it was my friend Tristan."

"Sorry, it's just us cops. Do you happen to know where Dr. Mertz is?" Schiller asked.

"No, he wasn't here when I got home from school," the girl replied.

"And you are?" Mack asked.

"Alison."

"You live here?"

"Yeah."

"We're working on a case and would like to talk to Dr. Mertz. Do you know how we might be able to get in touch with him?"

"My mom probably could tell you. I can give you her cell number, but she usually doesn't answer it when she's at work."

Schiller looked up from his notebook and asked, "Where's she work?"

"At Saint Luke's; she's a doctor there."

"What's her name?"

"Amanda Stearns."

"Okay, Schiller said, snapping the notebook closed and zipping it up. "Thank you."

The two cops turned to go back to their car but Mack stopped in mid-turn, looked over his shoulder as the door was swinging closed and said, "Alison, do me a favor. Please don't open the door when you're home alone until you know who's out on the porch. There are a lot of creeps runnin' around this town. We don't want to come back here trying to pick up the pieces when one of 'em grabs you."

Alison shrugged and closed the door. There was some satisfaction for Mack when he heard the deadbolt snap into place.

Bruce and Randy got in the car and headed toward St. Luke's. "I'll never understand why people just swing their doors open when a couple of mug-ugly guys like us are standing on the porch, especially sweet young things like Alison," Randy said.

"I know what you mean," Bruce replied, "but leave me off of your mug-ugly team, if ya don't mind."

"Huh, you're the captain as far as I'm concerned."

"Now that was just designed to hurt my very delicate feelers. I believe I might be offended," Bruce quipped, sniffing loudly.

"Yeah, whatever," Randy replied. "But what do ya think about our buddy Mertz being shacked up with another doctor?"

"I'd be interested to know when that little romance began. I might even bring that question into the conversation if we ever catch up with the good doctor."

As they weaved their way through traffic on the way to the hospital, Bruce brought the conversation back to the girl. "When you were the ripe old age of fifteen, did you worry about things like being abducted?"

"Nah, and I don't think I needed to either. If anyone would have grabbed me it would have ended up like the *Ransom of Red Chief*."

"That I don't doubt, but my point is that kids just don't spend much lime or energy thinkin' about the dangers of life."

"And good on 'em for that I say. What kind of life would it be if you went around being afraid of every shadow?"

They met with Amanda in the hospital cafeteria.

"I'm not 'stopping' to speak with you," said Amanda. "I've got a really full schedule so I'm only pausing for a moment. Let's cut right to the chase. What can I do for you?"

"Can you tell us where we can find Dr. David Mertz? We stopped by your condominium earlier today and your daughter told us that you could probably tell us where to find him."

She looked from Schiller to Mack through cold blue eyes before responding, "What's with you guys? Why do you keep harassing David? I don't have to tell you anything. Now if you'd excuse me, I'm going to go back to work." She marched off in the direction that she came, leaving the detectives standing in the cafeteria.

"Well," Mack quipped, "I think that went rather well, don't you?"

"Just about perfect," Schiller responded. "And aren't you proud of me for not giving her my speech about obstruction of justice?"

"Yes, I applaud your composure. And I'm pretty proud of myself for not slappin' that witch silly. So what do we do now?"

"Well, we could go back to Mertz's condominium and wait for him to show up. Or we could just bag it for today and try to pick up his trail tomorrow."

"I vote for option number two. I've had about all the citizen cooperation and interaction that I can stand for one day."

*Becky wished with all her soul that she could hit the off switch in her mind. Even a small gap in her cognitive state would be welcome. Losing awareness forever would be better. Instead, her mental anguish was increasing. Suddenly, the inside of her throat felt as if someone had scrubbed it with a wire brush, and pain was radiating from the backs of her hands and the inside of her elbows. She had wanted sensation. Be careful what you wish for, she thought. This wasn't exactly the sensation she had been seeking.*

*Sleep. Just a short nap. That would be appreciated.*

*That thought had no more than formed in her mind when the portal snapped. This time, it allowed only a view of the shaded face of the creature that had been holding a sword above Zach's head when she had last seen him.*

*"Appreciative to whom?" the creature shouted.*

*"What?" Becky responded, though only in her mind.*

*"To whom would you direct those feelings of appreciation if you were allowed to sleep?"*

*The first answer that occurred to her was, "God."*

*"Oh, so you would give thanks to God, would you," the monster shouted. "Don't you understand that it is God who put you here? It is God that holds the keys to this prison. And you would be appreciative to him for some small favor?"*

*"No!" Becky screamed in her mind. "It can't be God who has put me here. I've put myself here by turning my back on God."*

*The portal snapped closed, and Becky was again alone in the dark and heat.*

# 27

Zach started fishing at a spot where the stream's current had worn a large hole under the bank. A willow tree grew from the opposite back and its limbs leaned out over the water and shaded the hole. He tossed his baited hook into the swift water above the hole and watched as the offering was swept into the eddying swirl and under the willow. About halfway through the hole, the line stopped moving and, thinking he was snagged on one of the branches, Zach lifted the tip of the rod to apply some pressure. Immediately, the clicker on the old fly reel started chattering like crazy. The pressure on the line bent the rod almost double.

A bruiser of a fish was on the line. It was pulling, jerking, and shaking its head.

When the fish reached the shallow water at the tail-out of the hole, Zach got a glimpse of what he had hooked and his heart started pounding. It was at least twenty inches long and a bright chrome color. A brilliant line of scarlet ran horizontally down its side. This fish was huge and beautiful and Zach was sure it was going to come off before he could get it out of the water. "Oh, man," he said aloud, not knowing whether he was talking to himself or the fish. "Don't come off. Please stay on that hook!"

The fish got into the deep water of the next hole and stayed down on the bottom, pulling against the line. Zach splashed down the stream, chasing the biggest fish that he had ever fought. He played the trophy carefully, even gently, worrying the whole time that the fish was going to get loose. After three good runs and a lot of self-advise, the boy brought the fish up on a gravel bar. The large black spots on the back of the fish were beautiful against its bright silver body, and the red tinged with blue of the 'red band' was almost too perfect to be real. Blue and red hues colored the gill-plates. After looking at the fish for what Zach was afraid might be too long, he unhooked the trout and gently placed it back in the water. Holding it by the tail, he pushed and pulled it in the water to force oxygen into its gills and then grinned with excitement and pleasure as the perfect trout headed back to deeper water with a powerful swish of its big tail.

Zach kept fishing. The seven and eight inch fish that he caught on almost every cast were anti-climatic after that beautiful red-band, but they were welcome for dinner. Before long, he thought he had enough of the small brook trout to provide for a meal for himself and his grandfather.

Zach was headed back to the makeshift camp when he heard the approach of a helicopter. He spun in a circle looking for the machine on the horizon. When he spotted the craft, it was coming in low over the treetops on the west side of the meadow. He watched with a great sense of relief as the rescue bird landed beside the pickup. Zach's excitement sent him sprinting toward his grandfather.

He was still about a hundred and fifty yards away when the copter's door opened. To Zach's mortification, the first one out was the man in black. The man didn't even bother to duck as he went under the rotating blades of the helicopter and headed straight for Zach, whose excitement over the possibility of being rescued was instantly replaced by mortification.

Zach turned around and started running for the woods.

He sprinted into the willows that lined the creek, splashed across the stream, and didn't stop running at top speed until he was a quarter mile into the pine forest. He only stopped when he was completely out of breath.

He stood behind a large lodge pole pine tree and watched the trail he had just ran up, as he struggled to get air into his lungs. He stared until his eyes watered, trying to notice any sign of his pursuer. Leaning the fishing pole against the tree, Zach un-slung the rifle from his back and held it ready, convinced that he would, and could, use it when the man in black appeared.

The helicopter's rescue crew found Gabe stretched out on the grass in the shade of the pickup. He was unresponsive, his temperature high, and his respiratory rate rapid. Though the crew was made up of firefighters, not medics, they knew these were classic symptoms of severe dehydration and that he needed immediate medical attention.

Spreading the fire's fuel around on the small island, they gave it a thorough dosing with water from the stream. Once the firefighters were confident that the fire wouldn't spread, they loaded their patient into the helicopter and took off. The details of the situation were radioed ahead so that medical personnel would be available when the helicopter arrived back at the staging area. The information from Gabe's identification was also relayed so that steps for notifying his family could begin.

The crew on the helicopter had seen a young yellow lab lunging against a tether on the bumper of the pickup when they were landing. It had broken loose and run from the site, apparently terrified by the racket that accompanied the approaching craft. They had seen it a couple of more times when they were extinguishing the fire and loading Gabe, but it wouldn't come to them when they called it, and they had no choice but to leave it behind.

The racket of Zach's arrival had sent the creatures of the forest into hiding. Now, as Zach stood silently watching for any sign of being followed, those animals and birds began to return to their routines. A pine squirrel resumed his cone cutting in a nearby ponderosa. Each time a cone crashed into the underbrush beneath the tree, Zach was startled. A flock of chickadees reminded each other of their names while they hunted aphids in a small lodge pole pine. On the ground beneath a current bush, a rufus-sided towhee kicked and scratched the ground as it searched for seeds. Black on bronze chipmunks scolded each other as they scurried through the limbs of a blow-down tree hunting anything edible.

The scene was serene. Zach's emotions were not. The sound of the helicopter lifting off did nothing to lift the depression that had settled on the boy.

He kept watching the trail that he had come in on until he decided that his pursuer must have left on the helicopter. Zach tried to convince himself that it was safe to start back toward the campsite. He needed to see if there was anything left that he could use to survive while deciding what to do.

He was struggling to get the makeshift rifle sling back in place when movement to his right caught his attention. A large Manzanita bush that was about fifty yards away was shaking as if something had walked through it, but Zach couldn't see anything that would explain the motion. He stood, focusing on the area, trying to see or hear anything that would give him a clue. The movement slowed, then stopped, and Zach felt a chill ran up his spine.

The forest critters kept on with their routines, and Zach was able to convince himself that the motion had been caused by some birds, squirrels, or other small animals. He got the rifle in place, picked up the fishing pole, and took a step and a half when a patch of six foot tall jack pine trees to his left started shaking.

Zach threw the fishing pole down and ripped the rifle sling back over his head. The cord caught beneath his left ear lobe; in his frenzy to get it over his head, he gave himself a rope burn across his neck and ear, but the fiery wound didn't even register in his consciousness. With the rifle back in his hands, he again studied the surrounding forest for any sign of a threat. Minutes passed. Again, he saw nothing that would account for the movement in the brush. His heart was pounding hard and his breath was coming in short, shallow gulps as he jerked his head back and forth trying to watch every direction at once.

"Okay, okay," he told himself. "That was only some animal moving around. You have got to get a hold of yourself."

He left the fishing pole on the ground and kept the rifle in his hands as he took a few more steps. He was gaining confidence, and his breathing and heart rate had almost gotten back to normal when the man dressed in black jumped into the middle of the trail. Zach threw the rifle to his shoulder, brought the scope's crosshairs to bear in the middle of the black jumpsuit, and pulled the trigger. Nothing happened; no shot, not even the click of the hammer falling. The man standing in the trail tilted his head back and laughed a loud, haunting laugh.

Zach frantically tried to determine what was wrong with the rifle. He cupped his little finger on the rifle bolt grip and jerked. The chamber was empty when the bolt slid back, but a round advanced from the magazine and Zach let the bolt slam shut. He brought the rifle to his shoulder again. The target was gone.

The sound of laughter came from about a hundred yards to the north and then faded away. Zach slumped to his knees on the pine-needle strewn ground and wept, still clutching the rifle. His tears were born of a combination of fear, anger, and frustration. The drain of these emotions combined with the physical demands of the past day, and the night of almost no sleep, to produce complete exhaustion.

Zach was allowing that exhaustion to spin him down the funnel of sleep when he was jerked back to consciousness by the sounds of brush breaking and footsteps thumping on the hollow ground. He was struggling to get himself untangled from the underbrush, off the ground, and into a position to use the rifle when a ball of hair covered muscle ran over him and sent him sprawling. The rifle went flying from his hands, and panic distorted his vision and perception. He clamped his eyes shut and instinctively covered his face and neck with his arms.

The next thing that Zach knew was that the attacking beast had him pinned to the ground. Its sharp claws

were scratching his chest and stomach, and it was pushing its muzzle through his hands to get to his face and
neck. Hot breath and slobber splattered any exposed
skin, and Zach wondered if this is what it felt like to be
eaten alive. He rolled onto his side and into a fetal ball
as the animal continued its attack.

It could have been the whining or the stench of the
animal's breath or the fact that the ferocity of the attack was lessening that brought Zach back to the realm
of rational thought. Whatever the reason, reality arrived
and Zach realized that his attacker was Ace. Much more
relieved than embarrassed, he pushed the dog away
and sat up. Ace took off in his fastest low-butt-run and
ran two circles around Zach before jumping back in to
lick the boy's face some more.

*Instead of instantly snapping open, this time the por-
tal opened slowly. At first, Becky saw only a thread's
thickness of light. She watched with dread and anticipation as the opening gradually increased until she could
see the uppermost branches of some trees against a
blue sky. Ever so slowly, the view expanded until full trees
were in view. Then, on the ground beneath the trees, she
saw her son, Zach. He was sitting in the dirt; tear tracks
streaked his grimy face.*

*She tried to call out to him, to make some attempt
to comfort him, but she could make no sound. As she
struggled to make contact with her son, she noticed
that in the branches of the tree directly above Zach,
hid the tormentor. The monster was looking down at the
boy with nefarious delight. Then, slowly, the creature's
gaze shifted from Zach to Becky and for the first time she
was able to see his eyes—embers of glowing red. The
impersonation of evil tipped back his head and howled
in laughter.*

*The view through the portal went black from bottom to top, a reversal of its opening. Gradually, the entire view was blocked. Once again in total darkness, the image of those red eyes was imbedded in Becky's memory. Her silent screams echoed, but only in her mind.*

# 28

Meg was on the phone with a nurse at Saint Joseph's. Becky's condition had not changed. There was no indication of any response to stimulation, though the nurse said that there had been some more involuntary spasms, but, according to the nurses, those were common in this type of patient.

Discouraged from the thought of her daughter alone in her vegetative state, and depressed by the mental image of Becky caught in spasms, Meg had just hung up the phone when the door bell rang.

Two Sheriff's Deputies were standing at the sliding door when she answered. Her heart skipped a couple of beats, and she could feel the muscles in her lower abdominal area constrict. "Hello, officers. How can I help you?"

"Ms. Green? I'm Deputy Albers and this is my partner Deputy Moore. May we come in for a moment?"

Meg could feel her plastic smile melting when she opened the door a little wider and politely responded, "Certainly. Come right in and have a seat. May I get you something to drink? A soda or some coffee or anything?"

"Thank you, Ms. Green, but no," Deputy Albers said as he took a seat on one of the chairs she had indicated. "We just need a few minutes of your time."

Deputy Moore picked up the conversation at that point and said, "We'll cut right to the point. We're here about your husband. Have you heard from him in the last twelve hours or so?"

"Gabe is camping. Is he okay?" Meg hated the tone of panic that had crept into her voice.

"He's going to be fine. But he has been involved in a bit of a mishap. He has been taken by ambulance to Saint Charles Hospital in Bend. From the information relayed to us by the Forest Service, he has suffered a fairly serious concussion, and a broken leg. The break was a severe fracture, and he was badly dehydrated."

Meg's hand had gone up and covered her mouth while the deputy was speaking, but the move failed to stop a small guttural groan from escaping her lips. "What about Zach? Is he alright? Where is he?"

The two policemen looked at each other. "Ahh," Deputy Moore answered, "the guys who flew your husband out mentioned that there was a dog at the scene, but it was left behind."

"Dog?" Meg's voice rose in pitch and in volume as her words raced each other out of her mouth. "What're you talking about? Zach is our grandson. He was camping with my husband. Where is he?"

Deputy Albers responded, "We weren't advised of anyone at the site of your husband's accident but him. How old is the boy?"

"He's only thirteen."

220

"Are you sure that he was with your husband?"

"Yes I'm sure. Are *you* sure that he wasn't there with Gabe?"

"Ms. Green, we were not at the scene, but the report that we received from the guys that were there didn't say anything about a second person. We'll make sure that the right folks know, though, so they can get someone from search and rescue out there to look for him. They're going to need some information from you. You know, a description and stuff."

"Sure, but please hurry, it'll be dark in a couple of hours, and Zach is a city boy. He doesn't know anything about being out in the woods—especially at night."

Deputy Moore went to the patrol car and radioed their sergeant while his partner continued to try to keep Meg from going into hysterics. When he had explained the situation the sergeant ordered, "Get Ms. Green's cell phone number for me so I can relay it to the search and rescue people. I know they are going to want to talk to her; then, offer to take her to the hospital to see her husband. We need to make sure we keep her safe. The last thing we need is for her to take off into the woods to look for the kid. Then we'd have two people to look for."

Forty-five minutes later, the two deputies were transporting Meg to the hospital in their patrol car. She was in the back seat and she was praying...aloud. Both of these veteran cops had heard a lot of people talk to themselves while they were in the backseat of that car, and once in awhile some people would even talk to God. But they had never heard anything that resembled this before.

This lady was talking to God like she thought he was right in the backseat with her. There were none of the churchy sounding words, it simply sounded like an intense conversation that a person would have with a close friend. Moore and Albers looked at each other and then quickly away. Both of them felt they might be close to having an attack of hay fever and neither of them had allergies.

To the relief of the two deputies, Meg's phone chirped and interrupted her God connection. The call was from the commander of the search and rescue team that would be going in to the Winema National Forest to search for Zach. There were questions about the boy's height and weight and general physical condition. Then, there were the questions about his aptitude in survival skills. The final queries pertained to Zach's emotional stability.

"What does my grandson's emotional condition have to do with your finding him?" Meg asked.

"Well, we're not sure at this point that it does. We're just trying to get as much information as we can to make our job easier. Besides, your husband was picked up right beside his truck. We're real curious as to why your grandson wasn't there, too. Do you think he may have panicked and went after help when he saw his grandfather unconscious?"

"I don't know. I'm sure that's a possibility. That boy has been through a lot in the past couple of months, so it is hard to imagine what must be going through his mind. But I'd bet that he is very afraid."

"Why do you think that he would be frightened?"

"Come on, don't patronize me please. What kid wouldn't be scared if he found himself out it the middle of nowhere all by himself? Beyond that though, my husband had Zach out in that area a few months ago and the mere thought of seeing a herd of elk caused him to have a near melt down. That's how little he knows about being in the woods. I think they worked through some of the worst of that but I'm afraid that he might already be near hysteria being alone out there."

"I was not intending to sound like I was patronizing you. But it is important for us to know as much as possible about the mental state of your grandson. I'm just trying to get an idea of if he is merely afraid, or if he is hysterical. People who are in a state of panic behave completely differently than those who are able to remain calm. The biggest problem with a person in the throes of hysteria is that they are totally unpredictable. That makes the search much more difficult. But my crew is made up of a bunch of talented and professional people. We will find your boy."

Meg's voice went low and quiet when she replied, "I'm praying that you do, and fast."

Detectives Schiller and Mack were parked on the street in front of Dr. David Mertz's condominium at six in the morning. Their car was strategically placed to provide them a good view of the front door. It would be too hot to continue surveillance from the car past about eight o'clock, so the detectives were hoping that Dr. Mertz would get an early start to his day.

They had waited less than fifteen minutes when Amanda Stearns came out the front door. She was dressed in a well tailored suit, black with a gray pinstripe. The outfit accentuated her long legs. Her posture was perfect, and her stride was quick and deliberate. She marched directly to a white BMW that was less than a year old. Once in the vehicle, she drove away with the same crisp and aggressive movement that she had demonstrated in her walk.

"It looks like livin' with that gal would be a real pleasure," Bruce quipped.

"Yeah, as long as you knew how to click your heels together and salute crisply," Randy answered.

"It's nice the two of 'em found each other. There's no sense in them makin' two other people miserable."

"I'd guess that she was on her way to work. Man, I pity the poor nurses that work with her."

"Nurses? What about her patients?"

"The pharmaceutical companies probably love her, though. All her patients undoubtedly require a lot of tranquillizers and anti-depressants!"

The door to the condominium opened again fifteen minutes later and Alison came out. Though she had her mother's height and looks, her bearing and posture was the exact opposite. She walked slowly, almost with a shuffle. Her shoulders were rounded forward and she was looking at the ground. The clothes she was wearing were too large, to the point of looking sloppy.

"That girl has some self-esteem issues," Bruce commented.

"How could she help it, livin' with that bag of a mother?"

"You're really sweet on Amanda, aren't you? Old David best be watching out, or you'll be hornin' in on his territory."

"Yeah, right, cuddling up with that woman has all the appeal of hugging a friggin' boa constrictor."

Bruce drummed his fingers on the steering wheel as he watched Alison walk down the sidewalk. "Ya know, that girl didn't look beat down like that when we talked to her before. Something has got the girl upset."

The girl continued to walk toward the detective's car. Bruce rolled down the window and waited until she was even with them, then he spoke, "Hi, Alison."

The girl jumped from fright and it took her a moment to locate where the voice had come from. When she saw the detectives, she didn't say anything but kept walking.

Randy climbed of out the car and walked after her. "Hey Alison, where are you going? Can't you take a minute to answer a couple of questions?"

She kept on walking but did manage to say, "I'm going to school and you're going to make me late."

"Come on, we just need to know whether or not David Mertz is home."

"I talked to you guys yesterday and it got me grounded. So why don't ya just leave me alone?"

"Your mom grounded you for talking to us yesterday?"

"Yeah, for telling *you* where to find her, so kiss off."

"Okay, but all I need to know is whether or not David Mertz is home this morning."

"Yeah, the creep is there, but he's not going to open the door. He knows you guys are looking for him."

"Great, Alison, thanks. And I'm sorry for getting you in trouble. I won't tell David or you mom that you said anything." He handed her one of his business cards and said, "Give me a call if you ever want to talk about anything. See ya."

Alison had not stopped walking throughout the conversation, so Randy had to jog back to the car. He was just opening the car door to get back in when Bruce said, "Hey, look, here he comes."

Randy looked up in time to see David Mertz coming down the stairs. Bruce climbed out of the car and he and Randy started toward the doctor. He saw the detectives and they could almost hear his thoughts. He hesitated, started to turn back and go inside, then decided he wasn't going to humiliate himself by running and hiding, and kept walking toward them.

"Hey, Doc, how're you doin'?" Randy started in friendly tone. "Have ya got a few minutes?"

"Sorry, guys, I have an appointment I need to get to."

"We've just got a few things that we'd like to talk to you about. It'll only take a couple of minutes."

Mertz reached his car, a silver Mercedes, and started to open the door, but Detective Mack stepped in too close for the door to open. The doctor turned toward the detective, his face contorted in rage, as he said, "You'd better back off. I am sick and tired of you goons harassing me. There is no way that I'm going to talk to you without my lawyer being present."

Mack's voice was so quiet when he replied that his partner, who was only ten feet away, couldn't hear what he was saying. But he was close enough to Mertz for the doctor to hear him say, "Okay, then maybe you'd better call your lawyer. He can meet us down at the station where you can explain what's goin' on between you and your girlfriend's daughter."

At that, Mertz tried to ram Detective Mack with his shoulder, but Mack had anticipated the move and side-stepped it. The enraged doctor stumbled for a couple of steps. When he regained his balance, he spun and charged back, aiming a punch at the detective's head. Mack grabbed the swinging arm and used the doctor's momentum to slam him into the side of his car. A few seconds later, the doctor was in handcuffs, being led to the detective's vehicle.

"Well, Doc," Schiller said as they loaded their prisoner in the car, "it looks like you're gonna have time to talk to us after all. It sure does seem that you'd have learned that you can't go around attacking police officers after last time."

David Mertz's face was red as new brick, and spittle flew from his lips when he yelled, "The mayor is going to hear about this! I'll have your badges."

"I think I'd use my one phone call to talk to my lawyer if I were you," Schiller said. "I don't think the mayor is all that interested in what you have to say."

"You guys aren't going to think it's so funny when you're out of work," Mertz yelled back.

226

Neither detective responded to the continued ranting. The rest of the ride to the precinct was in silence.

With their prisoner in an interview room and safely out of earshot, Schiller asked his partner, "What happened back there? What did you say to this nut to make him go crazy like that?"

"I just played a hunch, and I think it may have paid off."

"What hunch?"

"Did you notice yesterday, when Mertz was not home, Alison's attitude and posture?"

"Not really, she seemed like a typical fifteen-year-old."

"Well, yesterday, she was standing straight and tall and coppin' an attitude. But, how about today, did she seem any different when we were talkin' to her?"

"I guess, I dunno. She seemed pretty beat down, like she had no self-esteem. Teenagers are like that, they're just moody, so what?"

"Probably nothing, but when our buddy was stiff arming us and trying to get in his car, I just got kind of a premonition and made a vague allegation about something going on between him and Alison. As you saw, he went for the bait way too well. I was saying it mostly just to rile him. But, the way he responded, I'm not too sure there isn't some truth to it. It seemed like he went way too crazy."

"So what'd we do now?"

"Well, when the doc's lawyer arrives, I think we should offer to forget about the assault on an officer charge, if he is willing to cooperate with us concerning his wife."

"I mean about your suspicions. Don't you think we should report that to Children's Services?"

"Yeah, we're going to do that, too."

# 29

Kay, a nurse in the long term care facility in Phoenix where Becky had been moved, had noticed that Becky never had any visitors. Without knowing why, since every indication was that this patient had no awareness, Kay began to take her breaks in Becky's room. She would talk to her a little, silly little bits of information about her family or her life, and she would read a chapter or two from the Psalms.

Aside from an involuntary shudder or spasm, there was never any response from Becky, but none was expected.

One day during Kay's afternoon break she sat reading Psalm 103 aloud. She had started to read and was to verse 4 when Becky began to convulse. The poor woman's normally lifeless body stiffened and her head arched back as her eyelids fluttered and her jaw clinched. Kay stopped reading, grabbed Becky's hand,

and started praying, "Please, Lord, release her from this terrible bondage. Heal her and give her peace."

*For the first time in what seemed to Becky like centuries, she had a sensation other than pain, heat, and despair. For the short period of time that it would take to draw a breath, she felt peace. Golden light surrounded her, and, though it didn't illuminate anything, it was so soothing. She remembered the only other time that she had experienced anything like this.*

*She had been eleven years old. It was at the summer camp that her parent's church sponsored, and she had responded to an invitation to receive Jesus as her savior. She was baptized and this same overwhelming peace had engulfed her for several days.*

*Gradually, the routine of life had swallowed the peace.*

*When she had first gotten home from camp, she was so excited about her new faith that she told everyone that she was going to go to Bible School and become a missionary when she grew up. She got nothing but encouragement from her parents, who were absolutely thrilled by her decision to follow Jesus Christ as Lord, though perhaps not so thrilled about the missionary thing.*

*Becky's descent from that spiritual high point was as unintentional as it was gradual. It started with innocent decisions like choosing to spend a few extra minutes in bed instead of getting up to read her Bible and pray. Then, it was deciding to skip church or youth group to go to a friend's house for a sleepover or party. Those subtle choices that everyone makes, and for most are without consequence, were the choices that undermined Becky's relationship with God.*

*By the time she was in high school, a pattern had developed. The choices were no longer that innocent or* accidental. She was finding, and even inventing, excuses for avoiding any event or activity that might bring her into contact with the things that pertained to God. Becky had grown to feel that those things were too rigid, too stifling. Anyway, she was sure that there would be plenty of time to do the 'church' thing when she was an adult.

When her mom and dad had realized that she was drifting away from them, and the things they held as crucial for life, they had no clue as to how to help her change course. Their efforts to point her back to God only seemed to motivate her to pull further away.

She met David Mertz while she was in college. He, too, had grown up in a family that attended church regularly. The Mertz family's purpose for belonging to a local congregation was considerable different than that of Becky's family, however. For the Mertz bunch, it was about socializing and networking, not about service and worship. David was convinced that a personal relation-ship with God was an impossible illusion. In his mind, that type of Christianity was a crutch for the weak, or as he enjoyed quoting, "An opiate for the masses."

Becky gradually embraced David's philosophy. It eased the latent guilt, though it failed to fill the void in her heart. In the rare times of honest introspection she knew that she had turned her back on the best relation-ship that she could have ever hoped for: A relationship with Jesus Christ.

And now, floating in this void and surrounded by the flotsam of regret and jetsam of torment, she saw that rare moment of peace from her childhood as nothing more than an additional torment to remind her that there was no going back.

Ace's enthusiasm helped Zach pull himself up off the ground. He grabbed the rifle and made sure that there was still a round in the chamber. When the stalker returned, Zach was going to be ready.

Once Zach was on his feet, he and Ace headed toward the truck. As he walked, he worked on a plan. He would salvage anything useful that he could carry from the camping supplies and equipment and then start hiking toward civilization.

He realized that there would be a search and rescue team coming for him, and knew that the best thing to do to assist them in locating him was to stay put. He also understood that staying at the truck would make it easy for the man in black to find him. Zach was positive that the creep would be back as soon as it was dark. In Zach's mind there was no choice but to get moving.

As they approached the tree line, Zach called Ace, and made sure that the dog didn't run out into the open until he had studied the clearing. When he was satisfied that there was nothing sinister waiting for them, he headed for the truck. Halfway across the meadow, he realized that the hood of the rig was up.

When he got to the truck, the hoses and belts had been slashed and wires cut. The damage was not the only vandalism, nor was it the most upsetting to Zach. The lid to the cooler had been ripped off and every container had been opened and its contents thrown out.

Ace ate one pile of food and then ran to the next until he had devoured all the discarded food.

The stuff in the cab of the pickup had been ransacked as well. The sleeping bags were slashed to ribbons, and the foam mattresses and duffels of clothing had been thrown into the stream. Zach's MP3 player was smashed on the ground beside the passenger side door of the truck, and broken discs littered the ground.

All Zach managed to salvage was a small flashlight and a pocket-sized New Testament Bible from the pocket in the driver's side door. There was also a box of granola bars stuffed under the seat that the vandal had overlooked.

He was happy with the granola bars and the mini-mag. He put the bible in his pocket.

Satisfied that he had gotten everything useful out of the truck, Zach took off, moving as fast as he could manage. He wanted to get as much distance between himself and this spot as possible before dark. He didn't take time to contemplate how his adversary had tracked from Arizona to Oregon, or how the guy arrived on the search and rescue helicopter. The vivid memory that person on the hood of the pickup was driving him to get away from the truck, and this place.

The sun was only about twenty degrees above the horizon when Zach crossed the stream and entered the trees on the east side of the meadow. The air was beginning to cool and a slight breeze at ground level was enough movement in the tree tops to produce a soothing cantata. Under different conditions, he may have enjoyed the music, but, as it was, he was too distracted to hear it.

Zach's plan was to head east, moving parallel to the main road for about a mile, then cut over and get on it. He hoped that the maneuver would throw the follower off his trail. Not being able to see for more than a few yards while in the dense trees was frightening, so Zach kept moving as fast as he could manage. Twenty minutes into his walk, both of his hands began to cramp, and he realized how tight a grip he had on the weapon and tried to relax. Fear that the guy in the black jumpsuit was going to jump out of the trees at any second made relaxing impossible.

Ace tore through the brush and jumped over logs as if hunting game. There was no indication that the dog missed Nute or Gabe. As Zach watched the dog's total abandon, he wondered if dogs had the capacity for abstract thought. It would be great to live only in the moment, Zach decided; with no guilt over making mistakes; no sense of wondering if what you were doing was the right thing; and no stress over what to do next. People spent so much time and energy worrying about things that they had little or no control over. Dogs appeared to be content to be nothing more than *dogs*, with no consideration of what anyone else thought, or what might happen fifteen minutes in the future. Who was the dumb animal?

Zach walked east for about an hour and then turned north expecting to intersect the road that he and his grandfather had driven when they arrived here. What the boy failed to remember was that the road that he was attempting to reach came in from the north. The course that he was on roughly paralleled the road he was attempting to reach. After he had walked for another twenty minutes, he came into a clearing expecting to find the way out of the woods. Instead, he found a vista of miles of trees, without a road in sight.

He stood looking out at the contour of the mountains. They looked like a carpet that had been crumpled by a giant. He saw only row after row of tree covered buttes. Under different circumstances, Zach may have seen the beauty of the view. As it was, all he felt was the panic of being alone. Without the road to follow, he had no idea of how to get out of this wilderness.

It was starting to get dark.

The guy in black was coming for him.

A sense of doom washed over Zach. He stood looking at the folds of trees that were ahead of him. Escape seemed impossible. Depression settled in and he wanted to fall on the ground and wait for whatever fate reached him first.

**234**

Ace came and settled on his haunches next to Zach, leaned against his leg, and whined. The contact pulled Zach out of the frump and reminded him that it was going to be dark soon and he had no shelter, no bedding, and no way to keep warm. And on top of everything else, he was hungry.

There was an outcropping of rocks on the other side of the clearing. Zach thought it looked like it might provide a good place to spend the night. He hurried to the spot and scrambled to clear an area large enough to allow him to lie down at the base of a large boulder. Using a piece of flat rock, he scraped a spot for a fire and made a circle of rocks around it. With the boulder protecting one side from a sneak attack, he'd only have to watch for the man in the jumpsuit in one direction. Zach gathered an arm load of limbs and then a handful of dry moss, twigs, and pitch. He piled the material the way that he had been taught.

Checking in the waterproof match container that his grandfather had given him, Zach counted nine matches. He carefully shook one out and struck it on the side of the container. The white top of the match broke off without igniting. The stick on the second match snapped in half. Zach was starting to get nervous. He had to have a fire, and he was wasting his precious matches.

To his relief, the third match struck and flamed up and Zach was able to ignite the collection of moss and pitch. Those materials, and a few twigs, were rapidly consumed by the flame, but it did not produce enough heat to get the larger pieces of wood to combust.

Zach gathered more moss and pitch and twigs and started over. Searching through his pockets for some paper, he found the small Bible. He tore out a handful of the pages out, crumpled them, and mixed them in with the rest of his tinder. The first match he used on this attempt blazed perfectly, and, within a few minutes, he had a nice fire going.

As much to keep busy as to make certain that there was enough fuel for the fire to last through the night, he gathered a large pile of limbs and bark.

The shadows had grown longer as he worked, and, when Zach finally settled in, it was nearly dark. He absently watched a pair of night hawks as they rode the last warm air currents of the day, and gathered their supper of flying insects, one bug at a time. Off to the south, a great-horned owl tested his voice with a couple of mournful hoots. Ace moved up against Zach. The eerie howling of a pack of coyotes came from a couple of ridges away and Ace shivered and whined as he leaned against Zach, who was glad for the companionship.

If the dog was afraid, Zach was petrified. The thought of wild animals coming for him was frightening. The threat from them attacking, however, was dwarfed by the memory of the glowing eyes that had stared at him through the windshield of the pickup.

He held the rifle across his legs, stared over the fire, and listened. Every night sound startled him. Small rustles in the underbrush, the occasional popping of the fire, and the persistent calls of the night animals, all held threats in Zach's overactive, obsessive, mind.

Ace's head pivoted at each sound. He kept his head cocked at an angle and his ears raised. When the sound of the coyote chorus erupted a little closer, the dog jumped up barking. He backed up until his haunches were up against the rock wall that was behind them, and then he showed his teeth and growled.

Zach brought the rifle to his shoulder and pointed it out in the darkness. Through the rifle's scope he saw nothing but black.

Almost two hours passed before David Mertz's lawyer arrived at the precinct. By that time, Randy and Bruce were irritated. Though there was plenty of paperwork for them to work on, they didn't like hanging around the office, and their appreciation hadn't been enhanced by being jerked around by this guy in a fancy suit, carrying a briefcase. Knowing that the lawyer that had left them hanging was a high-dollar shark named William Cornish didn't improve their attitude. Cornish had made a reputation, and a fortune, out of successfully defending rich and famous clients who had found themselves sideways to the law.

As unimpressed as the detectives were by being put on ice by the hotshot lawyer, Dr. Mertz apparently enjoyed the wait even less. When the door to the interview room, where Mertz was being held, opened to allow the lawyer in for the private consultation with his client, the doctor's voice came flooding out like water over a breached dam. The few words that escaped were all that were needed to indicate that the client was furious.

Fifteen minutes later, when the two detectives entered the room, Mertz had quieted down, though his expression indicated that the calm had not reached inside.

Bruce and Randy didn't mind. Their experience had taught them that angry interviewees often provided the most productive interviews.

Schiller and Mack started the interview by explaining that all they wanted was to ask David a few question about the circumstances surrounding the night of his wife's incident. They spoke to Cornish as if Dr. David Mertz was not in the room.

"We might be inclined to *not* pursue charges against your client's assault on Detective Schiller," Mack explained, "if he would cooperate with us by answering a few questions."

**237**

Mertz's jaw was set and his eyes were locked on the top of the table as his lawyer answered for him. "Dr. Mertz will be more than happy to provide any information he has. Obviously, he is as anxious as anyone to have the truth, surrounding the unfortunate event, come to light.

"What he is not interested in is being harassed by overzealous detectives. His life has had enough disruptions lately without having you people show up at his home to interrogate his friends. The man is in mourning, after all."

"Look," Detective Mack responded. "We are not members of a jury. You don't need to pretend that your client is some lily white choir boy when you're talking to us. We know that this scumbag's wife of nearly twenty years is lying in a coma because he refuses to allow her the small dignity of being taken off life-support. He's letting her suffer the ultimate indignity because he would rather be the center of an *attempted* murder investigation than an *actual* murder investigation. We are also well aware that he is playing house with another woman while all this is going on.

"So excuse us if we aren't too concerned with how our behavior might ruffle his delicate sensibilities."

David Mertz jumped to his feet and shouted, "I do not have to sit here and listen to this baboon ramble on, defaming my character!" He turned to his lawyer and growled, "Get me out of here, or I'll find someone who can!"

When Mertz stopped ranting to take a breath, Detective Schiller calmly interjected, "Yep, Mr. Cornish, the good doctor is correct. We don't need to be having this conversation at all. In fact, I think I'd rather make the arrest for assault right now and throw his sorry butt in the tank. He might be a little more interested in answering our questions after spending some time in the county lockup. There are a lot of the guys in there who would really enjoy spending some quality time with a doctor."

Cornish, still seated, turned to his client and crisply commanded, "Sit down. Acting like the south end of a northbound horse may work around your staff, but I think you'll find that it doesn't impress anyone in *this* room. And if you want to terminate my services, I will be more than happy to make my exit and leave you to these detectives. I can easily make my fees working with people who do not cause me undue heartburn."

Something about the lawyer's abrupt approach took the arrogance out of the doctor and he sat down.

"Thank you, Dr. Mertz," Cornish continued.

"So," Detective Mack said, "may we ask our questions?"

"Do we have your promise that there will be no arrest for assault? In addition, if you would persuade the D.A. to drop the assault charges against Dr. Mertz concerning the hospital security guard, I'm sure his cooperation would be superb."

"You know that we don't have any influence with a case where charges have already been filed. Whether or not we arrest Dr. Mertz for assault on a police officer depends on the level of cooperation we receive," Mack answered.

"That isn't—" Mertz started, but was immediately interrupted by an angry glance and upraised hand from Cornish.

"You can't blame us for trying. Ask your questions," Cornish said.

"First," Schiller began, "in the days just prior to the incident with your wife, did you ever see anyone in your neighborhood that looked out of place?"

Cornish nodded at Mertz, and the doctor looked puzzled and said, "What do you mean someone who looked out of place? I don't know everyone living around me, how would I know if they belonged in the neighborhood?"

"I'm talking about someone who dressed in a strange or unusual manner."

"Not that I remember. Why, did someone see some kind of a freak in the area?"

"Your son mentioned a man dressed in a black jump-suit to the officers that found your wife. We're just try-ing to run down every possible angle. Do you remember seeing anyone like that?"

"No. But I wasn't at home very much."

"Had your wife been unusually depressed or upset?"

"Our son, Zach, had gotten into trouble at school the morning that Becky overdosed. We had held a family meeting that did *not* go well. Yes, I'd say that she was very upset. But she appeared to be more mad than depressed."

"Did she have a history of suicidal tendencies?"

Mertz turned to Cornish and said, "These people know that Becky had previously attempted to kill her-self with an overdose. Do I have to submit to this asinine type of questioning? This is another prime example of their incompetence."

"Humor us," Mack said.

The lawyer tapped his pen on the table, clicked it a couple of times, and then said, "If you don't have any new questions I'm afraid this interview is over. Now we'll expect you to stand good on your end of the bargain and not make the arrest for assault."

Schiller stared at Mertz and his voice was filled with contempt when he continued, "Oh, we have a couple of new questions alright. And we'll try to overcome our incompetence as we ask them.

"Were you a boy scout when you were young?"

Cornish didn't wait for his client to react to the strange question. "What could whether or not Dr. Mertz was a boy scout possibly have to do with what happened to his wife?"

"Trust me, there's a connection. Besides, what could it harm to answer the question?"

"No," Mertz interrupted, "I was not in the scouts."

"Ever do any rock or mountain climbing, or sailing?"

"None of the above."

"How about your wife, was she ever involved in any of those activities?"

"Not hardly. She was afraid of heights and got sea sick running bath water. What does this have to do with anything?"

Detective Mack flipped his notebook closed, and Detective Schiller tapped his file folder on the table, signaling that the interview was over. Mack made it official by standing and saying, "Thank you for cooperating. As promised, we'll forget today's little altercation."

Cornish looked at Mertz and shrugged. Mertz took the cue, stood, and started toward the door.

"Oh," Schiller said as if he had just thought of it, "just one more question. When did you and Dr. Amanda Stearns become an item?"

Mertz would have been facing a new assault charge if his lawyer hadn't been between the doctor and the detective. As it was, Cornish pushed his client out the door.

In the hallway, Cornish got in Mertz's face and shouted, "Are you totally insane? You just wiggled out of one assault charge and now you're trying to get another. You need to lighten up!"

"I am through letting these Neanderthals push me around."

"You don't get it do you? These 'Neanderthals' as you call them are intelligent, well trained guys. And their goal is to put you in jail. Do NOT give them more motivation by being such an arrogant jackass! They know exactly how to pull your chain and you're letting them do it. I cannot believe that you are calling them Neanderthals when you're the one doing all the chest pounding. Now get out of here before I ask them to arrest you for excessive stupidity."

Randy and Bruce watched the drama from inside the interview room. They couldn't hear the exchange, but they could see from the posture of the two men that Cornish was telling his client how the cow ate the cabbage.

"So what did you think?" Randy asked Bruce. "Besides being a nut-case, did Dr. David Mertz have anything to do with his wife's overdose?"

"He had everything to do with it. By his own admission, he wasn't ever home. Ms. Mertz may have known that he was involved with another woman. Their kid was up to his nose-holes in trouble at school. And what'd the good old doctor do? He demonstrated his great skills as a husband and father by taking off, to meet the sweet Dr. Stearns, no doubt. But none of that is going to get the jerk convicted of attempted murder."

"That's for sure. But think about it. If every poor excuse for a dad was in the hoosegow, there wouldn't be many guys walkin' the streets. But you don't think he actually put the pills in her mouth?"

"Nah, do you?"

"No I guess I don't. I'm beginning to think she did that by herself. But that rope still bugs the heck out of me. Why did Ms. Mertz, or anyone else for that matter, tie the kid's door shut?"

"I think that she did that so the kid wouldn't come out of his room, find her and save her."

"I just can't buy that theory. What teenage kid is apt to wander into the room where his mother is taking a bath? And, if she wanted to keep him out, why not just lock the bathroom door?"

"I don't know, and it looks like we're never going to find out."

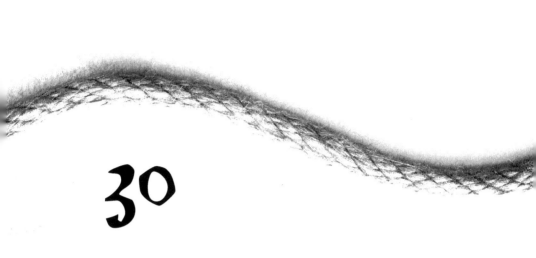

# 30

At the end of her shift, Kay was normally in a rush to leave work and get home to her family. However, on Tuesday night something drew her back to room 35. She had already punched her time card, gone to her locker and collected her purse. She was headed for the door when an overwhelming impulse pushed her back to Becky Mertz's room.

When Kay entered the small room, there was no change since her last visit. The patient lay with her eyes closed, mouth slightly open, engulfed in a tangle of tubes and wires. Monitors beeped and blinked.

Kay's back was sore and her feet were killing her. She knew if she sat down in the visitor's chair, it would be a battle to get her ample backside back up. What she wanted was to get home and get dinner started.

Annoyed at herself, she felt compelled to sit down. When she did, she sighed and said, "Well, Becky, I don't know why, but here I am. Is there something you wanted to tell me?"

Kay felt foolish asking someone in a coma a question, and she hoped that no one was listening. Her co-workers had already made enough snide comments about her talking and reading to these types of patients. Kay was adept at ignoring those remarks, but they still stung.

Not sure why she was there, Kay rummaged in her purse and pulled out her well worn New Testament. She flipped the pages until she found Luke Chapter 15 and read the story of the prodigal son aloud.

When she had finished reading the short parable, she felt relieved and released. She went out to her car and drove home. As she jockeyed her car through the rush hour traffic, she wondered why she had felt that reading to her patient had been so important.

*Becky's horrific black prison had become even more unbearable since the brief moment when Becky had been bathed in delicious golden light. Returning from that exquisite glimpse of tranquility intensified the torment.*

*In her absolute despair, she found herself doing something she had spent her adult life avoiding: Praying.*

*Her prayer was not a litany of requests. And it wasn't a chorus of pity over her condition. In fact, her prayer had two simple components. First, she pleaded for God's intervention in the life of her son. Second, she expressed her deep regret over wasting her life.*

*Even as she spoke to God, she found it profoundly odd that, after a lifetime of refusing to talk to him, she was trying to communicate with him from what she had decided was Hell.*

*While that strange thought was still in her mind, the portal blinked open. The man in black filled the opening.*

*He was leaning in when he shouted, "Ah, yes, call on the name of him who has sent you to this torment. But it is too late for you. You're mine. You chose me long ago and now you have me." A chilling laugh that contained no mirth echoed in Becky's ears after the portal had snapped closed.*

*In the darkest of darkness, a scene ran through Becky's mind: a dream or a vision, or both. Whatever, it was more realistic than reality. In this strange chimera, there was a young man clothed in tattered rags and covered with mud. His black hair and beard were matted with grime and he was surrounded, and covered, by filth from a herd of swine.*

*The pigs were snorting and rooting through the vile ground. Their sides were slabs of fat and they were covered in their own manure.*

*The man was pathetically thin and covered with dirt and crusted sores. The beady eyes of the hogs ignored him, but their huge nostrils flared while they used their snouts to push him out of the way. Hot, humid, breathe sprayed him as they rolled him back and forth in their attempts to get to some small bit of forage that the appalling man was trying to save for himself.*

*The largest hog, a black monster with stiff-bristle hair growing from its ears, rammed the man in his protruding ribs. While the man struggled to refill his lungs with air, the pig ripped the last small bit of green vegetation from the man's torn mud caked fingernails, and devoured the morsel with a loud snort.*

*The man lay in the stench of the hog wallow, breathing hard, with tears streaming down his face.*

*Becky focused on the man. As she stared in morbid fascination, she saw that man's face was slowly changing. As the gradual morphing progressed, it occurred to her that the face on which she was transfixed was*

247

*her own. Then, instantly, it was she that was laying in the sludge and muck, the pungent stench of hog ma-nure was in her nostrils, and the pain of broken ribs jolted through her.*

Gabe did not regain consciousness until he was in the hospital's surgical recovery unit. He remembered noth-ing of the helicopter ride from the mountain stream to the fire-watch command center, or the ambulance ride that took him to Saint Charles Hospital.

At the emergency room, they continued to adminis-ter the saline solution that had been started by the EMT in the ambulance. After x-rays confirmed that there were no broken bones other than his femur, he was taken to surgery for his broken leg. Pumped full of antibiotics in an attempt to ward off infection, they sent him to the recovery unit.

Gabe was only semi-conscious when the nurses brought Meg in. She held his hand and prayed while he fought to surface through the fog of pain and drugs and open his eyes.

"I must've died and went to heaven," he said when he was alert enough to speak. "Anybody as beautiful as you has got to be an angel."

"That bump on your head must have been worse than the doctors thought. You are talking sheer nonsense."

"Maybe that crack on the head knocked some sense into me."

"That'd be good," Meg answered through her tears.

"How'd I get here?"

"A Forest Service helicopter brought you out of the woods. Then an ambulance picked you up at the Forest Service incident command center and brought you here."

Gabe digested that information for a while. The drugs in his system were interfering with his thought process in obvious ways. "What day is it?" he asked.

"Thursday. But it's more like night. It's a little after nine o'clock."

Gabe closed his eyes and lay quietly for a few minutes, while he continued to try to get a hold on reality. His eyes popped open. In a startled voice, he said, "Where's Zach? Is he okay?"

"I was hoping that you might be able to give some insight into that," Meg's voice cracked as she answered. "When the rescue team found you, Zach wasn't anywhere to be found."

Gabe held his head in both hands and squeezed his eyes shut. Bits and pieces of memory started to snap together in his mind like pieces of a jigsaw puzzle. "The last thing I remember was him going downstream from the pickup. He was goin' to try to catch enough trout for supper. He had to have been right there when the Forest Service helicopter picked me up. Those guys didn't see him?"

"No one even knew he was out there until the County Sheriff's deputies talked to me. Last I heard, they were putting together a Search and Rescue team to go after him."

"He must be scared to death."

"He at least has the dogs with him. They should provide him some sense of security and companionship."

A knot formed in Gabe's throat. He closed his eyes and stammered, "Well, a dog anyway."

"What do you mean, 'a dog'?"

"Ace is with him."

"What about Nute? Why wouldn't Nute be with him?"

The anesthetic was interfering with his emotion control as much as with his thought process and Gabe's eyes were filled and his voice went quiet and high when he answered, "Nute was hit by a falling tree."

"Oh, Gabe, that's awful." Both of them were silent for a moment, and then Meg said through her own tears, "I hope he didn't suffer."

"He didn't. It was quick."

Meg nodded, and they fell silent again. Both of them were lost in their memories and grief for a few minutes before Meg said, "We *have* got to get to praying for Zach."

"I have been. And I'm not plannin' to quit now."


Ace stopped growling and barking and came back to lean against Zach. Both the dog and the boy spent half an hour concentrating on every noise, trying to sort out the sounds that were coming from the darkness. Little by little, they relaxed.

Eventually, after Zach had added several more pieces of wood to the fire, hunger managed to fight through the fear. Rummaging through his pockets he found the granola bars that he had gathered from the truck. He ripped one open, broke it in half, and gave half to Ace and ate the other. A second bar followed closely behind the first.

Zach's hunger had hardly been dented, but he thought he better save the other four bars. They were all the food that he had, and he didn't even have a guess as to how long it was going to take to walk out of this wilderness.

While Zach was thinking about how thirsty and hungry he was, exhaustion snuck up and took him captive. The warmth of the fire, combined with over forty hours with almost no rest, swirled him down into sleep. Ace stayed alert for a little longer, but, within a quarter hour, he was sleeping also.

As the pair slept, the fire burned down to coals and the full moon rose. A few thin clouds feathered their way across the moon, but they did not diminish its light. By the time the orb was a third of the way through its arch in the sky it was illuminating the landscape to almost as bright as day. The skimmed-milk white light left long shadows of darkness where trees or rocks stood in the way of the beams.

After about three hours of sleep, Zach awoke confused about where he was. When his memory kicked into gear, he bolted upright. He was straining to see into the shadows for any threat when he saw that the man in black was seated across the coals from him.

Zach's heart raced and he was afraid to take his eyes off his adversary while he patted the ground in an effort to locate the rifle. He had forgotten that the firearm was leaning against the boulder, out of reach, behind him. The frantic movement woke Ace, but the dog did not pay the least attention to the intruder.

On the other side of the fire, the man's mouth opened, and Zach expected to see rows of sharpened white teeth. Instead, there was a black hole that seemed to open into an abyss. The voice that came out of that void was a deep bass, and hollow.

"Zach. I'm coming for you. Soon. You're mine," the man said, and disappeared.

Then Zach glimpsed the back of the man with the shiny clothes. He was standing at attention in the coals, sword at the ready, blocking the enemy's line of attack. In an instant, he too was gone.

Zach grabbed Ace around the neck and hugged the dog this chest and shook with confusion and fear. His mind was going a hundred miles per hour.

He wanted to convince himself that all this was a dream or hallucination, but he was fairly certain that it wasn't; what he had witnessed was far more vivid than any dream he had ever had, and he didn't think people analyzed hallucinations.

He felt that he had just gotten a glimpse into a realm that was always there but was normally invisible; but, why would he be seeing something like that? Visions were for important people. As he contemplated his own question, the obvious answer was that he was going insane. He was pretty sure that crazy people saw things like this.

The problem was, what he had seen was as real and terrifying to him, regardless of whether it was a dream, a vision, or insanity.

Half an hour later, the fire was down to a single ember and Zach was getting cold. In order rekindle the fire, he would have to let go of Ace and reach right into the spot where the man in the bright clothes had been. What if the being was still there and Zach just couldn't see him? Would it kill Zach if he touched the guy?

After wrestling with fear for several minutes, Zach released his grip on Ace, and quickly placed some small sticks on the embers. When nothing happened he put several pieces of wood and a handful of needles with the twigs. It took awhile, but eventually a tendril of smoke curled up from the needles, and then a small flame started licking the new fuel.

The dancing flames and popping of the burning wood were encouraging, but Zach noticed that, though the immediate area around the fire was illuminated by the flames, the fire made it much more difficult to see what was out beyond the small area that it lit.

Perhaps not seeing what was out beyond the fire's reach was a benefit.

In the dirt and debris beside the flames lay the Bible that Zach had thrown aside after using a few of its pages for kindling. He picked it up. The missing pages made the book look like a person who was missing their front teeth.

He fumbled around in his pockets and found the small flashlight. He twisted the top of the mini-mag and focused the beam on the inside of the Bible.

The first words that caught his eye had been underlined and read, "...what must I do to be saved?" That phrase got his attention. It was exactly what he wanted to know; what did he need to do to be saved? He looked back in the book and there was the answer in the next phrase, "Believe on the Lord Jesus Christ and you will be saved."

Zach snapped the little book closed and turned off the flashlight. This was just too weird. How did he happen to open that book to that particular place?

The words kept running through his mind: Believe on the Lord Jesus Christ. Believe on the Lord Jesus Christ. What did that mean? He turned the flashlight on again and looked back in the little book. When he did, he noticed that someone, undoubtedly his grandfather, had written something on the margin of the page. It said "Hebrews 11." Assuming that the note was pointing to somewhere else in the book, he looked at the table of contents and found there was a part titled Hebrews. He turned there and started reading.

Hebrews 11 was a section about people who had faith in God and believed what God said. Their faith caused them to do things: Amazing things: A strange variety of things.

So if he decided to believe God, what was he supposed to do? As he sat contemplating that question, he noticed a note scribbled on this page. It said, "John 3:1-21."

Zach had stopped shaking, in fact, he wasn't even thinking about the man in the jumpsuit. He was too intent on this weird treasure hunt. He went back to the table of contents to see where this new clue would lead.

He read the story of Jesus and Nicodemus and sat thinking, confused. He kept going back to a couple of sentences that had been underlined. As far as he could figure, Jesus had told this Nicodemus guy that he needed to start a new life. A life that was so completely different that it was like being born all over again.

As Zach contemplated what it meant, he concluded that being born all over again might not be a bad idea. Maybe he wouldn't be such an oddball if he got to start over in a new family. The more he thought about it, the more he liked the idea.

No one had ever taught Zach how to pray. He had listened to his grandfather and grandmother, though, and it seemed like they pretty much just talked to God. It had always been strange to listen to them talking away like there was someone right there listening. All of a sudden, it didn't seem strange, and Zach gave it a try.

He didn't close his eyes or anything. He just started talking. Honestly. "God, I'm not sure you are really even there. But, if you are, I need to be saved. There is a crazy man in these woods that apparently wants to kill me or something. And even if I get away from him, I'll still be out in the forest without a clue of how to get back to civilization. I think Grumpa is the only one who knows how to find me, and he's hurt so bad that I don't know if he can tell anyone where I am.

"My life is pretty much a train wreck anyway. Mom is as good as dead. In fact, I think that she would be a lot better off if they just unplugged all the machines that are keeping her body alive and let her go. And my father, well, I don't think he remembers that I exist.

**254**

# Habits

"So, God, if you're someplace listening, I could stand some saving right about now. I'm trying to believe in you. But I guess I need some help with that, too."

The angel that had been standing guard over Zach turned to listen to him as he prayed. When Zach finished, the heavenly being pumped a huge fist in the air and shouted, "Praise King Jesus!"

Nothing in the earthly realm heard the praise, but in that other realm an answer came back from a mighty army singing in unison, "Salvation and glory and power belong to our God."

The being masquerading as a man in a black jumpsuit was writhing on the ground pressing his hands over his ears and gnashing his teeth.

When Zach finished talking, he looked back down at the Bible that was still open in his hands. There on the border of the page that he had last read was another note. It said, "I John 1:9."

It took Zach a few moments, even using the table of contents, to find the little part of the book that was labeled I John, but when he had he read it, tears began to run down both his cheeks. He immediately started talking to God again. "Oh God, I know I am a sinner. I've done so many things wrong. Please forgive me. Please clean me up."

The note in the margin of this passage was, "II Corinthians 5:17."

After reading that, Zach jumped to his feet and shouted into the night, "Oh, wow, that's the best. I'm new!"

Again, sounds of praises, silent to ears on Earth, resounded throughout the heavenly realm.

Zach tucked the little book into his pocket with care, regretting that he had torn pages from it. He added some more wood to the fire and lay back down by the blaze. Ace lay down beside the boy and they fell asleep.

As he slept, Zach had another dream. He saw the two men again, the one in black and the one awash with light. As before, the two were locked in combat. But in this battle, the bright shiny being was on the offensive and the dark figure was on the run. There were no missiles launched and the fight quickly ended when the being of the light landed a blow across the chest of his opponent with the flat side of his sword. The force of the strike sent the man rolling, and he was still tumbling end over end when he rolled out of sight.

A huge portion of Zach's fear was released as he watched his tormentor's defeat.

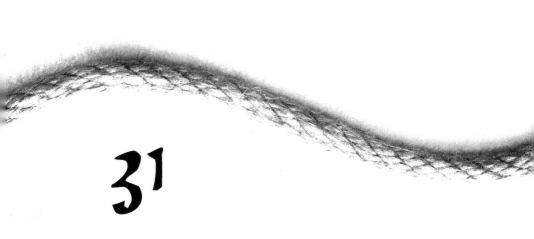

# 31

Officers Buck Rivera and Todd Evans had come out of briefing and were walking down the stairs of the precinct building. They were on their way to their squad car to go out on patrol when they met Detectives Bruce Schiller and Randy Mack going up the stairs.

There was enough testosterone in that stairwell to supply a pharmaceutical company for a month. The four lawmen stopped and faced each other, each man expecting one of the others to say something that would result in a brawl. As amazing as it was, no one cracked wise and all four of them stood in an awkward silence. Finally, Todd Evans spoke and said, "Hey, you guys ever get to the bottom of that overdose case?"

"Yeah, I think so," Detective Mack answered. "It looks like it really was a simple case of attempted suicide. Anyway, that's how it's going to go down on the books."

"What'd ya mean, 'attempted'?" Rivera asked. "That gal isn't still alive is she?"

"She is, sorta. She's in one of those long term care facilities, hooked up to enough machines to run a Detroit automotive plant, but in a technical sense at least, she's still alive."

"Man, I do not want to go out like that," Evans said.

"Nobody does, but most of us don't get to choose, do we?" Mack responded.

"That *is* the sorry truth," Evans added. "Do you know what happened to the kid that I sat with in the emergency room area?"

"He ended up with his grandparents somewhere in Oregon or Washington. Somewhere up there. It's a good thing they were there for him. That jerk of a father of his sure wasn't going to step up to the plate to take care of him. He's too busy with his new family."

Evans ran the end of the sole of his boot along the top of the stair he was standing on as he said, "I think that we all wanted to find out that he was responsible. I know I wanted him to go to jail, even if it was only for excessive jerk-itis."

"Yeah, I guess. But the whole deal was hinky from the start," Schiller added. "We never found a good explanation for the rope on the kid's door knob. And there were some other loose ends besides."

"What kind of things?" Rivera asked.

"I don't know. Things like, it looked like Ms. Mertz was arranging to take the kid and go to her parents. And then there was the deal with the husband renting the condo with that female doctor, things like that. Nothing concrete, but just little niggling things."

"How about the assault of the security guard at the hospital, are those charges gonna stand up?" Evans wanted to know.

258

Schiller looked up at the lights and focused on a couple of dead moths in the fixture covers as he responded, "The grand jury gave the green light for that to go to trial. But you know how backed up the courts are. It's hard to tell when that will get on the docket, if it ever does. My guess is that they'll plea it out, and the doctor will walk away with a little community service or something. Anyway, that's the deal."

"Okay," Mack said, heading on down the stairs, "thanks for the info. You guys have a good day."

As he and Buck walked across the parking lot to get in their patrol cars, Todd said, "Man, I wanted them to stick that chump of a doctor with murder charges. I *know* in my gut that he was responsible. I still want to nail him, but I don't know how."

"Yeah, me, too, and I bet those detectives missed something. But like you always say, we only catch the dumb ones. And while Mertz is a jerk, I guess he isn't *that* dumb."

*As Becky's mind continued to run the images of the dream through her senses, she felt the sticky, repulsive, muck fastened to her. She experienced the nausea of her empty stomach grinding on itself as a rebellion for having nothing in it. Pain from her broken ribs screamed at her with every breath.*

*In a moment of inspiration, she realized that the filth that she was wallowing in was her life and her possessions. The hunger that was gnawing away on her insides was her pursuit of status and social standing. The pain from her ribs represented her terrible choices. Her pride, ego, and vain ambition had landed her in a retched pig sty, and she it had taken disaster to awaken her to the fact.*

*That flash of insight was gone as quickly as it had come and she crawled out of the nasty filth and tried*

**259**

to remove some of it from o her exposed skin. The more she rubbed and scraped the more repugnant the dirt seemed to be. She continued to crawl and felt the skin peeling off her knees, then blood flowing down her shins. She looked down and stared in a morbid awe, as her bright red life's fluid mingled with the caked grime, and turned maroon.

Gnawing hunger broke her fascination with the bloody mud on her lower legs. Becky would have put anything that resembled nourishment into her mouth, but there was nothing that qualified. The ground stretching out from the pig sty was parched and cracked and without a hint of vegetation.

Despite the pain in her knees, and the agony of her empty stomach, she kept crawling. As she crept along, she tried to reason through this scene. Her logic assured her that she was still floating in the black nothingness of her prison, experiencing no physical sensation, and this whole ordeal in a sun scorched wasteland, covered with the feces of hogs, dying of hunger, aching from broken ribs, was some type of vision.

Her senses insisted otherwise.

Gabe had spent the night in bed, in the semi-dark of the hospital room, but he hadn't slept much. He might have been able to tune out the sounds of the ventilation system and the intrusive echoes of the staff's movements as they went about their duties. It was possible that he could have overcome, with the aid of the pain killers, the dull throb in his leg where the surgeon had put his femur back together with rods and screws. But there was no escaping the anxiety of knowing that Zach was all alone in the wilds of Central Oregon.

Despite all the hype the media carried about attacks from bears and cougars and coyotes, animal attacks were so rare as to not even be a consideration. What worried Gabe were the vastness of the area and the roughness of the terrain that Zach was in. You could walk for a week in some of the canyons in the area without crossing a logging road and there were spots that were so steep you could only navigate them with climbing gear.

If Zach stayed in the general vicinity of where they had set up camp the search and rescue team would find him without any problem. However, if for some reason he took off, trying to find his way out, or running from some phantom, it might take days for the crew to get to him.

Gabe had spent the night oscillating between praying for Zach's safety and conjuring up images of the disasters that his grandson might encounter.

When the bit of high desert landscape that was visible out the hospital room window began to lighten, Gabe was watching, cheering on the rising sun. He imagined that Zach was anticipating the sun's appearance more than he.

Gabe knew that here was little threat of the boy suffering hypothermia or frost bite. The weather was too mild, though the elevation where they had camped was just over seven thousand feet above sea level, and temperatures at dawn were typically below freezing, even in June and July. The real danger was in Zach's mind. Being alone in the vast wilderness of Central Oregon could play games with your mind.

The first faint rays of the morning sun were peeling up the eastern edge of the night's cover of darkness when Zach awoke. Ace was lying about a foot away with his nose pointed straight at Zach's face. The dog's muzzle was resting on his paws and his ears were cocked forward.

Had there been an observer, it would have appeared to them that the dog was sending the boy subliminal messages. The truth was that the dog was hungry and he knew there were tasty granola bars in the boy's pocket.

Zach sat up and looked around. Strange, he thought, everyone called this being lost, but he knew exactly where he was. What he didn't know, was where anything else was.

When he got onto his feet, every muscle in his body seemed to be screaming for attention at the same time. He had a stiff neck. His shoulder muscles felt tight. Every breath made his ribs ache. The joints in his hips burned. It felt like there was grit under his knee caps. There were knots in his calf muscles. And, his feet were sore. The funny thing was, though he was in more physical pain than ever before, inside, he felt better than he had in as long as he could remember. This was because, in spite of being out in the middle of a wilderness without much food and no water, inside a weight had lifted off his soul, and, for the first time in about forever, he wasn't afraid. It wasn't about him making the right decisions or doing the right things. Now it was about God doing something with his life.

Prayer had worked so well for Zach the previous day, he decided to talk to God some more. As the sun was turning the eastern sky an unlikely shade of pink he looked up into the expanse and opened up his heart, speaking what he felt and feeling surprised that so much of his emotions were based in thankfulness.

When he ran out of things to say to God, Zach reached into his pocket and fished out the little Bible. In the back were a group of poems labeled 'Psalms.' He read a few of them, and though he didn't understand much of what they said, he thought they were beautiful and fun to read. He read them aloud and thought they had the cadence of some of his favorite music.

He examined the little book before putting it back in his pocket and again felt a stab of remorse for having torn out the handful of pages when he started the fire.

Finding a boulder that was bathed by the early morning sun, Zach sat down and shared two more of the granola bars with an eager Ace. The snack bars weren't much more than a bite for either of them, but they were better than nothing. If there had only been something to drink with the bars it would have been great.

Zach stuffed the empty foil wrappers into his pocket, stood up, and stretched, trying to get some of the soreness out of his muscles. Walking to the middle of the opening, he stopped and turned in a full circle. After studying the entire tree line that surrounded the clearing, he had to admit to himself that he was disoriented. He didn't know what was north, south, east or west. Not that it mattered. He didn't know which direction he needed to go anyway. Panic swept over him as he tried to figure out which direction would take him toward civilization, or even back to the place where the helicopter had picked up his grandfather.

Fear came sweeping back into him. He struggled to find that peace that had filled him earlier and he cried out to God for relief. But it felt like an elephant was sitting on his chest. Taking in a deep breath seemed impossible. After a couple of minutes of short, shallow breathing, he began to feel dizzy. An intense pressure was building behind his eyes. The sounds of the forest were drowned out by the buzzing roar in his ears. Everything went black from the outside in.

The combination of the elevation, his hunger, and his fear had conspired to cause him to pass out. He was unconscious long enough for his breathing to return to normal.

263

Flat on his back looking into the deep blue of the sky, nausea swept over him. He sat up hoping to quell the need to vomit and everything started spinning again. He tucked his head between his knees and forced himself to breathe slowly and deliberately.

Gradually, things came back into focus.

Taking inventory, Zach found that his collapse in the dirt and rocks had resulted in only a small scrape to his left elbow. He had a pounding headache but no serious injuries. The oppressive fear began to recede.

Speaking out loud he said, "God, thank you for keeping me from smashing my head on one of these rocks when I fell. And Lord, please help me know what to do. I'm afraid, and I need you to get me out of here."

When he felt strong enough, he got back on his feet and was standing in the middle of the clearing trying to determine which way to go when a raspy squawk caught his attention. He had to turn around to locate the source of the racket. A great blue heron flapped its way across the sky. The big bird's wing beats were slow and awkward. The combination of the thick beak in front, and the long featherless legs that trailed along behind, made the bird look like something from the dinosaur era.

As Zach watched the heron's clumsy struggle, it suddenly stopped flapping and locked its wide wings. The bird's long neck stretched out and a graceful glide replaced the uncoordinated flight. The grayish-blue giant made a graceful turn and coasted out of sight behind the nearest hill to the south.

Zach's grandfather had introduced him to herons before. He remembered that they were wading birds and that one of their major food groups consisted of fish, frogs, and other aquatic animals. Based on that knowledge, he guessed that the bird's destination was the stream. If he could find the creek, all he would need to do was follow it upstream to the helicopter's landing zone. If anyone was going to come looking for him, that's where they would start.

Now Zach was as anxious to return to the spot where his grandfather's truck was parked as he had been to get away from the location a day earlier. Two things from the events of the previous night had changed his perspective.

First, as much as he had not wanted it to be true, it was obvious that the stalker could find Zach anywhere, at any time. Running and hiding were a waste of time and energy.

Second, despite the man's boasting and arrogance, something was keeping the lunatic from attacking. Had it been possible to cause physical harm, the perfect time would have been while Zach was sleeping. Yet he hadn't laid a finger on him then or on any of the other occasions when he had visited.

That he was not going to be able to find his way back to civilization without help was becoming obvious. He had walked into the woods for less than two hours, and already he had no idea which way to go to get out. No, he knew he had to get back to where the rescuers could find him.

Eager to get moving, he whistled for Ace. He had seen the dog follow his nose across the opening and into the trees, vacuuming up some invisible and interesting scents, after the heron flew past. When the yellow lab heard Zach's call, he came back like he was on a string.

"Come on," Zach said to the dog. "Let's get moving."

With the rifle slung on his shoulder and the dog casting back and forth ahead of him, Zach headed toward the spot where the heron's flight had taken it from view.

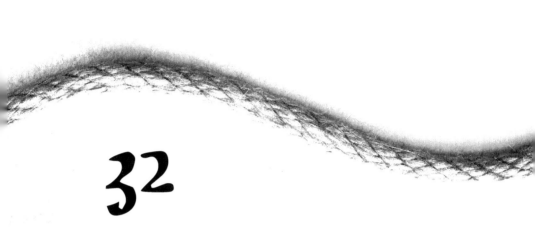

# 32

Becky crawled on, a slow excruciating inch at a time. The sun had baked the accumulation of grime onto her skin. Her awareness was limited to an arch of real estate that occupied the twelve inches immediately in front of her. She couldn't remember why, or to where, she was crawling.

A voice broke through the haze of her thinking. She thought she had heard this voice before, but it was too distant to recognize and too indistinct to understand. She stopped crawling and strained to listen. The voice was pleasant and almost felt soothing as it played across her scorched and tortured skin.

Becky sat back on her haunches and wiped at her eyes with the backs of her hands. She tried to adjust her eyes to the horizon, but everything was distorted by the darkness of her mind and the heat waves that rose from the ground.

*When the sound of the melodious voice reached her again, she thought that whoever was speaking was calling her name. She held her breath and strained, concentrating on the sound. Tears began to puddle up in her eyes and ran down her face as she struggled to see the source of the sound.*

*Through the blur of those tears, a figure came into focus, a man dressed in clothes of dazzling white. His arms were stretched toward her and she could see scars on his wrists. The man's eyes blazed with an intensity that, had it not been tempered with compassion, would have consumed her.*

*Then, it came to her ears, "Becky. Becky. I love you with a pure and everlasting love. Please come to me."*

*She struggled to her feet, reached out her arms toward him, and took a faltering step. Then she remembered the vile dirt that covered her and she stopped. How could she, in her retched condition, throw herself on him who was so spotless and clean? The terrible realization that she was too abominable to approach someone so perfect hit her and she collapsed on her face in the dust and wailed. She needed this man's touch, his embrace, but she was too dreadfully foul to accept it.*

*With that thought, her hallucination ended, and she was instantly thrown back into the black sensation-less void of her prison.*

Gabe's doctor had released him with a pair of crutches, instructions to take it easy, and a handful of prescription sheets for pain medication and antibiotics. He had been a bundle of impatient nerves while the discharge papers were being completed. Meg thought they might have to sedate him to get him to calm down for the wheelchair ride to the car. Once in the car, he began bombarding her with questions.

"Did the person in charge of the rescue team give you any indication as to when they might arrive at the meadow and begin the search?"

"She said that by the time the team was notified and assembled it was too late to get the helicopter back in the air. They felt that it was unsafe to fly after dark, especially with the unstable air associated with the thunderstorms that are moving through the area."

"Why didn't they send 'em in on the ground?"

"I think you know the answer to that. Apparently, the storm that hit where you were, affected a large area. Every forest service road in the area has about a bazillion trees blown down across them. She said it would be days, or maybe even weeks, before the roads were re-opened."

"So they're just gonna leave Zach out there to fend for himself while they monkey around? That makes me about as mad as a smashed cat."

Meg rolled her eyes and said, "Gabe, you know they're going to do everything they can to find him and get him out of there."

"Yeah, I know, but it's frustrating. If anything happens to that boy I'll never forgive myself for takin' him out there."

"You didn't know that storm was going to hit. You were doing what you thought was best. Can you at least try to not beat yourself to squash over this?"

"Yeah, yeah, I'll try. But you know how fast I can slip into depression. Anyway, right now I want to do whatever we can to help find Zach. Do you know where the command center is set up?"

"No, but I have the commander's cell phone number."

"Okay, I'm gonna call her. Do you know her name?"

"I don't remember. It's scribbled on the paper with her number. It's in my purse. Do you want me to pull over so I can find it?"

"Please. I could rummage through that satchel for three days and not find it. In fact, I'd probably have more luck finding Zach out there in the boonies. Even on these crutches."

Meg pulled to the shoulder of the road. In less than thirty seconds, she had located the sticky note with a phone number and 'J.D. Stihl' written on it. "Here," Meg said, handing the yellow paper to Gabe.

"Huh, Stihl. Poor gal, she's probably gone through life bein' called 'chainsaw'. I hope she doesn't live up to her name."

"She seemed cooperative enough when I talked to her. Why don't you give her a call and ask if there is anything we can do to help?" Meg said as she pulled the car back onto the road. "But try to be polite. You're likely to get a lot more information if you don't start rantin' and ravin' like a lunatic."

"Yeah, yeah, alright," Gabe mumbled as he punched the number into his cell phone. It rang three times before a raspy voice said, "J.D. here."

"Ms. Stihl," Gabe replied, "this is Gabe Green. I'm Zach Mertz's grandfather."

"Mr. Green, I'm glad you phoned. How are you feeling?"

The question caught Gabe off guard. He hadn't expected someone he'd never met to ask about his health. Then, he realized that he and J.D. Stihl had met. The problem was he had been unconscious at the time. After six or seven seconds of silence, he finally answered, "Uh, a lot better than when you saw me, I guess."

"Good," she replied. "I'd be seriously concerned if that weren't the case. You didn't look too good when our bird brought you in yesterday.

"I imagine that you called to find out about the search for your grandson."

Gabe found himself instantly liking this no-nonsense gal. "That's right. What's happening with the search?"

"We got the crew off the ground a couple of minutes ago. They'll touchdown in your meadow in about fifteen."

"How many are on the team?"

"It's a small bird, so it'll take two turns. Each run will include two trackers and a dog handler - plus the dog of course. Fortunately, we haven't got any fires in the area that are threatening to get out of control. So there's nothing competing for our attention at the moment."

"Sounds good. Can I come out to the command center and give you a hand."

"Mr. Green, there is nothing that you can do here that you can't do over the phone from home. I understand that you don't like it, but I bet you need to take it easy and let that leg heal. Not to mention that bump on your head."

"I'm fine. I need to be on site when you bring Zach out."

"Well, just so you know, we do not have all the comforts of home out here. No recliners, no refrigerators, not even any plumbing."

"Trust me, I'm use to roughing it and my injuries are not that serious. I really need to be there. Please give me directions to your location."

"Okay, okay, but first tell me which direction you think Zach is apt to go, and anything you know about the immediate area that might help us in the search."

"I can tell you that the crick has a nice gentle flow through the meadow but once it heads into the timber it falls fast. The terrain gets incredibly rough downstream and there are no roads near the water for miles.

"As to how Zach is goin' to act, I'm not sure. He's a city boy. He doesn't have much woods time behind him. If I had to guess, I'd say that he'll stay by the crick. But

**271**

then I'd have guessed that he'd have come runnin' yesterday when I was picked up, so my guessin' about what he's gonna do doesn't have a great track record. "

"None of the guys headed in there have ever been in this particular area before. Are they going to need any special type of gear if Zach's trail takes us downstream into that rough terrain you're talking about?"

"Yeah. They'll need some powerful legs and good lungs. I went down in there a few miles a couple of years ago lookin' for grouse and didn't think I was ever gonna haul my tired tail back outta there. Even my labs were woofin' before they got outta that hole and onto level ground. God put the land on edge right there."

"Okay. My guys are young and fit, so that shouldn't be a huge issue. Anything else we need to know?"

"Well, Zach was packin' a Ruger 10/22 rifle when I saw him last. I don't think he's dangerous with it, but your team should know he has it."

"Thanks for the info, but that chopper is going to be putting down real soon, and I need to get on the line with the search and rescue team. If you're still bent on coming out here to get in my way, I'll patch you over to someone who can tell you how to get here by road. And why don't you give them your cell number so we can call if we have any news or need any more information before you arrive."

The assistant that Ms. Stihl connected Gabe to provided directions to the field command center.

Gabe convinced Meg, and it didn't require much convincing since she wanted to be as close as possible to Zach, that he was well enough to go.

The detectives were leaving the precinct building, heading for lunch, when Randy Mack's phone rang. It was Alison Stearns wanting to meet face to face.

**272**

Alison was waiting inside the front doors of her school like she had promised. She looked young, and frightened.

After speaking with the principal, Bruce got them in a private office

Mack leaned forward with his elbows on his knees and said, "Okay, Alison, what was it that you needed to talk to us about?"

She was looking at the floor and playing with a lock of her blonde hair with her right index finger. Mack thought she might start crying before she said, "I'm scared."

"What are you afraid of?" Mack asked.

"My mom's boyfriend, David."

"Has he hurt you or your mom?"

"No, but last night they had a big argument. They were yelling at each other and David tipped over a chair and threw some stuff. He, like, kind of went nuts or something. I know you guys think he tried to kill his wife, and I got to thinking that my mom might be next."

"Did he threaten her?"

"Not that I heard. But he was just so crazy."

"What were they fighting about?"

"I'm not sure. I was in my room when it started but came out when I heard the yelling and stuff. Do you think he might hurt us?"

"I don't know," Mack replied. "Have you asked your mom about that?"

"Yeah, but she like just blows me off. She says that the whole deal with David's wife is all just a big misunderstanding and that he's harmless."

"Did you hear anything that would tell you what the fight was about?"

"I don't know. They fight all the time about money and David has been whining about losing patients because of what people are saying about him trying to kill his wife. There was something about the payments on

David's house and how much the lawyer costs. I usually try not to listen, but when I heard all the crashing I had to make sure that Mom was alright."

"Have you ever heard David, or your mom, say anything that caused you to think that he might have harmed his wife?"

"He was at our place when he found out that she was hurt. I was getting ready for school when he listened to the messages on his cell phone that morning. He started running around yelling that he had to get to the hospital. Mom asked him what was going on, and he said that he was afraid that his son had killed his wife."

Schiller had been quietly taking notes throughout the interview, but when he heard that statement, he stood up and said, "David Mertz said that he thought his son had killed his wife?"

"I don't remember exactly what he said, but it was something like, 'That stupid kid has killed his mother'."

Schiller sat back down and his eyes locked with Mack's while he asked, "Did you ever hear him say anything else about his son?"

The detectives watched Alison as they waited for her response. They could tell that she had more to say but was hesitant, or embarrassed to say it. Her face had gotten red and she was wringing her hands when she quietly said, "Well, sometimes, you know, I could hear Mom and David through the wall. I was already in my bedroom that night when he got to our place. They were loud."

"What night are you talking about?" Mack asked to clarify.

"The night before we found out that the jerk's wife was in the hospital."

"What did you hear him say?"

"He was all freaking out about what his son had done. I heard him say that the idiot had totally screwed up and now he was going to have to fix it."

"Did he say anything about what he was going to do to fix it?"

"Not that I remember. He was just ranting about how expensive the lawyers were going to be and how the stupid kid of his would never get into a decent college. That's when he told Mom that he was done with his wife and son and asked her if he could move in with us."

"He hadn't been living with you and your mom before that?"

"No. He'd only come to visit once or twice a week. Usually for just for a couple of hours; but once in awhile he'd stay the night."

"How'd you feel about that relationship?"

"I hated it."

"Why?"

"Well, for one thing, the guy is a total jerk. Not to mention he's married. How gross is that? And I want my mom and dad to get back together. That's not going to happen with this loser hanging around."

"Do you think that your mom knew he was married when he first started coming around?"

"Like, *yeah*, totally. They were sneaking around like junior high kids. It was so bogus. They tried to tell me that they worked together and they were just friends, like I'm that stupid."

Schiller tried to bring the interview back on track by asking, "Did you ever meet the Mertz boy?"

"No. But I have wondered about him a couple of times. I mean, his mom's a vegetable or whatever and his dad is playing house with my mother. Where is he? Do you guys have him in jail or something?"

"No, he's not in jail. Is there anything else you can tell us about David or his son that might help us in our investigation? You sounded pretty upset when you called and asked to talk to us."

"No. I don't think so. I guess I just got to thinking about everything and got spooked. Do you think he might kill us or something? He was really wigged out last night."

Mack and Schiller stood up and Mack said, "No, I don't think he's going to hurt you or your mom. But you did the right thing by calling us, thank you. If he does anything else to scare you or you think of any more details about the night when Ms. Mertz went to the hospital, please call."

When the two detectives were back in their car and headed to a sandwich shop to pick up their lunch, Mack asked Schiller, "So what was your take on that?"

"I'm not sure. It was strange. But she did accidentally cause me to think that Mertz didn't have anything to do with his wife's overdose."

"You mean the way she described his reaction to the news?"

"Yeah, that and what she overheard the night before he got the news. It sure didn't sound like he knew anything about what was going on back at home."

"She really got my interest with that 'He killed his mom' thing."

"Yeah, but it sounded like our friend the doctor was just doin' some more of his whining. Still, we should probably get back together with Rivera and Evans and run the idea by them. Especially considering how much you like those guys."

"They're not so bad once you get past the fact that they're arrogant idiots. I can stand talking to 'em again if you can. But we got to put this case to bed one of these days. We've got a ton of hours into it and haven't got much of anything to show for the effort."

"Yeah, well, the chief must be kind of interested, what with the connection to the mayor. I think that's why we're not getting any grief over the amount of time we've put in on it. Anyway, this just might be the lead we need with this thing."

"I don't think so, but I guess we need to go through the motions."

A phone call and a couple of hours later, the two detectives and the two patrol officers were seated in a booth in a coffee shop.

"So what's up with the Mertz case now?" Evans asked.

"Well, we got a phone call from the daughter of Dr. Mertz's new girlfriend. She wanted to talk to us, and, when we met, she told us that Mertz had made some vague reference to the Mertz kid trying to kill his mother. We just wanted to run that possibility by you guys, since you spent some time with the kid, and get your take on that."

Evans answered, "Well you're wasting your time. I can tell you right now that there ain't no way that kid could have had anything to do with what happened to his mother. When we got to the house that night he was locked out and trying really hard to get back in."

"So you don't think that could have been an act to direct suspicions away from him?"

"If it was, the boy deserves and academy award. No, it wasn't an act. Besides, what possible motive could the boy have had to off his mother? And how could he have managed to get the pills into her?"

Rivera had been quiet throughout the meeting but chimed in at this mention of motive. "Did you check motive on the doc?"

"No. As hard as he's been working at keeping the woman alive, it's hard to imagine that he had been trying to kill her."

"Well, have you looked into his motivation for keepin' her alive?"

The look that passed between the two detectives made it obvious that they had not checked that detail and now realized that they probably should have. "No," Mack admitted, "but I think we will. It does seem odd, doesn't it?"

"Yeah, it's especially odd knowing that the bum had shacked up with his girl friend while his wife was in the hospital, caught between the land of the living and the zone of the dead. It seems like it would be more convenient for him to have her dead."

"We were assuming that he was trying to keep her alive to avoid murder charges. But once it began to look like no charges were going to be brought against him, we never thought about why he was still keeping her alive."

"My gut is telling me that it has something to do with life insurance," Rivera added. "I can't think of any other reason for the dumb smuck to insist that she be kept on life support."

"Ya know," Mack replied, "I wouldn't be surprised to find out that you're right. I'll look into that. Thanks for sparking the thought. Not that it is apt to make much difference, other than to confirm that the guy is a total loser."

Rivera snorted through his nose and said, "There's no need to confirm that."

Once Mack and Schiller were back in their office it didn't take them long to determine that Officer Rivera's suspicions were correct. Twenty-two months prior to

Becky Mertz's overdose, she had purchased a million dollar life insurance policy that named David Mertz as the sole beneficiary. A standard clause in the policy voided payment if death resulted from suicide within the first two years.

Mack tapped the computer screen that showed the clause and told Schiller, "I'd wager all the overtime on my next paycheck that Mertz gets his wife off the life support equipment once that two year period lapses."

"You ain't gonna get me to sucker in on that deal," Schiller replied. "I wouldn't be surprised if he was at the hospital at midnight of the last day of the two years to pull plug of the life support equipment in person as soon as the calendar clicks."

"When is that two years up?" Mack asked as he shuffled through papers on his desk, looking for a calendar.

Schiller pushed off his desk and leaned back in the rolling chair, hands linked behind his head, as he coasted backward. "I just did the math, the two years was over yesterday."

"Well, then we don't have long to wait to see what he's going to do. Do you think it'd be smart to ask the staff at the care facility to notify us if Mertz pays his wife a visit?"

"Yeah, I think that would be an excellent idea. Let's make a swing by there right now."

# 33

As painful and miserable as the brief mental excursion into skin-puckering, baked on, filth had been, Becky would have been glad to trade a reality in that world for the torture of the black existence to which she had returned.

She was racking her brain, trying to remember what had produced that dream. Perhaps she would be able to recreate the sensation if she could remember how it had begun. Regardless of how she strained to center her focus on a particular subject, it seemed that maintaining a thought was becoming more and more difficult. Her mind would grab the tag end of an idea, but before she could mentally tug on the concept more than once or twice, it would dissipate into the colorless void that surrounded her.

It had started with a conversation, she thought. Who could she have been having a conversation with; there was no one else here. There was nothing here, only this emptiness. Had she conversed, through the portal, with the man in black? No, he had spoken to her, but she had never spoken back had she? He laughed at her. She remembered that cruel fiendish laugh.

The memory came to her like a bolt of lightning. She had been praying and it had agitated her tormentor. And she was going to try it again.

Someone from her past had told her that praying was nothing more than having a conversation with God. Could she talk to God? What right did she have to talk to the creator and ruler of the universe? What could she possibly have to say to him that wouldn't be idiotic? And why would he listen. She had spent her entire adult life avoiding him.

Another memory spun its way into her mind. An invitation, or a quote from someone, "Come to me all who are carrying a heavy burden, and I will give you rest." Who said that? Becky tried to recall. Was it God who said that? It would be fabulous to gain some rest. How could a person who was doing nothing besides floating or drifting in a huge sea of blackness—without contact with anything— need rest? But she did.

"God, I want to come to you," Becky said in her mind. Could he hear her when she wasn't able to make any sound? "I need rest but I can't walk or run or even crawl, so how do I get to you?"

Nothing resulted from her mental plea. No cosmic transport. No clap of thunder. Not even the ridiculing appearance of the tormentor. The disappointment of no response was devastating. Had she been capable, she would have pulled into a fetal ball and wept.

When Zach left the clearing and entered the timber, heading in the direction that he had watched the heron fly, the landscape made an abrupt change. The soft soil, whose primary component had been pumice, turned to shale stone and the flat terrain became steep. Among the trees, large moss and lichen covered boulders jutted up out of the ground. Trees knocked down in the storm were everywhere.

Walking on the loose shale and negotiating through, and over, the down trees made progress slow and difficult. The distance that the big grey-blue bird had covered in minutes—even with its awkward wing beat—was going to take Zach an hour or more to traverse.

The sound of fast flowing water was an encouragement, and a torment. It confirmed that this was the direction to the stream, but it also reminded him of his thirst. Thick brush and debris hid the water from view, but there was no doubt that it was there.

Rocks and blow downs weren't a hindrance to Ace. He was busy tearing around, investigating the smells beneath the thick tangle of limbs of every freshly downed tree, and in each crevice in the boulders. It wasn't clear what he was hunting for, but it was obvious that he thought he would know it when he found it. Zach hoped that the dog didn't discover a porcupine, or a bear. A bear would be very bad.

The farther into the ravine he dropped, the steeper it got and the more difficult it was to make forward progress. Every step had to be deliberate, which made moving tedious. Twice he slipped and kept from sliding to the bottom only by grabbing on to the abundant current bushes that were growing on the slope. The makeshift rope sling on the rifle that he had over his shoulder almost hung him the second time he fell. The welt from the rope burn across the bottom of his ear stung like crazy.

Frustrated and hot, sweaty and thirsty, Zach began to think that it had been an error to try to reach the stream at this spot. He turned around with the thought of climbing back out of this hole and looking for an easier place to go down. He was unnerved at how near vertical the last hundred feet of his descent had been. Going back up on this shale slide was not a viable option.

He had slumped to the ground in discouragement. He knew he had to attempt to muster enough energy to continue toward the creek; he had to have water. Ace ran up to investigate why they had stopped. The dog's slobber-covered tongue was hanging at least six inches out of his mouth, and he panted and pushed on Zach in an attempt to get the boy to pet him. This ordeal might have been stressing Zach, but it was all just a big adventure to Ace.

Sitting in the dirt, trying to get a dog to leave him alone, with the sound of the rushing water tantalizing his growing thirst, Zach was ready to give up. "God," he said out loud, "this is too hard. Last night I thought I was new; today, you seem far away and I seem like the same old worthless Zach."

With his eyes blurring from tears, he pulled the little book out of his pocket and flipped through the pages. Near the back of the book, in a section labeled 'Psalm 46' a highlighted passage caught his eye and he read that God is 'an ever-present help in trouble.' "God," Zach said, "I have plenty of trouble and I need that help."

Something was biting him on the leg! He jerked his left pant leg up and found a black centipede attached to the tan skin on his calf. Dust rolled out Zach's pant leg and sock top as slapped at the biting bug. Ace jumped back, tilted his head to one side and barked at the boy's strange antics.

The incident helped Zach understand his grandfather's frequent question about bugs in his britches and the thought brought him a smile and helped pull him out of this slide into depression. He pulled himself to his feet and carefully resumed his downward climb. A few months earlier his thoughts would have been filled with fear of venom from the insect bite. Now the thought didn't enter his mind.

He made it about three small steps before the shale stone beneath his feet slid out from under him and he went tumbling into the ravine. He unsuccessfully tried to grab brush or limbs as he fell, but he didn't get stopped until he was lying in a jangle of boulders and wood beside the stream.

The air had been knocked out of him during his tumble and while he was trying to get his breath, the ribs on the left side of his rib cage hurt so much that he was sure that he was going to die.

When he was finally able to get some air into his lungs, the expansion of his chest sent so much pain surging through him that he blacked out.

When he regained consciousness he lay as still as he could. The throbbing gradually lessened. As the pain became bearable, the sound of gurgling water teased Zach. Thirst eventually overcame the fear of the stirring up the injury. He held his ribs as tightly as he could and began to wriggle toward the creek. By the time that he reached the water, he was drenched with sweat.

First, he took a cautious sip. The water tasted so cold and sweet that he plunged his face into the ice cold water and drank until his stomach was tight. Once his thirst was quenched, he inched his way across the rocks toward a sandy spot beside the stream. Every movement racked him with pain. A few times, he cried out in sharp yelps that were answered by whines from Ace.

By gritting his teeth and praying for strength, he managed to make progress until he made it to the relative comfort of the sand.

If he held as still as he could and concentrated on breathing shallow breaths, the pain wasn't quite as excruciating. The warmth of the sun and the noise of the rushing water and the hopelessness of the situation lulled Zach into dozing.

After a few minutes of snoozing, something roused him from his nap. When he opened his eyes, the first thing that he saw was the guy in the black jumpsuit.

The man was sitting on a log on the other side of the stream. His back was to Zach. When the tree he was on had fallen it had uprooted the root-wad, so the log was about thirty inches off the ground, leaving the man's feet to swing in the air. He looked like a content kid on a piece of school playground equipment.

Zach clenched his teeth at the pain in his ribs and was trying to get the rifle's sling from around his neck when the man spoke. "So, you'd shoot a fellow in the back, would you? That's a fine way for a good Christian chap to act, isn't it? And what harm have I done you? I haven't but tried to help you and this is the thanks I get?"

The man's calm voice froze Zach for a moment and he forgot about the rifle. "What do you mean you've tried to help? You've chased me, and harassed me, and threatened me, is what you've done. How is that helping?"

"Well, I came in on the helicopter that took your grandfather out of here, didn't I? You know, he'd be dead by now if I hadn't led that crew to him. And I tried to get you out of the pickup the other night during that storm. I'd have rescued you right then if you hadn't gone so crazy."

"You weren't trying to help. You were trying to kill me, like you did my mom."

"I did not try to kill your mom. I was trying to help her like I'm trying to help you. She's much better now, by the way. I'd be happy to get you out of here to go see her, if you'd just settle down and cooperate a little."

"She's out of the coma?"

"She is. And she's calling for you. She's really worried about you, don't you know. Why don't you just come with me? I'll take you to her."

"How are you going to get me out of here? I think my ribs are broken. Every movement feels like it's going to kill me. Breathing is about all I can manage."

"Oh I can get you out alright. And it will be painless. But I don't think you're quite up to it yet. You probably will be though, as soon as my assistant arrives."

"You have a helper out here somewhere?"

"Technically, he's not an assistant, or a helper. But I'm pretty sure he'll get the job done for me." The man jumped off the log and said, "You'll see what I mean. Soon. I'll be back to give you the details," he said as he walked into the thick currant and wild rose bushes and out of sight.

Zach was trying to make sense out of the words when he heard movement in the brush behind him. Thinking that it was his tormentor circling around, or the assistant that had been mentioned, Zach turned around and got the rifle to where he could use it.

His ribs were screaming at him by the time he was facing the direction that the noise was coming from and the rifle stock was on his shoulder.

In Zach's peripheral vision, he saw Ace's head come up off his paws. The dog's nose started working to iden-tify some scent that was coming to him through the still air. A low growl came out of deep in his throat. The lab slowly rose to his feet and continued to snarl in a low rumble as the hair across his hackles stood on end.

Zach tried to keep one eye on the dog and one eye on the bushes from which the noise was coming. He felt the hair on the back of his neck and arms bristle. The dog had paid no attention to the man in black on any of his previous visits, which caused Zach to think that whatever, or whoever, was approaching was new.

The wild roses and snowberry bushes on the other side of the stream were shaking and their leaves were rattling when something pink came into view among the tops of the bushes. Zach couldn't decide what he was seeing until the strange object wrapped around a bunch of rose hips that were at the top of the bush. Then the tongue, rose hips, and the top of the rose bushes disappeared into the tan-on-black muzzle of a bear. Zach's already pounding heart beating even faster.

The massive black head, with its rounded ears and small jet-black eyes, emerged from the brush no more than twenty-five feet from Zach and Ace. Zach put the scope's crosshairs on the side of the bear's head, just below the ear, but was afraid to squeeze the trigger. What if the shot just wounded the bear and made him mad?

The view through the scope was nothing but coarse black hair and Zach moved his eye away from the lens so that he could see the whole bear.

Ace had stopped growling and was on his belly, shaking and whining softly.

The bear froze for a second and then lifted his nose and pointed it at Zach and Ace. The nostrils twitched as he tested the scent. In an instant, the bear was on his hind legs, his neck and shoulders bowed, and his front legs rounded in front of him like a wrestler's. He woofed and feinted a charge, took a step back, and woofed again.

Zach and Ace held as still as they could, knowing that they were no match for this three hundred and fifty pound bruin. Zach was silently asking God to turn the beast around.

After five seconds, that seemed like they lasted a day and a half, the bear spun and disappeared into the dense brush. There was a lot of crashing for a second, then complete silence.

Zach put the rifle down, hugged his aching ribs, and trembled. Ace quivered as he nuzzled against the boy and whined.

Gabe and Meg needn't have worried about being able to find the command center. They had turned off the pavement and driven less than a mile on the Forest Service road, that they had been instructed to take, when a Search and Rescue vehicle passed them. They got in behind that rig, though it was traveling considerably faster than they would have liked on the washboard gravel road, and followed it right to the camp.

By the time that Gabe had pulled himself out of their rig, and Meg and handed him his crutches, a young man in a Forest Service uniform was there to meet him. The name tag on the guy's shirt said 'Courtright' and he came over to Gabe, hand extended, and said, "Mr. Green, we're glad to see you in the land of the living, even if you do have to use the sticks," pointing to the crutches. "I'm sure you want to talk to J.D., she's right over here."

"That's right," Gabe answered nodding in her direction, "and by the way this is my wife, Meg."

"Nice to meet you, I'm Ian Courtright."

Ian began walking slowly toward a large windowless trailer that had 'Incident Command Center' stenciled on its side. As he walked he said, "The rescue crew set down about an hour ago. I'll leave it to J.D. to bring you up to speed on what they found so far. Here she is now," Ian said as he pointed in the open back door of the trailer.

A middle-age well tanned woman with short cropped salt and pepper hair looked up from a lap-top computer and smiled when she made eye contact with Gabe. "Well, she said, you look a heap better than when I saw you last." Her focus shifted to Meg as she continued, "But are you sure that it's a good idea for you to be out here? Don't you think that you should be taking it easy?"

Gabe ignored the question and said, "You must be Ms. Stihl. I guess you know that I'm Gabe. This is Zach's grandmother, Meg."

"Nice to meet you Meg, please call me J.D., grab a seat," J.D. said pointing to some canvas camping chairs. I'll let you know what we've got so far."

The forester waited until everyone was situated and then said, "Both of the search teams are now on the ground at the site where we picked you up. One group has been there over an hour, the other less than fifteen minutes. At this point, about all we know is that your pickup is still there, but it appears to have been looted or vandalized. Can you think of any reason why your grandson would tear up your camping gear?"

Gabe looked puzzled as he answered, "What'd ya mean vandalized? No, Zach wouldn't have a reason to vandalize anything."

"I don't know what happened, but the first team in reported that sleeping bags were torn up and duffle bags and mattresses were washed up in the shallows downstream of your pickup. They also said that it looked like a lot of the stuff from in your cooler had been scattered all over. There were wrappers strewn around the area, but the foodstuffs were gone."

"Do you suppose that it was raccoons, or coyotes, or some critters like that?" Gabe asked.

"I'm not sure. I wouldn't put it past a 'coon to raid the ice chest, but I've never heard of them tearin' up sleeping bags and such?"

"Well, I can't imagine why Zach would tear that stuff up," Meg interjected.

Gabe shook his head and said, "No, I'm sure it wasn't Zach. But I can't fathom why anyone else would messin' around with our gear."

J.D stood up and headed toward the trailer that housed the electronic equipment. "You guys go ahead and stay put. It's about time for the team leaders to call and give another report. I'll be back out to give you an update as soon as I have one."

Meg sat looking at the breeze ruffle the upper branches of the nearby ponderosa pine trees. Gabe was making an unsuccessful attempt at ignoring the pain that was throbbing in his leg. Both of them were pleading with God for protection for Zach. The trauma, and drama, of the situation rekindled the raw wounds surrounding their daughter and her condition. Each of them included Becky in their petitions.

J.D. came out of the trailer and took her place in the chair that faced Meg and Gabe. "So. The team that went upstream from your pickup hasn't found anything of interest. The other group went down stream. They've picked up a trail that they believe to be Zach's. In fact, they think they found where he built a fire and spent the night. The makeshift campsite is a couple miles from your pickup and they estimate it's about a mile from the stream.

"We aren't sure why he headed that direction. Do you have any clues?"

Gabe focused on some invisible image in the brilliant sky before saying, "I'm still tryin' to figure out why he wasn't waiting at the pickup. The only thing I can come up with is that I think he is suffering from some hallucinations. He may have had another one and went goofy."

"Hallucinations? He has hallucinations? What kind of hallucinations?"

"I dunno. He told me on more than one occasion that he has seen some dude that is all dressed in black. Zach claims that this guy keeps showin' up and makin' all kind of threats. The last time was night before last when I was lyin' unconscious in the pickup. When I came to, he was completely rattled."

"Interesting," J.D. said. "How do you know that they're hallucinations? Could someone actually be following the boy?"

"I don't think so. No one else has seen the guy and there are never any tracks, or other evidence. And, besides, how likely is it that there was someone stalkin' Zach? Especially in that storm the other night? I mean, if there was anyone around they would have been tryin' to find someplace to ride the storm out, not harassin' a kid."

"Well, if he is delusional, it'll make our job a lot more difficult," J.D. said. "The hardest people to find are those who are not functioning rationally. The problem is that there is no way to predict what they are going to do. In a typical search, if we can't find tracks and the dogs don't pick up a good scent trail, we'll try to anticipate where the person is going to go. That is next to impossible if the person has some type of mental disability, or is operating in a state of total panic."

When Mack and Schiller were a block and a half away from the entrance to the care facility parking lot, a silver Mercedes pulled out of the lot and drove toward them. As they passed, the detectives saw Dr. David Mertz behind the steering wheel of the car. Mack and Schiller looked at each other and nodded.

# 34

Without warning, Becky felt the intensity of the heat change and reality shift. Then, she was back in the desert, experiencing the chaffing of the dried filth on her skin, and the dirt and pebbles grinding into her knees. Feeling a presence, she looked up and the man was standing in front of her. His arms were extended, offering an embrace. The intensity of his eyes cut through to her heart.

She struggled to her feet, reached out her hands, and stumbled toward him. Remembered her repugnant condition, she hesitated and he called to her, "Becky, my daughter, don't worry about the dirt and grime, I'll cleanse it. Just come here and enter my embrace."

A frantic howling rose behind her to drown out the voice. Becky could feel the force of the being behind her willing her to turn around. His voice was full of power and authority, and the tormentor ordered her, "Turn around *wench! You are mine. You have no right to turn to him. You've rejected him all your life; he'll not have you now. How can you think that he'll greet you with anything other than the destruction you deserve? You're going to stay with me. My domain is where you belong."*

*It is true,* Becky thought. *After a lifetime of rebellion, I have no right to any mercy.* She faltered, started to turn around, and, out of desperation, she threw herself forward to the one who was quietly calling.

She was immediately wrapped in a cool embrace. Looking down, she was startled and thrilled to see that the filth, dirt, and grime that had covered her were gone. Her vile rags were replaced by a garment of the purest white. He gently slipped a band of polished gold on her finger and a new pair of sandals on her feet.

Tears poured out of her eyes and sobs of joy filled her throat.

A touch of impossible gentleness, from hands incredibly strong, dried her eyes and the fullest and sweetest voice ever heard said, "Welcome home Becky, welcome home. Come recline at my table and I will serve you."

"No, Lord, let me serve you."

"Oh, Becky, you will serve; in time you will certainly serve. Now, however, enjoy my presence. We have a lot to talk about."

"Is this real? Will I awaken in that other place, that place of torment?"

"This is the only reality. You will never again know pain or sorrow."

The bear was no sooner gone than the man in black was back on his log perch. This time he was facing Zach.

"How'd you like your visitor, my assistant?" the man asked.

**294**

Zach didn't bother to lift the rifle and answered, "You mean the bear? He's yours?"

"Yeah, sort of, anyway. Let's just say that he and I have an understanding. Cute little guy, isn't he? You and your pup are lucky that I didn't send him in for a taste of you. That little pea-shooter you're packing would have done nothing but make him mad."

"I don't think you sent that bear at all. He didn't act like he knew we were anywhere around until he picked up our scent."

"Think what you want. It doesn't change the facts. Would you like me to have him come back for another visit?"

Zach's ribs were hurting too much, it was too hard to breath, and he was too flustered to carry on a debate and he said, "You're just trying to frighten me. That bear is long gone. Why don't you follow it?" He put the Ruger rifle to his shoulder to emphasize his point. Looking through the scope, he couldn't find his tormentor but started pulling the trigger anyway, spraying the foliage on the other side of the stream with the bullets as quickly as he could pull the trigger. He fired until the ten rounds were gone. Popping the empty clip out of the rifle, he replaced it with a full one.

On his back in the sand, he felt frightened, frustrated, and foolish. There was no way that he was going to get out of this canyon. He was either going to be eaten by bears, die from his broken ribs, or starve to death, unless the visitor came back and killed him first.

His circumstances refueled his desperate depression, and Zach suddenly found himself thinking of his mother. This must have been what his mother felt like, he thought. Living with his father must have been trial enough. When he added to her misery by getting in trouble at school, followed by acting like a complete jerk, it must have been more than she could handle.

For the first time, Zach began to understand why she had tried to kill herself. He had been angry at her for what he had viewed as an act of a coward, but now he could see that suicide may have been her only reasonable option. The anger-filled home in Arizona must have felt as hopeless to her as this isolated hole in the wilderness of Oregon did to him. There had been no other option for her. Or, he reasoned, for him.

Ace was licking the tears from Zach's face when the sound of breaking brush and rustling leaves came from the other side of the stream. The dog began growling and the hair across his shoulders stood on end. A grunt came from across the creek and Ace barked deep in his throat as he launched himself toward the sound.

Zach couldn't see anything through the dense underbrush, but the sounds told him that the bear was back, and Ace had decided that he'd had enough of it, and attacked. There was a lot of growling and barking followed by a sickening yelping from Ace, then silence.

Zach was lost in a state of panic and trying to decide what he could do to help Ace when he heard, "So. Now, do you still think the bear has left? I can have him come back and give you a chance to wrestle with him? Your dog wasn't too successful. Maybe you and your little gun could do better."

"Is Ace dead?"

"Well, let me just say that he has had better days."

"What do you want from me? Why are you tormenting me?"

"Zach, I don't want anything from you. What could you possibly have that I want? I'm just trying to help you."

"Help me? You think that Ace getting killed by a bear is helping me?"

"That was your fault. You're the one who wanted the bear to come back, remember?"

"I did not say I wanted it to come back. You're twisting everything. What are you doing here, anyway?"

"I'm here to tell you how to escape this mess and be reunited with your mother."

"Yeah, okay, tell me."

"This is going to sound scary at first, but it's actually quite easy, Zach. Just put the gun barrel in your mouth and pull the trigger. You won't feel a thing, I promise. The next thing you know you'll be with your mom."

"What? Kill myself and I'll be with my mom? You said she was better."

"Oh, Zach, did you misunderstand? She *is* better. She's dead. That's always better. And you can be better, too."

J.D. came back out of the trailer and took her place in the folding chair facing Gabe and Meg. "I just talked to the team that's tracking Zach. They heard a lot of gunfire a few minutes ago, nine or ten shots really close together. How much ammo does he have with him?"

"I'm not sure. Did your guys say anything about finding any of the clips for the rifle in the pickup?'

"No."

"Well, there were four clips. I assume that he stuffed them all in his pocket when he took off. That'd give him forty rounds."

"Do you have any idea why he'd burn through ten rounds as fast as he could pull the trigger?"

"I have no idea. Did your guys say how far away they were from the shots?"

"They weren't sure, but they guess-timated that they were less than a mile away."

"And they're gonna go right in?"

"Apparently the terrain is quite steep so it's going to be slow going, but, yes, they're moving that direction."

The receptionist's eyes went wide when Mack asked for Becky Mertz's room number. "I don't think you can see Ms. Mertz at the moment," she stuttered at the pair of detectives.

When Schiller whipped out his badge and said, "Just give us the room number," the poor gal went completely white, but she complied.

Detectives Mack and Schiller hurried down the hall toward Becky Mertz's room and found a scene that could only be described as chaotic. Nurses and nurses' aides were scrambling around like they were conducting a fire drill.

A guy wearing scrubs came out of the room, and Mack grabbed him by the arm and showed him his shield. "What's goin' on in there?"

"The patient coded. They're in there trying to perform CPR on her, but it doesn't look like it's going to work. I think we've lost her."

Mack let the guy go and turned to Schiller. Both detectives raised their eyebrows, and Schiller said what they were both thinking, "If Mertz had them disconnect the life support, why would they be trying to save her?"

The detectives leaned against the hallway wall and waited for things to settle down enough for them to ask some questions. After about fifteen minutes, a middle aged women who appeared to be in charge came out of the room and Schiller asked, "What happened?"

The woman stopped and gave them an icy stare that sent them fishing for their shields. Satisfied that they weren't Looky-Lous trying to catch a glimpse of someone else's misery, she said, "An aide went into the room and the patient's heart monitor had flat lined. We tried to resuscitate her, but we were unsuccessful."

"Her husband had not requested that she be disconnected from the life-support equipment?"

"No. She wasn't disconnected from any equipment. Her heart simply stopped beating. But that was no surprise. The mystery was why it kept beating as long as it did."

"Was her husband here?"

"What, when she coded? Not that I know of. In fact, as far as I know, her husband had *never* visited her. That's another thing that I find odd. The rumor is that he was the one that had insisted that she be kept on the life support system when everyone knew that she wasn't ever going to recover. But then he paid absolutely no attention to her."

"Would anyone here know if someone had been in her room today?"

"Kay might. She's a nurse who had kind of adopted Ms. Mertz. She would go in and talk to her and read to her on breaks and lunch and stuff."

"Can you tell us where we might be able to find this nurse?"

"I'll have her paged. You guys can just wait here."

Mack turned to his partner and said, "We both know that the guy, in the Porsche we met right before we got here, was David Mertz. It seems like a long stretch to think that it is coincidental that she died within minutes of his one and only visit."

Schiller glanced at the ceiling as he replied, "Coincidence is like a skinny cook. You can't trust either one."

Kay appeared timid as she approached and spoke to the two detectives. "Hi, my name is Kay. My supervisor said that you had some questions about Becky that I might be able to answer."

Schiller put on a rare nice guy persona and said, "Yeah, no big deal, we were just curious as to whether or not Ms. Mertz had any visitors today?"

Kay shook her head and answered, "I don't think she has had a visitor since her parents went back to Oregon, and that was last month. You could stop at the front desk and ask the receptionist. She doesn't miss much that goes on around here."

The receptionist was no help. She was sure that there had not been a visitor by her that, she did not recognize, the entire day.

Mack and Schiller silently headed to the dead woman's room. They were convinced that, even though no one had seen him, Mertz had something to do with his wife's death. The men were both thinking the same thing and spoke the thought at the same time, "We need to ask the medical examiner for an autopsy."

The medical examiner was not enthusiastic about the idea and said, "This woman has been dead, without her body knowing it, for weeks. Why in this green world would you want me to do an autopsy? You think the county has money to pile up and burn? Or maybe you think I don't have enough to do."

"It's not that, Doc," Mack responded. "Suffice it to say that this poor lady's husband is a real piece of work, and he stands to benefit substantially, via a life insurance policy, now that she's dead."

"That makes no sense. He would have had the right to have her taken off the life support equipment at any time. Why not have her doctor shut down the machines?"

Mack shook his head and said, "I've been doin' this job for quite awhile now, and it doesn't happen all that often, but once in a while I get a hunch, and I have got a hunch about this. Over the years, I've learned to follow those hunches. So just humor us. Do an autopsy and look for drugs in quantities that are unusual in a patient like this."

"Okay, if you say so. But I think we're wastin' time and money. How would her husband get the drugs and know how to administer them?"

"The dude's a doctor."

The M.E. shook his head, turned to the ambulance crew that had loaded the body on a stretcher, and said, "Drop her off at my place instead of the funeral home."

Zach tried to concentrate on what his next action should be, but found that he was too bombarded by an array of emotions to complete a rational thought.

The grief brought on by hearing that his mother was dead was the big surprise. He had mourned for her when the doctors first said that she was brain-dead and had no hope for recovery. He had expected the news of the formality of her heart stopping to produce relief rather than this immense sorrow.

At the same time, anger over the bear's attack on Ace surged inside of him. Part of him wanted the beast to return and provide an opportunity for revenge, even while possibility that the animal might return and attack him was terrifying.

Zach struggled to his feet and headed for the spot where Ace and the bear had met. The spot where the two animals had collided was obvious as it was well marked by the torn up ground and broken brush. A stark red blood smear on the side of a log, white where the bark had fallen off, indicated that Ace hadn't escaped the confrontation without serious injury.

The boy sat down in the dirt and started crying. As intolerable as the grief, anger, and pain were, worse was the hopelessness. He could see no way of escape. How did this feeling fit in with the 'all things were new' stuff that he had read about in his grandfather's Bible? This set of emotion wasn't anything new. He'd been feeling this turmoil of despair most of his life. He didn't want to feel it anymore.

The unmistakable sound of a helicopter flying over-head made Zach think that even his oppressor had left him.

The advice of the man in the black jump suit began to gain merit. A simple pull of the trigger would allow him to escape the entire mess, forever.

Zach was trembling, and tears were running down his face, as he slowly maneuvered the rifle so that the muzzle rested under his chin. He calculated the angle of the bullet, trying to picture the path of the projectile. He didn't want to botch this. The path of the little hollow-point bullet had to end in his brain.

*Zach's mom was watching her son struggle. Absent were the fear, panic, hurt, and frustration that she would have experienced prior to her homecoming. As she observed from this realm of light, love, and learning, she experienced only anticipation. She was eager to see how her Lord was going to use this situation to manifest his glory. There was no question of 'if' the only unknown was 'how'.*

"Gabe, Meg," J.D. said as she sat down across from them again, "we just received another call from the rescue team. Your grandson's trail indicates that he has dropped off the plateau and headed for the stream. As you told us, it is extremely rough terrain and they're finding it necessary to proceed in a slow and cautious manner. Still, they are confident that they will reach him within the hour, unless of course he keeps moving, which they are quite confident that he won't."

"And what makes them think that he isn't gonna keep movin'?" Gabe asked.

"We don't know for sure, but we think that he has moved into a place that is almost impossible to get out of without climbing gear. Our helicopter has flown over the ravine and sent us some real-time photos. Across the stream, there is a sheer rock wall. Upstream, the creek runs through a boulder patch that, from the air at least, appears to be impossible. He could travel downstream, but that would take him in the opposite direction from where it appears he is trying to go, so we are hoping that he won't choose that route, but instead, try to climb back out the way he went in, which would be extremely difficult to do. That shale is a lot harder to negotiate going up than it is when you are going down."

Meg, who had been quiet throughout most of the interaction asked, "Was there any sign of Zach in those pictures from the helicopter?"

"No," J.D. answered. "But that area is so thick with brush and trees that getting a glimpse of him from the air would be next to impossible."

"I know the exact spot you're talkin' about," Gabe said. "The land downstream from there belongs to the Nature Conservancy group. If Zach decides to go down into there, he won't as much as hit a loggin' road before he gets to the Sycan Marsh, and that's at least twenty miles, as the crow flies. Going around the rock slides and down trees will double that distance."

"Yeah, judging from the photos the helicopter is sending, those are some of the roughest miles in Central Oregon. It appears that the creek bed is made up of boulders the size of old Buicks," J.D. replied as she stood and started back to her computer. Halfway back to the trailer she stopped and turned back to Gabe and Meg, "Mr. Green, you should go home and rest. Excuse me for saying it, but you look like cra...em...you're looking very pale. You don't need to worry; we'll phone you with any information as soon as we get it."

"I don't care what I look like, pale or not, I wanna be here when you bring Zach out. Once your search team gets him, do you think they'll bring him here?"

"Most likely they'll fly him here, but it that depends on a lot of factors. The circumstances, and his condition, will dictate our actions once we contact the boy."

Meg asked, "Will you tell us as soon as you hear anything else?"

"I will," J.D. promised before she disappeared into her trailer.

While the Forest Service continued their rescue routine, Gabe and Meg prayed.

Zach wondered if he'd feel anything when he pulled the trigger. Was it true that you didn't hear the shot? As he thought, he began to feel a sense of calm. This was what he was supposed to do. It just felt right. His tears stopped, and his heartbeat and breathing had slowed down.

He looked up through the limbs of a huge ponderosa pine and was amazed at how blue the sky was behind that dark green.

A white-breasted nuthatch was hopping down the trunk of the ponderosa, hunting a lunch of bugs, just above Zach's head. Zach decided that the bird's erratic upside-down movement was a good last thing to see.

With the rifle on his chest, the end of the barrel pushing into his chin above his Adam's apple, Zach put his thumb through the trigger guard and began to apply pressure to the trigger. His thumb slowly tightened against the slender curve of the trigger. He squeezed until he could feel his pulse in his thumb.

Nothing happened.

He lay confused, with a metallic taste in his mouth. Through a strange combination of disappointment and relief, he realized why the gun wasn't firing. He had forgotten to disengage the rifle's safety.

As he was maneuvering the rifle in to reach the safety button, he heard whining in the bushes nearby. Zach glanced to his right and saw Ace limping toward him. The dog's head was down, his eyes were full of pain, and it was obvious that every step was a struggle.

Zach laid the rifle aside, sat up, and called, "Ace, Ace, come here boy." The dog let out a painful yip as he moved closer and put his head on Zach's thigh.

There were three long parallel gashes down the length of Ace's left side. The bear's claws had opened the dog's skin to the bone. Blood and dirt coated the animal's reddish-yellow fur.

"What'd are we going to do?" Zach muttered to the dog as he tried to push the gaping skin back together. He hardly felt his own rib pain as he went to the stream, stripped off his shirt, and dipped the cloth in the ice cold water. He took the wet rag back to the dog and tried to wash out the wounds. Ace whimpered as blood oozed from the wound. The dog's eyes were bright with pain and expectation. The slow blood flow made Zach think the dog would not bleed to death.

"Lord," Zach cried. "Please don't let Ace die. None of this is his fault. He didn't do anything wrong!"

Zach's pleading was interrupted by a yell that came from across the stream and echoed down the hillside, "Zach, Zach Mertz!"

The sound startled Zach and Ace, but they both kept still and listened to the sound of rocks clattering and brush snapping above them. Then, the voice came again, "Zach, are you down there?"

**305**

Zach looked at the rifle lying in the sand where he had tossed it when Ace saved him from shooting himself. Then, he looked at the dog's ripped skin and around at the impassable terrain. Who was coming for him now? He didn't want to fight. He was too exhausted to run. And he did not want Ace to bleed to death. Surrender seemed the easiest option. "Over here," he hollered. "We're over here."

"Stay put, son, we'll be there in a minute," a voice different from the first answered.

Zach whispered to Ace, "Stay put? Like we can go someplace? What kind of torture are these guys bringing with them?"

J.D. was moving fast, and had an excited look on her face, as she came out of the tent. "We've got him! The search team has reached Zach," she told Gabe and Meg in an excited voice.

"Is he alright?" Meg asked.

"He's a little bunged up. And it's going to take the team awhile to get him out of the hole that they found him in, but they think he's going to be fine."

Tears were pouring from Gabe's closed eyes, and down into his beard as he said, "Thank you, thank you," over and over. J.D. knew he wasn't thanking her.

# 35

The helicopter landed. Gabe was on his crutches standing next to Meg as the rotor-wash stirred dust and dirt and sent debris into the air. Both of the grandparents were trying to shield their eyes against the blowing grit. They would have turned away and closed their eyes, but both were too anxious to see Zach.

The crew lifted Ace out of the craft first. The fact that the dog's body was wrapped in field dressing didn't even register with Gabe or Meg as they waited for Zach to be off-loaded.

Zach was still in the rescue litter and covered with grime and needles and blood but none of that detracted from their excitement. The sight of their grandson strapped into the basket-like stretcher was frightening, but both Gabe and Meg were flooded with relief when they saw his face and realized that his eyes were open, and he was alert.

There were only a few minutes for asking the "are you alright?" questions before the rescue crew picked Zach up to load him in the ambulance that was on hand to transport him to the hospital. As he was being carried to the waiting vehicle, Zach, fear tangible in his voice, asked his grandfather, "Is he here?"

"Is who here?"

"The guy who wears the black jump suit, is he with these guys?"

Gabe looked at Meg before answering, "We haven't seen anyone like that around here."

"Watch out for him. He is evil. And please pray that he won't be at the hospital," Zach said as the doors of the ambulance were closed.

J.D. had been standing off to the side while Zach was placed into the ambulance. As it drove away, she asked, "What was he talking about? Who's evil?"

Gabe shrugged and stared at the ground as he answered, "I guess it's more of that hallucination stuff I told you about. The boy is fixated on the guy that he thinks he sees."

"That's pretty odd. You will probably want to get him in to see a counselor about that."

J.D. turned to Meg, "Meanwhile, though, Meg, you need to get this big galoot home and in bed before we have to ship *him* back to the hospital."

"Getting him home would probably be a great idea," Meg replied. "But I think we'd better get up to the hospital to see what they're going to do with Zach."

Gabe slapped himself on the forehead with the palm of his hand and said, "Oh, man, what are we gonna do with Ace? He really needs to go to the vet's?"

"Ian is headed to town in about half an hour. I can have him drop the dog at the veterinarian's office if you'll call ahead and make the arrangement. But can't you let the boy's parents take care of that?" J.D. pointed at Gabe and continued, "That guy needs to get some rest."

Gabe interrupted, "We don't want to impose, but it would be a huge help if Ian would be willing to drop Ace at the Rosland Animal Hospital. And this 'galoot' as you called me, is fine. I'm not so sure about the boy."

They got Ace situated in the Forest Service rig and then Gabe and Meg thanked J.D. while she walked beside them on the way to their car. When they were buckled in and headed out the rough gravel road Gabe said, "We've got to send a letter commending J.D. and her crew to her supervisor. They did a fantastic job!"

"Yeah, that'd be good. Everyone was so helpful."

They drove along in silence for ten minutes before Meg said, "Do you really think he's a demon or evil spirit or something?"

Gabe was lost in a wave of pain, and replied, "What? Who?"

"You know—the guy in the black jump suit."

"Oh. Yeah. I haven't wanted to admit it, even to myself, but yeah, I think he is."

"So, what're we going to do about him?"

"Pray and pray and pray. What else *is* there to do?"

"I don't know. Maybe we're going to need to get Zach in to see a psychiatrist or someone."

"This is a spiritual issue. He doesn't need a shrink."

"There are Christians who suffer from mental illness you know; and there are God loving doctors who treat them. Don't close your mind to the possibility."

"Okay, but right now I think the priority is making sure that he is alright physically. Let's worry about that other stuff later."

Meg was quiet for several miles. She looked at Gabe to make sure that he wasn't sleeping. He was staring out the window, so she asked, "Have you ever seen anyone like this guy that Zach has been talking about?"

"No. Why? Have you?"

"No, I haven't, but you don't seem too surprised about what he says he sees. I just thought maybe you'd seen demons, or whatever, too."

"Demons aren't all he's seen."

"What? How do you know?"

"He's talked about seeing someone that he described as a shiny guy, or someone with bright shiny clothes. I think that may have been an angel."

"Gabe, now you are freaking me out. What are you talking about?"

They were coming to the intersection that brought them out onto the highway, and Gabe didn't answer until Meg had pulled onto the pavement and brought the rig up to cruising speed. Then, he said, "You remember my Uncle Jake, don't you? He's supposed to have seen angels, and demons, and all kinds of creepy stuff. I think that Zach has somehow inherited that same ability."

Meg had heard the stories about Uncle Jake. She'd always thought that they were mostly the result of overactive imaginations. "Do you really believe that stuff?" she asked.

"Yeah, I think I do. There are a lot of stories in the Bible where angels and demons talk to people. I don't know why that it would only be true then and not now."

"It's just too weird, that's all. And in the Bible didn't the angels or whatever have some special message? What is the message that Zach is supposed to be getting?"

Gabe was holding his head with both hands. "How would I know? All I know right now is that my leg is throbbing and I have a king-sized, bruiser, of a headache. If Uncle Jake was still alive I'd call him and talk to him 'bout all this. But, remember, he got croaked about a year ago. In fact, the events leading up to his murder supposedly included a lot of supernatural stuff."

"Yeah, I remember, but the whole deal seems too bizarre. Anyway, could we at least talk to Pastor Terry?"

"Let's ask Zach how he feels about it before we start advertising. I don't want him turned into some kind of a freak show."

Meg sighed and tapped her finger tips on the steering wheel as she focused on the road in front of her. "I just don't want anything else bad to happen to him."

"I know, neither do I. I'll talk to Zach about this whole deal as soon as I can and we'll go from there. Meanwhile, let's pray for wisdom."

When they arrived at the hospital, Gabe was glad to see that the shift had changed since he had been there earlier. The doctors and nurses attending Zach were not the same ones that had worked on Gabe's leg.

The receptionist informed them that a doctor had already examined Zach and he had been sent to the x-ray department so they could take pictures of his chest. Gabe and Amy squirmed in the waiting room's uncomfortable chairs, glanced through a stack of six-month-old magazines and tried to be patient while they waited for him to be brought back to his cubicle.

They heard the gurney coming before they saw it. A squeaking wheel announced its progress as it rolled down the hallway. When it rounded the corner, Zach looked like a frightened four year old. The faded hospital gown that they had put him in and thin blanket that covered him made him look small, cold, and scared.

Meg got to her feet and Gabe on his crutches as soon as they saw Zach. They went to either side of the noisy gurney and escorted their grandson and the x-ray technician back into cubical twenty-eight. The tech said,

"The doctor will be in after she looks at the pictures," and went through the curtain.

Meg took Zach's hand and asked, "Are you alright?"

"My ribs hurt a lot."

"Did the doctor tell you anything yet?"

"She said that she thought I had a couple of broken ribs. That's why they sent me for the x-rays."

"If they're broken, they won't do anything about it but give you some pain meds," Gabe said. "It use'ta be that they'd tape you all up when your ribs were broke but they don't do that anymore."

There were a few minutes of awkward silence as the three of them avoided eye contact then Zach said, "I'm sorry," and started to cry.

"Don't be sorry," Gabe replied. "You didn't do anything wrong. It sure wasn't your fault that the storm caught us."

"I'm sorry that mom died," Zach was able to choke out.

Meg gripped the boy's hand harder and said, "What do you mean, your mom died?"

Zach was beginning to sob; with each sob, he winced from the pain in his ribs. He struggled to regain his composure before answering, "That guy told me that Mom had died."

"You mean the guy in the black jumpsuit?" Gabe asked.

Zach nodded.

"I don't think you hav'ta take too much stock in what he told ya," Gabe responded looking at the floor.

"I think he was telling me the truth. I think he knows that Mom is dead."

"Oh, Zach, how could some guy out in the woods have that information? Don't you think we would have been notified?" Meg asked.

"Grandma, I don't know how he knew or any of that, but I'm telling you, this guy knew what he was talking about."

Meg patted his hand and said, "Tell you what, I'll go out and phone down to Phoenix and talk to her nurse and we'll find out for sure."

After Meg had gone outside to use her cell phone, Gabe leaned over Zach's bed and asked, "Zach, who do you think this guy is?"

"At first I had no idea. I thought he was just some weird freak. Now I know that he's someone evil."

"Like the devil? Do you think he might be Satan?"

"I don't know anything about that Grumpa, but he knows way too much, and he can do way too much. Do you know that he tried to get me to kill myself. He said that shooting myself was the only way to make everything better. I just about did it, too. If Ace hadn't come whimpering out of the brush as I started to pull the trigger, I'd have killed myself."

"But why Zach? Is life that hopeless for you?"

"I know it sounds really dumb now, but while I was lost, and the pain in my ribcage was making every breath feel like a knife was stabbing through me, a bear had come along and ripped Ace to pieces – and I thought that bear was going to come for me. Then this guy shows up and starts talking about how good and easy it would be to kill myself. And he told me that Mom was dead. He made it sound like a really good idea to just kill myself."

"You thought he was evil, and it seemed like a good idea to follow his advice?"

"I hadn't figured out how bad he was by then. It was all so confusing."

"When did you figure it out?"

"In the helicopter. I was praying to God that the guy wouldn't show up, and it just hit me. It was like God peeled back a layer of reality and showed me that this guy that was harassing me was nothing but evil."

"Wait a minute. I didn't think you believed in God and there you were prayin' to him?"

"Well, that's another part of the story. I started reading in your little Bible while I was lost. You know, the one that was in the pickup, and I saw that part about needing to be born into God's family, and it just made sense to me. I prayed that God would take me into his family. And he did."

Gabe was standing with tears running down his face, almost too emotional to talk, when the curtain was pulled back and Meg stepped into the cubicle. Her face was soaked, too. Gabe looked at her and said, "You heard what Zach said?"

Meg shook her head, took a tissue from the dispenser that was next to the sink and blew her nose and dried her face before saying, "No. But he is right. Becky has passed away."

Gabe let go of one crutch and hugged her with one arm and said, "Oh, Meg, I'm sorry."

"Don't be sorry. We've known all along that she was gone. And I suppose it's terrible to say, but I'm relieved."

"No, that's not terrible, I know what you mean. I just pray that the faith that she expressed as a girl was real."

Right, then the doctor came into the room and looked at the tears in each of their eyes and said, "Well, it looks like you folks could use some good news, and it happens that I have some. Zach, three of your ribs are broken, but they are still in place so we don't have to worry about any of them puncturing your lungs.

"You're going to have a lot of pain for awhile, but I'll give you a prescription that will help you cope with that. Aside from the ribs, everything looks good.

**314**

"Do you have any questions for me? If not, you can go ahead and get dressed; if the pain gets worse or if you have any other problems, give me a call." He handed a prescription paper to Gabe and left the room.

Meg looked at the clothes that they handed Zach for him to put on and said, "Oh, Zach, I'm sorry you have to put on those filthy things. I could run to the store and get you something."

"It's alright, Grandma. I don't mind. I just want to get out of here."

Gabe pulled the curtain aside and stepped out into the hallway and said, "Come on, Meg, give the man some privacy while he dresses."

While they waited for Zach to get his clothes on, Gabe whispered to Meg, "He became a follower of Jesus while he was out there by himself!"

"What? That's great! How'd that happen?"

"I guess he was readin' some of the places that I've marked in that little New Testament that I always have in the truck."

Half the weight of the news of Becky's death was lifted from Meg's heart, and she whispered, "Praise God. That is an absolute miracle."

Alison Stearns called Detective Randy Mack.

"You asked me to call if I heard anything more about that whole deal with David's wife," Allison said. Well, I think I might have heard something. I'm not sure if it means anything or not, but David creeps me out. Anyway, he and my mom were having a big fight last night...something to do with the payments on David's house. Mom was telling him that he should rent it out to help cover the payments, but the creep was shouting that we needed to stop leasing the condo and move into the house."

"What's that have to do with Becky Mertz?"

"That's the deal, in the middle of this big arg, David says, 'It doesn't matter, by this time next week Becky will be out of the picture and I'll have enough money to pay off the house. Then we can move in there'."

Mom got real snotty and said, "She's been lying in that coma for eight weeks, what makes you think something is going to change in the next few days?"

Then David said, "Because I'm going to make sure that it does."

"What did your mom say to that?"

"She asked him to just wait for her to die. But he said that she might live for months or even years and he'd lose the house by that time."

Mack was scribbling all this down, but he knew none of it would stand up in court, but it might be good enough for a search warrant allowing him a shot at finding whatever drug might have been administered to cause Becky's heart to quit beating. "Did you ever hear him say anything about why he didn't just request that she be removed from the life support equipment?"

Alison's voice sounded excited when he answered, "Yeah, during the fight, Mom ask him that."

"So what'd he say?"

"He said that his practice had suffered enough because of the accusations the police were making about him poisoning her in the first place. He thought that he'd lose even more clients if word got out that he had her unplugged."

"Alison, if David ever ends up in court would you be willing to tell a judge and jury what you're telling me? Before you answer, you need to know it could make you very unpopular with your mom. And it might make David want to kill you"

"I don't care about them anyways. I'm moving out the first chance I get. But, if I had to talk in court, would the lawyers be mean to me like on those television programs?"

"Yeah, the defense attorney may try to make you look bad so that the jury doesn't believe you. We would have you all ready for that though, but how old are you?"

"Sixteen."

"Ya know that chance for you to move out might not come along for a long while."

"I don't care. David needs to go to jail for everything he's done."

"How do you know he's really done anything? All this might just be a bunch of big talk."

Alison went quiet, and Mack began to think that she may have hung up on him. Then, she quietly said, "What he did to me wasn't just talk."

"Alison—"

"I'm done talking about that, please just arrest him."

Mack heard the click of the connection being broken and threw his notepad down on his desk. "I knew it. That guy is a first class scumbag!"

Schiller had returned to his desk just in time to see the tirade. "What's going on now?" he asked.

"That jerk of a doctor, David Mertz, is diddlin' his girlfriend's daughter. We've got to get the Sex Crimes Unit involved in this mess."

With Gabe on crutches and Zach so stove up and sore that he couldn't carry anything heavier than a ballpoint pen, all the carrying fell to Meg when they went to the airport. They look like a living advertisement for male chauvinism. But they made it to Phoenix for Becky's memorial service without being accosted by a single feminist group.

The service was small and sad. If Becky had had many friends, most of them had forgotten about her during the two months of her coma. The minister had not known Becky. The eulogy was generic and short. The mourners included Gabe, Meg, Zach, Kay the nurse, and a score of others that came quietly and left quickly.

Gabe was surprised to see Detectives Mack and Schiller at the service. They stayed long enough to tell Gabe that they were no longer pursuing Becky's death as a murder. They did, however, say that the detectives from the Sex Crimes Division felt that the case they had against David was a slam dunk.

David was in police custody so they could only speculate as to whether or not he would have attended if he had been able.

For Gabe, Meg, and Zach, the service was anticlimactic. They had each said goodbye to Becky when they had left her a month earlier.

The air of the pre-dawn fall morning held a crisp bite. A great-horned voiced a lonely 'whoo' and his sad note set off the music of a family of marauding coyotes. Ace listened to the desert song dogs from the warmth of his dog house then laid his muzzle back across the three parallel scars on his side and went back to sleep.

Gabe had his study books fanned out on the counter. He was putting the finishing touches on the material that he would present to the adult Bible study class at church the next morning.

Zach was across the room, frowning as he read through a section of an Oswald Chambers devotional book. The frown was not a product of disagreement but of attempting to understand.

Soon, both of them would close their books and spend some time in prayer. Then, they would hook the boat trailer to the pickup and go to a nearby lake to spend the last Saturday of trout season trolling for rainbow trout.

## Habits

As they drove through the first rays of dawn, Gabe said, "You did a great job in that cross-country race yesterday afternoon."

"Thanks. It was fun."

Far away, the figure of a man wearing a black jump suit shrugged, pulled a coiled length of rope over his shoulder, and started walking, away.

5515433R0

Made in the USA
Charleston, SC
26 June 2010